EIGHT WORLDS OF
C. M. KORNBLUTH

EIGHT WORLDS OF
C. M. KORNBLUTH

C. M. KORNBLUTH

INTRODUCTION BY BUD WEBSTER

WILDSIDE PRESS

EIGHT WORLDS OF C. M. KORNBLUTH

"Introduction" and "Bibliography" copyright © 2010 by Bud Webster. They originally appeared, in slightly different form, in the February 2009 issue of *Jim Baen's Universe*.

"The Cosmic Expense Account" originally appeared in *The Magazine of Fantasy & Science Fiction*, January 1956. "The Adventurer" originally appeared in *Space Science Fiction*, May 1953. "The Altar at Midnight" originally appeared in *Galaxy Science Fiction*, November 1952. "The Marching Morons" originally appeared in *Galaxy Science Fiction*, April 1951. "The Little Black Bag" originally appeearered in *Astounding Science Fiction*, July 1950. "Theory of Rocketry" originally appeared in *The Magazine of Fantasy & Science Fiction*, July 1958. "Make Mine Mars" originally appeearerd in *SF Adventures*, November 1952. "Time Bum" originally appeearered in *Fantastic*, January/February 1953.

CONTENTS

INTRODUCTION

Cyril With an M (or, I'm As Kornbluth as Kansas in August)

By Bud Webster

Cyril M. Kornbluth wasn't born with an M in his name. According to Frederik Pohl (who ought to know), he added it when he decided to write in collaboration with his wife, Mary. Just how many of Kornbluth's fifty or so stories were, in fact, written that way I don't know; it's entirely possible that, like Henry Kuttner and his spouse Catherine L. Moore, the collaborations were subtle and indirect as often as they were active exchanges.

Kornbluth was born in 1923. He made his first bones at age 17, selling "Stepsons of Mars" — a collaboration with Richard Wilson under the pseudonym Ivar Towers — to Pohl's *Astonishing Stories* for the April, 1940 issue, and followed this with his first solo story, "King Cole of Pluto" (as S. D. Gottesman) in the May, 1940 *Super Science*, also edited by Pohl.

If you're paying close attention, you should have noticed two things by now: first, that CMK wasn't at all adverse to using pseudonyms, both with others and by himself, and that he hung around with the baddest literary gang this side of the Algonquin Hotel, the Futurians.

I'm going to assume that you already know about the Futurians. If you don't, I suggest you Google them directly; without argument, they were the single most important group — fan or pro — in the early history of science fiction. I'm not exaggerating here, even a little bit. The Futurians produced a significant number of writers, editors, and agents, not to mention an equally significant number of feuds, dalliances, schisms, and life-long friendships. Frankly, I suspect that it would be impossible to overestimate their influence on the burgeoning field of magazine science fiction, and they would continue to do so as individuals well into the 1970s.[1]

Kornbluth was a good fit with the Futurians, for all that he was in his

---

[1]   For those of you whose interest is piqued, allow me to point you to a couple of books written by those who were there: *The Way the Future Was*, by Frederik Pohl, an indispensable personal history by one of the most important figures in SF; and *The Futurians*, by Damon Knight, hardly a figure of lesser stature.

mid-teens when he first began hanging around them. He was opinionated, brash, wry and witty, and boiling with the compulsion to contribute to science fiction, not just read it. And that he did, for all that his catalog isn't as extensive as many of his fellows': 90 or so short stories, a dozen novels, much of it in collaboration with one or another writer (mostly Pohl, or another Futurian). Take a look at one single year in the biblio at the end of this book: more than two dozen stories in 1941 alone, and in many cases, two stories in the same issue under different names. This, clearly, was a man trying to prove himself.

Numbers aren't everything, however. In fact, an author's prolificacy is meaningless in the long run if s/he has little of sum and substance to say; look at Lionel Fanthorpe or Barbara Cartland. They certainly filled their editors' in-boxes, but how widely are they read now?

Kornbluth was all about sum and substance, crafting near-perfect little gems that could cut you to ribbons if you didn't handle them carefully. The contents of *The Best of C. M. Kornbluth* (ed. Frederik Pohl, Ballantine 1976) give the reader plenty of opportunities for such self-injury, all of them as rewarding as they are cynical, as entertaining as they are scornful.

No accident, this. In his introduction to the above, Pohl described his old friend as "a sardonic soul," and said his work "… relates to the essential hypocrisies and foolishnesses of mankind." Well, yeah. Even a brief examination of his stories — "The Marching Morons," "The Little Black Bag," and his novel *The Syndic* are typical — offer a particularly jaundiced view of the Great Unwashed.

This factor has a particular and peculiar effect on the reader: either you get it, and you have a really good time, or you don't — and you end up scratching your head and wondering what all the fuss is about. I'm serious about this; the reader who "gets" Kornbluth will more than once find him/herself snorting and saying, "Yeah, ain't *that* th' truth!"

That's a bit of an oversimplification, of course. Even if you don't agree with Kornbluth's amused contempt at the majority of the Human Race, his skill as a writer is engaging and admirable. I'm far less of a gleeful pessimist than he was, and he's always been one of my favorites.

Take one of his most famous stories, for example. If there is a typical Kornbluthian story, it is "The Marching Morons" (originally in the April, 1951 issue of *Galaxy*). It begins with a character sincerely near and dear to Kornbluth's heart, a potter. The opening scene works as well as it does primarily because Mary Kornbluth, his wife, was a potter and ceramicist, and the details are spot-on as a result.

The character isn't just any potter, though, I should point out. Not only is he skilled in shaping and glazing his wares, he's also an engineer/physicist, and almost certainly a half-dozen or more other brainy-mug specialties. So is the secretary of the man who ostensibly buys his pots, although the buyer himself is ... well, a moron.

And that's the point of this gleefully dark little yarn. The human race has split into proto-Eloi and proto-Morlocks, with the (comparative) handful of brains actually running things while the morons take the credit and drive their noisy, flashy cars. All is well, until the potter — in search of mineral deposits to use in making glazes — digs up "Honest John" Barlow, a real estate mogul who went to the dentist for an impacted wisdom tooth (note the irony there) and was accidentally thrown into a state of suspended animation.

What was, in the past, an accident with no foreseeable solution turns out to be child's play for the non-morons of the future, and Barlow is awakened to find his old world gone to dust, and this new one faced with the Problem: what to do with the moronic portion of the population? What, indeed, and if you haven't yet read this nasty little tale, I won't spoil it for you; it's way more fun if you read it for yourself.

As I mentioned, Frederik Pohl knew Kornbluth from an early age, and the two men took to writing early on. He told me:

> I think Cyril wanted to be a writer at an age when most of us did, in his early teens. His first efforts, or at least the first I knew anything about, weren't stories. They were poems.

Pohl himself was no stranger to poetry, and in fact, his first professional publication was the verse "Elegy to a Dead Satellite: Luna," published in the October, 1937 issue of *Amazing* under the name Elton V. Andrews. The two youngsters acquired a book by one of Kornbluth's teachers which gave the rules for writing just about every type of poem there is, and they were determined to try their hand at all of them:

> We made a good start, actually writing haiku (we spelled it hokku), a villanelle, a sestina, two sonnets (one Petrarchian and one Shakespearian) and I think a couple of others. We bogged down when it came to the chant royale (the chant royale is *hard*) and, like most of the other Futurians, we decided to try our luck with science fiction. At that time I think Cyril was maybe 14, and I three or four years later.

The plain truth is that there is precious little of the sympathetic in Kornbluth's work, and not a drop of sentimentality. There is, if you want it, plenty of bitterness, but that alone wouldn't mean much: if you look hard enough, there's no lack of acerbic wit out there in Fantasyland, even in those writers not particularly known for it. Bitterness by itself is just a bad taste; what makes Kornbluth's prose memorable and gratifying is the skill with which he expresses his bitterness, and that *is* a rarity.

I'm talking about elegance. Elegance of prose, more specifically. Not just an economy of words, although that can be part of it, but using the optimum word or phrase for the task at hand. I could give you example after example: Bradbury's "It was a pleasure to burn;" Vonnegut's "Billy Pilgrim was unstuck in time;" Cordwainer Smith's ... well, take your pick.

Kornbluth is *eat-up* with elegance, it's there almost everywhere you look. Not necessarily poetry, mind you — despite his early experimentation, there's little of the poetic in his work — but there is, nevertheless, an elegance born of his innate (and integral) sardonicism. Consider this, from "The Marching Morons:"

> Lying twisted and broken under the acceleration, [he] realized that some things had not changed, that Jack Ketch was never asked to dinner however many shillings you paid him to do your dirty work, that murder will out, that crime pays only temporarily.
> The last thing he learned was that death is the end of pain.

Only Kornbluth could have expressed the death of a soulless and cynical character so elegantly, at least in the still mostly-Campbellian science fiction field of 1951. Perhaps it's just as valid, though, to say that only Kornbluth would have found it desirable to do so.

I said above that there was little if any poetry in his writing, but that's not strictly true across the board. Like all fine writers, Kornbluth defies attempts to stuff him into convenient pigeonholes, even mine. He did it rarely, he did it for specific and precise effect, and he did it without fanfare or flash, as in this from "The Remorseful" (from *Star Science Fiction Stories 2*, ed. Frederik Pohl, Ballantine 1953):

> It does not matter when it happened. This is because the Visitors were eternal; endless time stretched before them and behind, which mentions only two of the infinities that their "lives" included. Precisely when they arrived at a particular planetary system was to them the most trivial of irrelevancies. Eternity was theirs; eventually they would have arrived at all of them.

Lovely. Just lovely. No sentiment, nothing wistful or nostalgic or lugubrious; just a few lines of quiet prose admirably constructed to express a concept using the optimum words for the task at hand. Elegance.

What of the man behind this elegance, though? That's rather complicated, I'm afraid, and not a little unfortunate as well. Pohl, probably Kornbluth's closest friend and his frequent collaborator, is perhaps the least likely to express a negative estimation, even though he was lampooned severely in *Gunner Cade*[2], which was written during one of their occasional rifts. He says in his introduction to *The Best of C. M. Kornbluth*:

> There is a character in the book who is pitifully corrupt and whiningly ineffectual. It is not an accident that the character's name is what Judy's first daughter called me when she was first learning to talk: Threadwick.

"Sardonic," indeed. Others weren't nearly so forgiving. In a letter to Isaac Asimov dated after Kornbluth's death, John W. Campbell said, "His anger against the ways of the culture he didn't fit too well produced cumulative bitterness in him."

Author and critic Barry Malzberg goes even further:

> Kornbluth's nastiness is remarked on by everyone who knew him at all. He was deeply embittered by his experience in the War and by his economic struggles after the War. Don Wollheim ... told me, "Cyril was so bitter in his last year that you knew that either the world would have to go away or he would. There was no compromise possible."

(Wollheim himself was at least once a Kornbluth collaborator. The January 1953 *F&SF* contained "The Mask of Demeter," by Cecil Corwin and Martin Pearson; Corwin was a frequent pseudonym of Kornbluth's, and Pearson was Wollheim. How the story — actually, a story fragment — came to be published at all is one of a number of deplorable incidents Kornbluth suffered during his short life. It was sold to Boucher and McComas not by either of the authors, or by Kornbluth's agent, the ever-present Pohl, but by an agent who had no rights to it.[3] Need-

---

2   By Kornbluth and Judith Merril writing as Cyril Judd, originally serialized in three parts beginning with the March 1952 *Astounding*, and published later the same year in book form by Simon & Schuster

3   Rumor has it that said agent was Wollheim himself; I have not been able to confirm this, and if it's true, there seems to be no evidence that DAW

less to say, Kornbluth knew nothing of it until it appeared, and found it extremely difficult to collect his due; all in all, it was just another brick in the wall.)

That such a body of work as Kornbluth left behind was written by a man so cynical and angry is remarkable, frankly. It puts him in a class with Anthony Burgess and Kurt Vonnegut, without their literary pretensions (don't forget that Vonnegut, for all his rejection of the genre, began his career selling to *Galaxy* and *Wonder Stories* like every other sci-fi hack he so despised).

His noteworthiness wasn't limited to his sour outlook, though. His stories may lack sentimentality, but they certainly don't lack humanity. The titular object in "The Little Black Bag" transforms its finder, Dr. Full, from a shattered drunk into a man again capable of feeling something other than a desperate need for another bottle of wine, back into a physician with the firm intent to use the contents of the magic case to do once again what he had always done best: heal the sick. Simple bitterness wouldn't give an author the range to create that character and make him breathe; it takes a clear understanding of, as well as a real affection for, people.

Kornbluth himself might have been horrified to hear me say that, but nevertheless I'm convinced that he had more love for his fellows than he was ever comfortable expressing, either in fiction or in person.

The exception to this was almost certainly his family. Clearly he and his wife Mary loved each other deeply; the year following his death, she assembled a slim anthology, *Science Fiction Showcase* (Doubleday 1959), containing stories by a number of his friends including Futurians Damon Knight, James Blish, and the ever-present Pohl, as well as Bradbury, Philip K. Dick, and Theodore Sturgeon among others as a tribute to her late husband. It is a quiet, but heart-felt little book, well worth the reading even now, a half-century later.

CMK was an infantryman in WWII, fighting in the Battle of the Bulge and winning the Bronze Star. However, his injuries stayed with him for the rest of his too-short life, adding yet another brick to that already daunting wall.

After the war, he went into journalism, working his way up to the position of editor of the Chicago office of Trans-Radio Press and busting

---

acted as agent — legit or otherwise — for anyone else except himself. I will point out, though, that the only reprint of "The Mask of Demeter" in an anthology was in Wollheim's *Prize Science Fiction*, published by McBride in 1953.

his hump to find that elusive thing that all penny-a-word scriveners lusted for and few found: a regular paycheck as a writer. He went back to writing fiction full-time in 1951, producing almost all of his best-known work, including a number of novels both solo and in collaboration.

Although he was making better money than before, the memories of his days with the miss-meal cramps loomed like the Sword of Damocles over his head, and he looked for something within his range of skills. Pohl relates:

> Although Cyril was doing reasonably well in economic terms, a writer's income comes in lumps of various sizes at irregular times, and (with two kids) he felt the need of a more regular income. He was offered an assistant editor job on *F&SF*, which he liked a lot. (He was delighted with some of the pieces he passed along to Bob Mills, particularly Fritz Leiber's "The Silver Eggheads.")

Unfortunately, his involvement with the magazine was not fated to be a long one. Early in the spring of 1958, he was scheduled to meet with Mills in New York City. It had snowed heavily at his home in Levittown, and he rushed to shovel out his drive before running to the station to catch his train. He was struck by a heart attack on the platform, and died there, age 35.

His death came at an age when most writers are just beginning to hit their stride and create mature, lasting bodies of work. Considering the maturity and complexity of the stories and novels he left behind, it's humbling to contemplate what he could have produced given even another few decades. Not only was he popular with the readers, but with the critics as well. In his Hugo-winning history of science fiction, *Trillion Year Spree* (Atheneum 1986), Brian Aldiss calls Kornbluth's passing "… a minor disaster …"; of his erudition and (if I may repeat myself) elegance of language, Damon Knight said:

> Kornbluth must have been born with a lexicon in his mouth. Legend has it that once, when a motherly stranger bent over him in his perambulator and made the sounds that are usually made to babies, Kornbluth remarked, "Madame, I am not the child you think me."

The three books which make up the two volumes of that most excellent collection, *The Science Fiction Hall of Fame* (eds. Robert Silverberg and Ben Bova, Doubleday 1970 and 1973), contain stories which were chosen by the members of the SFWA as being worthy of the Nebula had it existed when those stories were originally published. Although he died before the founding of the Science-Fiction and Fantasy Writers of America and thus would never win the Nebula, Cyril M. Kornbluth is represented twice therein with — what else? — "The Little Black Bag" and "The Marching Morons."

Summing up a remarkable author like Kornbluth in a few words is a difficult task, one best left (in this case, anyhow) to someone who knew him well, and whose understanding of the man and his work is far greater than mine could ever be, so I will leave you with the words with which Frederik Pohl ended his appreciation of his friend and colleague in *The Best of C. M. Kornbluth*:

> As a person he was what he was as a writer: bright, sardonic, and immensely rewarding. Cyril had a great deal to say, and he said it all tersely, wittily, and with grace. I do not think we shall soon see his like again.

Nor do I. You have this book now in your hands, which is a Good Thing; if you are otherwise unfamiliar with this outstanding man's books and stories, I urge you to haunt the used bookstores and convention dealers' tables, and to assiduously pour over the offerings of the on-line booksellers for his titles. It will not be a waste of your time or money.

THE COSMIC EXPENSE ACCOUNT

The Lackawanna was still running one cautious morning train a day into Scranton, though the city was said to be emptying fast. Professor Leuten and I had a coach to ourselves, except for a scared, jittery trainman who hung around and talked at us.

"The name's Pech," he said. "And let me tell you, the Peches have been around for a mighty long time in these parts. There's a town twenty-three miles north of Scranton named Pechville. Full of my cousins and aunts and uncles, and I used to visit there and we used to send picture post cards and get them, too. But my God, mister, what's happened to them?"

His question was rhetorical. He didn't realize that Professor Leuten and I happened to be the only two people outside the miscalled Plague Area who could probably answer it.

"Mr. Pech," I said, "if you don't mind — we'd like to talk some business."

"Sorry," he said miserably and went on to the next car.

When we were alone, Professor Leuten remarked: "An interesting reaction." He was very smooth about it. Without the slightest warning he whipped a huge, writhing, hairy spider from his pocket and thrust it at my face.

I was fast on the draw too. In one violent fling I was standing on my left foot in the aisle, thumbing my nose, my tongue stuck out. Goose flesh rippled down my neck and shoulders.

"Very good," he said, and put the spider away. It was damnably realistic. Even knowing that it was a gadget of twisted springs and plush, I cringed at the thought of its nestling in his pocket. With me it was spiders. With the professor it was rats and asphyxiation. Toward the end of our mutual training program it took only one part per million of sulfur dioxide gas in his vicinity to send him whirling into the posture of defense, cranelike on one leg, tongue out and thumb to nose, the sweat of terror on his brow.

"I have something to tell you, Professor," I said.

"So?" he asked tolerantly. And that did it. The tolerance. I had been prepared to make my point with a dignified recital and apology, but there were two ways to tell the story and I suddenly chose the second.

"You're a phony," I said with satisfaction.

"What?" he gasped.

"A phony. A fake. A hoaxer. A self-deluding crackpot. Your Functional Epistemology is a farce. Let's not go into this thing kidding ourselves."

His accent thickened a little. "Let me remind you, Mr. Norris, that you are addressing a doctor of philosophy of the University of Gottingen and a member of the faculty of the University of Basle."

"You mean a Privatdozent who teaches freshman logic. And I seem to remember that Gottingen revoked your degree."

He said slowly: "I have known all along that you were a fool, Mr. Norris. Not until now did I realize that you are also an anti-Semite. It was the Nazis who went through an illegal ceremony of revocation."

"So that makes me an anti-Semite. From a teacher of logic that's very funny."

"You are correct," he said after a long pause. "I withdraw my remark. Now, would you be good enough to amplify yours?"

"Gladly, Professor. In the first place —"

I had been winding up the rubber rat in my pocket. I yanked it out and tossed it into his lap where it scrabbled and clawed. He yelled with terror, but the yell didn't cost him a split second. Almost before it started from his throat he was standing one-legged, thumb to nose, tongue stuck out.

He thanked me coldly, I congratulated him coldly, I pocketed the rat while he shuddered and we went on with the conversation.

I told him how, eighteen months ago, Mr. Hopedale called me into his office. Nice office, oak panels, signed pictures of Hopedale Press writers from our glorious past: Kipling, Barrie, Theodore Roosevelt and the rest of the backlog boys.

What about Eino Elekinen, Mr. Hopedale wanted to know. Eino was one of our novelists. His first, Vinland the Good, had been a critical success and a popular flop; Cubs of the Viking Breed, the sequel, made us all a little money. He was now a month past delivery date on the final volume of the trilogy and the end was not in sight.

"I think he's pulling a sit-down strike, Mr. Hopedale. He's way overdrawn now and I had to refuse him a thousand-dollar advance. He wanted to send his wife to the Virgin Islands for a divorce."

"Give him the money," Mr. Hopedale said impatiently. "How can you expect the man to write when he's beset by personal difficulties?"

"Mr. Hopedale," I said politely, "she could divorce him right in New York State. He's given her grounds in all five boroughs and the western townships of Long Island. But that's not the point. He can't write. And even if he could, the last thing American literature needs right now is another trilogy about a Scandinavian immigrant family."

"I know," he said. "I know. He's not very good yet. But I think he's going to be, and do you want him to starve while he's getting the juvenilia out of his system?" His next remark had nothing to do with Elekinen. He looked at the signed photo of T. R. "To a bully publisher" and said: "Norris, we're broke."

I said: "Ah?"

"We owe everybody. Printer, paper mill, warehouse. Everybody. It's the end of Hopedale Press. Unless — I don't want you to think people have been reporting on you, Morris, but I understand you came up with an interesting idea at lunch yesterday. Some Swiss professor."

I had to think hard. "You must mean Leuten, Mr. Hopedale. No, there's nothing in it for us, sir. I was joking. My brother — he teaches philosophy at Columbia — mentioned him to me. Leuten's a crackpot. Every year or two Weintraub Verlag in Basle brings out another volume of his watchamacallit and they sell about a thousand. Functional Epistemology — my brother says it's all nonsense, the kind of stuff vanity presses put out. It was just a gag about us turning him into a Schweitzer or a Toynbee and bringing out a one-volume condensation. People just buy his books, I suppose, because they got started and feel ashamed to stop."

Mr. Hopedale said: "Do it, Norris. Do it. We can scrape together enough cash for one big promotion and then the end. I'm going to see Brewster of Commercial Factors in the morning. I believe he will advance us sixty-five per cent on our accounts receivable." He tried on a cynical smile. It didn't become him. "Norris, you are what is technically called a Publisher's Bright Young Man. We can get seven-fifty for a scholarly book. With luck and promotion we can sell in the hundred thousands. Get on it." I nodded, feeling sick, and started out. Mr. Hopedale said in a tired voice: "And it might actually be work of some inspirational value."

Professor Leuten sat and listened, red-faced, breathing hard.

"You betrayer," he said at last. "You with the smiling face that came to Basle, that talked of lectures in America, that told me to sign your damnable contract. My face on the cover of the Time magazine that looks like a monkey, the idiotic interviews, the press releasements in my name that I never saw. America, I thought, and held my tongue. But from the beginning it was a lie!" He buried his face in his hands and muttered: "Ach! You stink!"

That reminded me. I took a small stench-bomb from my pocket and crushed it.

He leaped up, balanced on one leg and thumbed his nose. His tongue was out four inches and he was panting with the terror of asphyxiation.

"Very good," I said.

"Thank you. I suchest we move to the other end of the car."

We and our luggage were settled before he began to breathe normally. I judged that the panic and most of his anger had passed. "Professor," I said cautiously, "I've been thinking of what we do when and if we find Miss Phoebe."

"We shall complete her re-education," he said. "We shall point out that her unleashed powers have been dysfunctionally applied —"

"I can think of something better to do than completing her reeducation. It's why I spoke a little harshly. Presumably Miss Phoebe considers you the greatest man in the world."

He smiled reminiscently and I knew what he was thinking.

La Plume, Pa. Wednesday 4A.M. (!)
Professor Konrad Leuten
c/o The Hopedale Press
New York City, New York

My Dear Professor,

Though you are a famous and busy man I do hope you will take time to read a few words of grateful tribute from an old lady (eighty-four). I have just finished your magnificent and inspirational book How to Live on the Cosmic Expense Account: an Introduction to Functional Epistemology.

Professor, I believe. I know every splendid word in your book is true. If there is one chapter finer than the others it is No. 9, "How to be in Utter Harmony with Your Environment." The Twelve Rules in that chapter shall from this minute be my guiding light, and I shall practice them faithfully forever.

Your grateful friend,
(Miss) Phoebe Bancroft

That flattering letter reached us on Friday, one day after the papers reported with amusement or dismay the "blackout" of La Plume, Pennsylvania. The term "Plague Area" came later.

"I suppose she might," said the professor.

"Well, think about it."

The train slowed for a turn. I noticed that the track was lined with men and women. And some of them, by God, were leaping for the moving train! Brakes went on with a squeal and jolt; my nose bashed against the seat in front of us.

"Aggression," the professor said, astonished. "But that is not in the pattern!"

We saw the trainman in the vestibule opening the door to yell at the trackside people. He was trampled as they swarmed aboard, filling, jamming the car in a twinkling.

"Go to Scranton," we heard them saying. "Zombies."

"I get it," I shouted at the professor over their hubbub. "These are refugees from Scranton. They must have blocked the track. Right now they're probably bullying the engineer into backing up all the way to Wilkes-Barre."

We've got to get off!" he said. We were in an end seat. By elbowing, crowding, and a little slugging we got to the vestibule and dropped to the tracks. The professor lost all his luggage in the brief, fierce struggle. I saved only my briefcase. The powers of Hell itself were not going to separate me from that briefcase.

Hundreds of yelling, milling people were trying to climb aboard. Some made it to the roofs of the cars after it was physically impossible for one more body to be fitted inside. The locomotive uttered a despairing toot and the train began to back up.

"Well," I said, "we head north."

We found U.S. 6 after a short overland hike and trudged along the concrete. There was no traffic. Everybody with a car had left Scranton days ago, and nobody was going into Scranton. Except us.

We saw our first zombie where a signpost told us it was three miles to the city. She was a woman in a Mother Hubbard and sunbonnet. I couldn't tell whether she was young or old, beautiful or a hag. She gave us a sweet, empty smile and asked if we had any food. I said no. She said she wasn't complaining about her lot but she was hungry, and of course the vegetables and things were so much better now that they weren't poisoning the soil with those dreadful chemical fertilizers. Then she said maybe there might be something to eat down the road, wished us a pleasant good day and went on.

"Dreadful chemical fertilizers?" I asked.

The professor said: "I believe that is a contribution by the Duchess of Carbondale to Miss Phoebe's reign. Several interviews mention it." We walked on. I could read his mind like a book. He hasn't even read the interviews. He is a foolish, an impossible young man. And yet he is here, he has undergone a rigorous course of training, he is after all risking a sort of death. Why? I let him go on wondering. The answer was in my briefcase.

"When do you think we'll be in range?" I asked.

"Heaven knows," he said testily. "Too many variables. Maybe it's different when she sleeps, maybe it grows at different rates varying as the number of people affected. I feel nothing yet."

"Neither do I."

And when we felt something specifically, when we felt Miss Phoebe Bancroft practicing the Twelve Rules of "How to be in Utter Harmony with Your Environment" we would do something completely idiotic, something that had got us thrown — literally thrown — out of the office of the Secretary of Defense.

He had thundered at us: "Are you two trying to make a fool of me? Are you proposing that soldiers of the United States Army undergo a three-month training course in sticking out their tongues and thumbing their noses?" He was quivering with elevated blood pressure. Two M.P. lieutenants collared us under his personal orders and tossed us down the Pentagon steps when we were unable to deny that he had stated our proposal more or less correctly.

And so squads, platoons, companies, battalions and regiments marched into the Plague Area and never marched out again.

Some soldiers stumbled out as zombies. After a few days spent at a sufficient distance from the Plague Area their minds cleared and they told their confused stories. Something came over them, they said. A mental fuzziness almost impossible to describe. They liked it where they were, for instance; they left the Plague Area only by accident. They were wrapped in a vague, silly contentment even when they were hungry, which was usually. What was life like in the Plague Area? Well, not much happened. You wandered around looking for food. A lot of people looked sick but seemed to be contented. Farmers in the area gave you food with the universal silly smile, but their crops were very poor. Animal pests got most of them. Nobody seemed to eat meat. Nobody quarreled or fought or ever said a harsh word in the Plague Area. And it was hell on earth. Nothing conceivable could induce any of them to return.

The Duchess of Carbondale? Yes, sometimes she came driving by in her chariot, wearing fluttery robes and a golden crown. Everybody bowed down to her. She was a big, fat middle-aged woman with rimless glasses and a pinched look of righteous triumph on her face.

The recovered zombies at first were quarantined and doctors made their wills before going to examine them. This proved to be unnecessary and the examinations proved to be fruitless. No bacteria, no Rickettsia, no viruses. Nothing. Which didn't stop them from continuing in the assumption embodied in the official name of the affected counties.

Professor Leuten and I knew better, of course. For knowing better we were thrown out of offices, declined interviews and once almost locked up as lunatics. That was when we tried to get through to the President direct. The Secret Service, I am able to testify, guards our Chief Executive with a zeal that borders on ferocity.

"How goes the book?" Professor Leuten asked abruptly.

"Third hundred thousand. Why? Want an advance?"

I don't understand German, but I can recognize deep, heartfelt profanity in any language. He spluttered and crackled for almost a full minute before he snarled in English: "Idiots! Dolts! Out of almost one third of a million readers, exactly one had read the book!"

I wanted to defer comment on that. "There's a car," I said.

"Obviously it stalled and was abandoned by a refugee from Scranton."

"Let's have a look anyway." It was a battered old Ford sedan halfway off the pavement. The rear was full of canned goods and liquor. Somebody had been looting. I pushed the starter and cranked for a while; the motor didn't catch.

"Useless," said the professor. I ignored him, yanked the dashboard hood button and got out to inspect the guts. There was air showing on top of the gas in the sediment cup.

"We ride, professor," I told him. "I know these babies and their fuel pumps. The car quit on the upgrade there and he let it roll back." I unscrewed the clamp of the carburetor air filter, twisted the filter off and heaved it into the roadside bushes. The professor, of course was a "mere-machinery" boy with the true European intellectual's contempt for greasy hands. He stood by haughtily while I poured a bottle of gin empty, found a wrench in the toolbox that fit the gas-tank drain plug and refilled the gin bottle with gasoline. He condescended to sit behind the wheel and crank the motor from time to time while I sprinkled gas into the carburetor. Each time the motor coughed there was less air showing in the sediment cup; finally the motor caught for good. I moved him over, tucked my briefcase in beside me, U-turned on the broad, empty highway and we chugged north into Scranton.

It was only natural that he edged away from me, I suppose. I was grimy from working under the gas tank. This plus the discreditable ability I had shown in starting the stalled car reminded him that he was, after all, a Herr Doktor from a real university while I was, after all, a publisher's employee with nebulous qualifications from some place called Cornell. The atmosphere was wrong for it, but sooner or later he had to be told.

"Professor, we've got to have a talk and get something straight before we find Miss Phoebe."

He looked at the huge striped sign the city fathers of Scranton wisely erected to mark that awful downgrade into the city.

WARNING!
SEVEN-MILE DEATH TRAP AHEAD.
SHIFT INTO LOWER GEAR.
$50 FINE. OBEY OR PAY!

"What is there to get straight?" he demanded. "She has partially mastered Functional Epistemology even though Hopedale Press prefers to call it 'Living on the Cosmic Expense Account.' This has unleashed certain latent powers of hers. It is simply our task to complete her mastery of the ethical aspect of F.E. She will cease to dominate other minds as soon as she comprehends that her behavior is dysfunctional and in contravention of the Principle of Permissive Evolution." To him the matter was settled. He mused: "Really I should not have let you cut so drastically my exposition of Dyadic Imbalance; that must be the root of her difficulty. A brief inductive explanation —"

"Professor," I said, "I thought I told you in the train that you're a fake."

He corrected me loftily. "You told me that you think I'm a fake, Mr. Norris. Naturally I was angered by your duplicity, but your opinion of me proves nothing. I ask you to look around you. Is this fakery?"

We were well into the city. Bewildered dogs yelped at our car. Windows were broken and goods were scattered on the sidewalks; here and there a house was burning brightly. Smashed and overturned cars dotted the streets, and zombies walked slowly around them. When Miss Phoebe hit a city the effects were something like a thousand-bomber raid.

"It's not fakery," I said, steering around a smiling man in a straw hat and overalls. "It isn't Functional Epistemology either. It's faith in Functional Epistemology. It could have been faith in anything, but your book just happened to be what she settled on."

"Are you daring," he demanded, white to the lips, "to compare me with the faith healers?"

"Yes," I said wearily. "They get their cures. So do lots of people. Let's roll it up in a ball, Professor. I think the best thing to do when we meet Miss Phoebe is for you to tell her you're a fake. Destroy her faith in you and your system and I think she'll turn back into a normal old lady again. Wait a minute! Don't tell me you're not a fake. I can prove you are. You say she's partly mastered F.E. and gets her powers from that partial mastery. Well, presumably you've completely mastered F.E., since you invented it. So why can't you do everything she's done, and lots more? Why can't you end this mess by levitating to La Plume, instead of taking the Lackawanna and a 1941 Ford? And, by God, why couldn't you fix the Ford with a pass of the hands and F.E. instead of standing by while I worked?"

His voice was genuinely puzzled. "I thought I just explained, Norris. Though it never occurred to me before, I suppose I could do what you say, but I wouldn't dream of it. As I said, it would be dysfunctional and in complete contravention of the Principle of Permissive."

I said something very rude and added: "In short, you can but you won't."

"Naturally not! The Principle of Permissive!" He looked at me with slow awareness dawning in his eyes. "Norris! My editor. My proofreader. My by-the-publisher-officially-assigned fidus Achates. Norris, haven't you read my book?"

"No," I said sharply. "I've been much too busy. You didn't get on the cover of Time magazine by blind chance, you know."

He was laughing helplessly. "How goes that song," he finally asked me, his eyes damp, "'God Bless America'?"

I stopped the car abruptly. "I think I feel something," I said. "Professor, I like you."

"I like you too, Norris," he told me. "Norris, my boy, what do you think of ladies?"

"Delicate creatures. Custodians of culture. Professor, what about meat eating?"

"Shocking barbarous survival. This is it, Norris!"

We yanked open the doors and leaped out. We stood on one foot each, thumbed our noses, and stuck out our tongues.

Allowing for the time on the train, this was the 1,961st time I had done it in the past two months. One thousand, nine hundred and sixty-one times the professor had arranged for spiders to pop out at me from books, from the television screen, from under steaks, from desk drawers, from my pockets, from his. Black widows, tarantulas, harmless (hah!) big house spiders, real and imitation. One thousand, nine hundred and sixty-one times I had felt the arachnophobe's horrified revulsion. Each time I felt it I had thrown major voluntary muscular systems into play by drawing up one leg violently, violently swinging my hand to my nose, violently grimacing to stick out my tongue.

My body had learned at last. There was no spider (this time; there was only Miss Phoebe: a vague, pleasant feeling something like the first martini. But my posture of defense this 1,962nd time was accompanied by the old rejection and horror. It had no spider, so it turned on Miss Phoebe. The vague first-martini feeling vanished like morning mist burned away by the sun.

I relaxed cautiously. On the other side of the car so did Professor Leuten. "Professor," I said, "I don't like you any more."

"Thank you," he said coldly. "Nor do I like you."

"I guess we're back to normal," I said. "Climb in." He climbed in and we started off. I grudgingly said: "Congratulations."

"Because it worked? Don't be ridiculous. It was to be expected that a plan of campaign derived from the principles of Functional Epistemology would be successful. All that was required was that you be at least as smart as one of Professor Pavlov's dogs, and I admit I considered that hypothesis the weak link in my chain of reasoning. . . ."

We stopped for a meal from the canned stuff in the back of the car about one o'clock and then chugged steadily north through the ruined countryside. The little towns were wrecked and abandoned. Presumably refugees from the expanding Plague Area did the first damage by looting; the subsequent destruction just happened. It showed you what would just happen to any twentieth-century town or city in the course of a few weeks if the people who wage endless war against breakdown and dilapidation put aside their arms. It was anybody's guess whether fire or water had done more damage.

Between the towns the animals were incredibly bold. There was a veritable army of rabbits eating their way across a field of clover. A farmer-zombie flapped a patchwork quilt at them, saying affectionately: "Shoo, little bunnies! Go away, now! I mean it!"

But they knew he didn't and continued to chew their way across his field.

I stopped the car and called to the farmer. He came right away, smiling. "The little dickenses!" he said, waving at the rabbits. "But I haven't the heart to really scare them."

"Are you happy?" I asked him.

"Oh yes!" His eyes were sunken and bright; his cheekbones showed on his starved face. "People should be considerate," he said. "I always say that being considerate is what matters most."

"Don't you miss electricity and cars and tractors?"

"Goodness, no, I always say that things were better in the old days. Life was more gracious, I always say. Why, I don't miss gasoline or electricity one little bit. Everybody's so considerate and gracious that it makes up for everything."

"I wonder if you'd be so considerate and gracious as to lie down in the road so we can drive over you?"

He looked mildly surprised and started to get down, saying: "Well, if it would afford you gentlemen any pleasure —"

"No; don't bother after all. You can get back to your rabbits."

He touched his straw hat and went away, beaming. We drove on. I said to the professor: "Chapter Nine: 'How to be in Utter Harmony with Your Environment.' Only she didn't change herself, Professor Leuten; she changed the environment. Every man and woman in the Area is what Miss Phoebe thinks they ought to be: silly, sentimental, obliging and gracious to the point of idiocy. Nostalgic and all thumbs when it comes to this dreadful machinery."

"Norris," the professor said thoughtfully, "we've been associated for some time. I think you might drop the 'professor' and call me 'Leuten.' In a way we're friends —"

I jammed on the worn, mushy brakes. "Out!" I yelled, and we piled out. The silly glow was enveloping me fast. Again, thumb to nose and tongue out, I burned it away. When I looked at the professor and was quite sure he was a stubborn old fossil I knew I was all right again. When he glared at me and snapped: "Naturally I withdraw my last remark, Norris, and no gentleman would hold me to it," I knew he was normal. We got in and kept going north.

The devastation became noticeably worse after we passed a gutted, stinking shambles that had once been the town of Meshoppen, PA. After Meshoppen there were more bodies on the road and the flies became a horror. No pyrethrum from Kenya. No DDT from Wilmington. We drove in the afternoon heat with the windows cranked up and the hood ventilator closed. It was at about Meshoppen's radius from La Plume that things had stabilized for a while and the Army Engineers actually began to throw up barbed wire. Who knew what happened then? Perhaps Miss Phoebe recovered from a slight cold, or perhaps she told herself firmly that her faith in Professor Leuten's wonderful book was weakening; that she must take hold of herself and really work hard at being in utter harmony with her environment. The next morning no Army Engineers. Zombies in uniform were glimpsed wandering about and smiling. The next morning the radius of the Plague Area was growing at the old mile a day.

I wanted distraction from the sweat that streamed down my face. "Professor," I said, "do you remember the last word in Miss Phoebe's letter? It was 'forever.' Do you suppose . . . ?"

"Immortality? Yes; I think that is well within the range of misapplied F.E. Of course complete mastery of F.E. ensures that no such selfish power would be invoked. The beauty of F.E. is its conservatism, in the kinetic sense. It is self-regulating. A world in which universal mastery of F.E. has been achieved and I now perceive that the publication of my views by the Hopedale Press was if anything a step away from that ideal would be in no outward wise different from the present world."

"Built-in escape clause," I snapped. "Like yoga. You ask 'em to prove they've achieved self-mastery, just a little demonstration like levitating or turning transparent, but they're all ready for you. They tell you they've achieved so much self-mastery they've mastered the desire to levitate or turn transparent. I almost wish I'd read your book, professor, instead of just editing it. Maybe you're smarter than I thought —"

He turned brick red and gritted out: "Your insults merely bore me, Norris."

The highway took a turn and we turned with it. I braked again and rubbed my eyes. "Do you see them?" I asked the professor.

"Yes," he said matter-of-factly. "This must be the retinue of the Duchess of Carbondale."

They were a dozen men shoulder to shoulder barricading the road. They were armed with miscellaneous sporting rifles and one bazooka. They wore kilt-like garments and what seemed to be bracelets from a five-and-ten. When we stopped they opened up the center of the line and the Duchess of Carbondale drove through in her chariot only the chariot was a harness-racing sulky and she didn't drive it; the horse was led by a skinny teenage girl got up as Charmian for a high-school production of Antony and Cleopatra. The Duchess herself wore ample white robes, a tiara and junk jewelry. She looked like your unfavorite aunt, the fat one, or a grade-school teacher you remember with loathing when you're forty, or one of those women who ring your doorbell and try to bully you into signing petitions against fluoridation or atheism in the public schools.

The bazooka man had his stovepipe trained on our hood. His finger was on the button and he was waiting for the Duchess to nod. "Get out," I told the professor, grabbing my briefcase. He looked at the bazooka and we got out.

"Hail, O mortals," said the Duchess.

I looked helplessly at the professor. Not even my extensive experience with lady novelists had equipped me to deal with the situation. He, however, was able to take the ball. He was a European and he had status and that's the starting point for them: establish status and then conduct yourself accordingly. He said: "Madame, my name is Konrad Leuten. I am a doctor of philosophy of the University of Gottingen and a member of the faculty of the University of Basle. Whom have I the honor to address?"

Her eyes narrowed appraisingly. "O mortal," she said, and her voice was less windily dramatic, "know ye that here in the New Lemuria worldly titles are as naught. And know ye not that the pure hearts of my subjects may not be sullied by base machinery?"

"I didn't know, madame," Leuten said politely. "I apologize. We intended, however, to go only as far as La Plume. May we have your permission to do so?"

At the mention of La Plume she went poker-faced. After a moment she waved at the bazooka man. "Destroy, O Phraxanartes, the base machine of the strangers," she said. Phraxanartes touched the button of his stovepipe. Leuten and I jumped for the ditch, my hand welded to the briefcase handle, when the rocket whooshed into the poor old Ford's motor. We huddled there while the gas tank boomed and cans and bottles exploded. The noise subsided to a crackling roar and the whizzing fragments stopped coming our way after maybe a minute. I put my head up first. The Duchess and her retinue were gone, presumably melted into the roadside stand of trees.

Her windy contralto blasted out: "Arise, O strangers, and join us."

Leuten said from the ditch: "A perfectly reasonable request, Norris. Let us do so. After all, one must be obliging."

"And gracious," I added.

Good old Duchess! I thought. Good old Leuten! Wonderful old-world, with hills and trees and bunnies and kittens and considerate people . . .

Leuten was standing on one foot, thumbing his nose, sticking out his tongue, screaming: "Norris! Norris! Defend yourself!" He was slapping my face with his free hand. Sluggishly I went into the posture of defense, thinking: Such nonsense. Defense against what? But I wouldn't hurt old Leuten's feelings for the world.

Adrenalin boiled through my veins, triggered by the posture. Spiders. Crawling, hairy, horrid spiders with purple, venom-dripping fangs. They hid in your shoes and bit you and your feet swelled with the poison. Their sticky, loathsome webs brushed across your face when you walked in the dark and they came scuttling silently, champing their jaws, winking their evil gemlike eyes. Spiders!

The voice of the Duchess blared impatiently: "I said, join us, O strangers. Well, what are you waiting for?"

The professor and I relaxed and looked at each other. "She's mad," the professor said softly. "From an asylum."

"I doubt it. You don't know America very well. Maybe you lock them up when they get like that in Europe; over here we elect them chairlady of the Library Fund Drive. If we don't, we never hear the end of it."

The costumed girl was leading the Duchess's sulky onto the road again. Some of her retinue were beginning to follow; she waved them back and dismissed the girl curtly. We skirted the heat of the burning car and approached her. It was that or try to outrun a volley from the miscellaneous sporting rifles.

"O strangers," she said, "you mentioned La Plume. Do you happen to be acquainted with my dear friend Phoebe Bancroft?"

The professor nodded before I could stop him. But almost simultaneously with his nod I was dragging the Duchess from her improvised chariot. It was very unpleasant, but I put my hands around her throat and knelt on her. It meant letting go of the briefcase but it was worth it.

She guggled and floundered and managed to whoop: "Don't shoot! I take it back, don't shoot them. Pamphilius, don't shoot, you might hit me!"

"Send 'em away," I told her.

"Never!" she blared. "They are my loyal retainers."

"You try, Professor," I said.

I believe what he put on then was his classroom manner. He stiffened and swelled and rasped toward the shrubbery: "Come out at once. All of you."

They came out, shambling and puzzled. They realized that something was very wrong. There was the Duchess on the ground and she wasn't telling them what to do the way she'd been telling them for weeks now. They wanted to oblige her in any little way they could, like shooting strangers, or scrounging canned food for her, but how could they oblige her while she lay there, slowly turning purple? It was very confusing. Luckily there was somebody else to oblige, the professor.

"Go away," he barked at them. "Go far away. We do not need you any more. And throw away your guns."

Well, that was something a body could understand. They smiled and threw away their guns and went away in their obliging and considerate fashion.

I eased up on the Duchess's throat. "What was that guff about the New Lemuria?" I asked her.

"You're a rude and ignorant young man," she snapped. From the corner of my eye I could see the professor involuntarily nodding agreement. "Every educated person knows that the lost wisdom of Lemuria was to be revived in the person of a beautiful priestess this year. According to the science of pyramidology —"

Beautiful priestess? Oh.

The professor and I stood by while she spouted an amazing compost of lost-continentism, the Ten Tribes, anti fluoridation, vegetarianism, homeopathic medicine, organic farming, astrology, flying saucers, and the prose poem of Kahlil Gibran.

The professor said dubiously at last: "I suppose one must call her a sort of Cultural Diffusionist. . . ." He was happier when he had her classified. He went on: "I think you know Miss Phoebe Bancroft. We wish you to present us to her as soon as possible."

"Professor," I complained, "we have a road map and we can find La Plume. And once we've found La Plume I don't think it'll be very hard to find Miss Phoebe."

"I will be pleased to accompany you," said the Duchess. "Though normally I frown on mechanical devices, I keep an automobile nearby in case of — well! Of all the rude!"

Believe it or not, she was speechless. Nothing in her rich store of gibberish and hate seemed to fit the situation. And fluoridation, organic farming, even Khalil Gibran were irrelevant in the face of us two each standing on one leg, thumbing our noses, and sticking out our tongues.

Undeniably the posture of defense was losing efficiency. It took longer to burn away the foolish glow. . . .

"Professor," I asked after we warily relaxed, "how many more of those can we take?"

He shrugged. "That is why a guide will be useful," he said. "Madame, I believe you mentioned an automobile."

"I know!" she said brightly. "It was asana yoga, wasn't it? Postures, I mean?"

The professor sucked an invisible lemon. "No, madame," he said cadaverously. "It was neither siddhasana nor padmasana. Yoga has been subsumed under Functional Epistemology, as has every other working philosophical system, Eastern and Western — but we waste time. The automobile?"

"You have to do that every so often, is that it?"

"We will leave it at that, madame. The automobile, please."

"Come right along," she said gaily. I didn't look on her face. Madam Chairlady was about to spring a parliamentary coup. But I got my briefcase and followed.

The car was in a nearby barn. It was a handsome new Lincoln, and I was reasonably certain that our fair cicerone had stolen it. But then, we had stolen the Ford.

I loaded the briefcase in and took the wheel over her objections and we headed for La Plume, a dozen miles away. On the road she yelped: "Oh, Functional Epistemology and you're Professor Leuten —"

"Yes, madame," he wearily agreed.

"I've read your book, of course. So has Miss Bancroft; shell be so pleased to see you."

"Then why, madame, did you order your subjects to murder us?"

"Well, Professor, of course I didn't know who you were then, and it was rather shocking, seeing somebody in a car. I, ah, had the feeling that you were up to no good, especially when you mentioned dear Miss Bancroft. She, you know, is really responsible for the re-emergence of the New Lemuria."

"Indeed?" said the professor. "You understand, then, about Leveled Personality Interflow?" He was beaming.

"I beg your pardon?"

"Leveled Personality Interflow!" he barked. "Chapter Nine!"

"Oh. In your book, of course. Well, as a matter of fact I skipped —"

"Another one," muttered the professor, leaning back.

The Duchess chattered on: "Dear Miss Bancroft, of course, swears by your book. But you were asking no, it wasn't what you said. I cast her horoscope and it turned out that she is the Twenty-seventh Pendragon!"

"Scheissdreck," the professor mumbled, too discouraged to translate.

"So naturally, Professor, she incarnates Taliesin spiritually and," a modest giggle, "you know who incarnates it materially. Which is only sensible, since I'm descended from the high priestesses of Mu. Little did I think when I was running the Wee Occult Book Shoppe in Carbondale!"

"Say," said the professor. He made an effort. "Madame, tell me something. Do you never feel a certain thing, a sense of friendliness and intoxication and good will enveloping you quite suddenly?"

"Oh, that," she said scornfully. "Yes; every now and then. It doesn't bother me. I just think of all the work I have to do. How I must stamp out the dreadful, soul-destroying advocates of meat eating, and chemical fertilizer, and fluoridation. How I must wage the good fight for occult science and crush the materialistic philosophers. How I must tear down our corrupt and self-seeking ministers and priests, our rotten laws and customs —"

"Lieber Gott," the professor marveled as she went on. "With Norris it is spiders. With me it is rats and asphyxiation. But with this woman it is apparently everything in the Kosmos except her own revolting self!" She didn't hear him; she was demanding that the voting age for women be lowered to sixteen and for men raised to thirty-five.

We plowed through flies and mosquitoes like smoke. The flies bred happily on dead cows and in sheep which unfortunately were still alive. There wasn't oil cake for the cows in the New Lemuria. There wasn't sheep-dip for the sheep. There weren't state and county and township and village road crews constantly patrolling, unplugging sluices, clearing gutters, replacing rusted culverts, and so quite naturally the countryside was reverting to swampland. The mosquitoes loved it.

"La Plume," the Duchess announced gaily. "And that's Miss Phoebe Bancroft's little house right there. Just why did you wish to see her, Professor, by the way?"

"To complete her re-education . . ." the professor said in a tired voice.

Miss Phoebe's house, and the few near it, were the only places we had seen in the Area which weren't blighted by neglect. Miss Phoebe, of course, was able to tell the shambling zombies what to do in the way of truck gardening, lawn mowing and maintenance. The bugs weren't too bad there.

"She's probably resting, poor dear," said the Duchess. I stopped the car and we got out. The Duchess said something about Kleenex and got in again and rummaged through the glove compartment.

"Please, Professor," I said, clutching my briefcase. "Play it the smart way. The way I told you."

"Norris," he said, "I realize that you have my best interests at heart. You're a good boy, Norris and I like you n —"

"Watch it!" I yelled, and swung into the posture of defense. So did he.

Spiders. It wasn't a good old world, not while there were loathsome spiders in it. Spiders.

And a bullet shot past my ear. The professor fell. I turned and saw the Duchess looking smug, about to shoot me too. I side-stepped and she missed; as I slapped the automatic out of her hand I thought confusedly that it was a near miracle, her hitting the professor at five paces even if he was a standing target. People don't realize how hard it is to hit anything with a hand gun.

I suppose I was going to kill her or at least damage her badly when a new element intruded. A little old white-baked lady tottering down the neat gravel path from the house. She wore a nice pastel dress which surprised me; somehow I had always though of her in black.

"Bertha!" Miss Phoebe, rapped out. "What have you done?"

The Duchess simpered. "That man there was going to harm you, Phoebe, dear. And this fellow is just as bad —"

Miss Phoebe said: "Nonsense. Nobody can harm me. Chapter Nine, Rule Seven. Bertha, I saw you shoot that gentleman. I'm very angry with you, Bertha. Very angry!"

The Duchess turned up her eyes and crumpled. I didn't have to check; I was sure she was dead. Miss Phoebe was once again in Utter Harmony with Her Environment.

I went over and knelt beside the professor. He had a hole in his stomach and was still breathing. There wasn't much blood. I sat down and cried. For the professor. For the poor damned human race which at a mile per day would be gobbled up into apathy and idiocy. Good-by, Newton and Einstein, good-by steak dinners and Michelangelo and Tenzing Norkay; good-by Moses, Rodin, Kwan Yin, transistors, Boole and Steichen . . .

A redheaded man with an Adam's apple was saying gently to Miss Phoebe: "It's this rabbit, ma'am." And indeed an enormous rabbit was loping up to him. "Every time I find a turnip or something he takes it away from me and he kicks and bites when I try to reason with him —" And indeed he took a piece of turnip from his pocket and the rabbit insolently pawed it from his hand and nibbled it triumphantly with one wise-guy eye cocked up at his victim. "He does that every time, Miss Phoebe," the man said unhappily.

The little old lady said: "I'll think of something, Henry. But let me take care of these people first."

"Yes, ma'am," Henry said. He reached out cautiously for his piece of turnip and the rabbit bit him and then went back to its nibbling.

"Young man," Miss Phoebe said to me, "what's wrong? You're giving in to despair. You musn't do that. Chapter Nine, Rule Three."

I pulled myself together enough to say: "This is Professor Leuten. He's dying."

Her eyes widened. "The Professor Leuten?" I nodded. "How to Live on the Cosmic Expense Account?" I nodded.

"Oh dear! If only there were something I could do!"

Heal the dying? Apparently not. She didn't think she could, so she couldn't.

"Professor," I said. "Professor."

He opened his eyes and said something in German, then, hazily:

"Woman shot me. Spoil her racket, you call it? Who is this?" He grimaced with pain.

"I'm Miss Phoebe Bancroft, Professor Leuten," she breathed, leaning over him. "I'm so dreadfully sorry; I admire your wonderful book so much."

His weary eyes turned to me. "So, Norris," he said. "No time to do it right. We do it your way. Help me up."

I helped him to his feet, suffering, I think, almost as much as he did. The wound started to bleed more copiously.

"No!" Miss Phoebe exclaimed. "You should lie down."

The professor leered. "Good idea, baby. You want to keep me company?"

"What's that?" she snapped.

"You heard me, baby. Say, you got any liquor in your place?"

"Certainly not! Alcohol is inimical to the development of the higher functions of the mind. Chapter Nine —"

"Pfui on Chapter Nine, baby. I chust wrote that stuff for money."

If Miss Phoebe hadn't been in a state resembling surgical shock after hearing that, she would have seen the pain convulsing his face. "You mean . . . ?" she quavered, beginning to look her age for the first time.

"Sure. Lotta garbage. Sling fancy words and make money. What I go for is liquor and women. Women like you, baby."

The goose did it.

Weeping, frightened, insulted and lost she tottered blindly up the neat path to her house. I eased the professor to the ground. He was biting almost through his lower lip.

I heard a new noise behind me. It was Henry, the redhead with the Adam's apple. He was chewing his piece of turnip and had hold of the big rabbit by the hind legs. He was flailing it against a tree. Henry looked ferocious, savage, carnivorous and very, very dangerous to meddle with. In a word, human.

"Professor," I breathed at his waxen face, "you've done it. It's broken. Over. No more Plague Area."

He muttered, his eyes closed: "I regret not doing it properly . . . but tell the people how I died, Norris. With dignity, without fear. Because of Functional Epistemology."

I said through tears: "I'll do more than tell them, Professor. The world will know about your heroism. The world *must* know. We've got to make a book of this your authentic, authorized, fictional biography and as Hopedale's west-coast agent I'll see to the film sale —"

"Film?" he said drowsily. "Book . . . ?"

"Yes. Your years of struggle, the little girl at home who kept faith in you when everybody scoffed, your burning mission to transform the world, and the climax here, now! as you give up your life for your philosophy."

"What girl?" he asked weakly.

"There must have been someone, Professor. We'll find someone."

"You would," he asked feebly, "document my expulsion from Germany by the Nazis?"

"Well, I don't think so, Professor. The export market's important, especially when it comes to selling film rights, and you don't want to go offending people by raking up old memories. But don't worry, Professor. The big thing is, the world will never forget you and what you've done."

He opened his eyes and breathed: "You mean your version of what I've done. Ach, Norris, Norris! Never did I think there was a power on Earth which could force me to contravene the Principle of Permissive Evolution." His voice became stronger. "But you, Norris, are that power." He got to his feet, grunting. "Norris," he said, "I hereby give you formal warning that any attempt to make a fictional biography or cinema film of my life will result in an immediate injunction being — you say slapped? — upon you, as well as suits for damages from libel, copyright infringement and invasion of privacy. I have had enough."

"Professor," I gasped. "You're well!"

He grimaced. "I'm sick. Profoundly sick to my stomach at my contravention of the Principle of Permissive —"

His voice grew fainter. This was because he was rising slowly into the air. He leveled off at a hundred feet and called: "Send the royalty statements to my old address in Basle. And remember, Norris, I warned you —"

He zoomed eastward then at perhaps one hundred miles per hour. I think he was picking up speed when he vanished from sight.

I stood there for ten minutes or so and sighed and rubbed my eyes and wondered whether anything was worth while. I decided I'd read the professor's book tomorrow without fail, unless something came up.

Then I took my briefcase and went up the walk and into Miss Phoebe's house. (Henry had made a twig fire on the lawn and was roasting his rabbit; he glared at me most disobligingly and I skirted him with care.)

This was, after all, the pay-off; this was, after all, the reason why I had risked my life and sanity.

"Miss Phoebe," I said to her taking it out of the briefcase, "I represent the Hopedale Press; this is one of our standard contracts. We're very much interested in publishing the story of your life, with special emphasis on the events of the past few weeks. Naturally you'd have an experienced collaborator. I believe sales in the hundred thousands wouldn't be too much to expect I would suggest as a title — that's right, you sign on that line there — How to be Supreme Ruler of Everybody . . ."

THE ADVENTURER

For every evil under the sun, there's an answer. It may be a simple, direct answer; it may be one that takes years, and seems unrelated to the problem. But there's an answer—of a kind. . . .

President Folsom XXIV said petulantly to his Secretary of the Treasury: "Blow me to hell, Bannister, if I understood a single word of that. *Why* can't I buy the Nicolaides Collection? And don't start with the rediscount and the Series W business again. Just tell me *why*."

The Secretary of the Treasury said with an air of apprehension and a thread-like feeling across his throat: "It boils down to—no money, Mr. President."

The President was too engrossed in thoughts of the marvelous collection to fly into a rage. "It's *such* a bargain," he said mournfully. "An archaic Henry Moore figure—really too big to finger, but I'm no culture-snob, thank God—and fifteen early Morrisons and I can't begin to tell you what else." He looked hopefully at the Secretary of Public Opinion: "Mightn't I seize it for the public good or something?"

The Secretary of Public Opinion shook his head. His pose was gruffly professional. "Not a chance, Mr. President. We'd never get away with it. The art-lovers would scream to high Heaven."

"I suppose so. . . . *Why* isn't there any money?" He had swiveled dangerously on the Secretary of the Treasury again.

"Sir, purchases of the new Series W bond issue have lagged badly because potential buyers have been attracted to—"

"Stop it, stop it, *stop* it! You know I can't make head or tail of that stuff. Where's the money *going*?"

The Director of the Budget said cautiously: "Mr. President, during the biennium just ending, the Department of Defense accounted for 78 per cent of expenditures—"

The Secretary of Defense growled: "Now wait a minute, Felder! We were voted—"

The President interrupted, raging weakly: "Oh, you rascals! My father would have known what to do with you! But don't think I can't handle it. *Don't* think you can hoodwink me." He punched a button ferociously; his silly face was contorted with rage and there was a certain tension on all the faces around the Cabinet table.

Panels slid down abruptly in the walls, revealing grim-faced Secret Servicemen. Each Cabinet officer was covered by at least two automatic rifles.

"Take that—that traitor away!" the President yelled. His finger pointed at the Secretary of Defense, who slumped over the table, sobbing. Two Secret Servicemen half-carried him from the room.

President Folsom XXIV leaned back, thrusting out his lower lip. He told the Secretary of the Treasury: "*Get* me the money for the Nicolaides Collection. Do you understand? I don't care how you do it. *Get* it." He glared at the Secretary of Public Opinion. "Have you any comments?"

"No, Mr. President."

"All right, then." The President unbent and said plaintively: "I don't see why you can't all be more reasonable. I'm a very reasonable man. I don't see why I can't have a few pleasures along with my responsibilities. Really I don't. And I'm sensitive. I don't *like* these scenes. Very well. That's all. The Cabinet meeting is adjourned."

They rose and left silently in the order of their seniority. The President noticed that the panels were still down and pushed the button that raised them again and hid the granite-faced Secret Servicemen. He took out of his pocket a late Morrison fingering-piece and turned it over in his hand, a smile of relaxation and bliss spreading over his face. *Such* amusing textural contrast! *Such* unexpected variations on the classic sequences!

The Cabinet, less the Secretary of Defense, was holding a rump meeting in an untapped corner of the White House gymnasium.

"God," the Secretary of State said, white-faced. "Poor old Willy!"

The professionally gruff Secretary of Public Opinion said: "We should murder the bastard. I don't care what happens—"

The Director of the Budget said dryly: "We all know what would happen. President Folsom XXV would take office. No; we've got to keep plugging as before. Nothing short of the invincible can topple the Republic. . . ."

"What about a war?" the Secretary of Commerce demanded fiercely. "We've no proof that our program will work. What about a war?"

State said wearily: "Not while there's a balance of power, my dear man. The Io-Callisto Question proved that. The Republic and the Soviet fell all over themselves trying to patch things up as soon as it seemed that there would be real shooting. Folsom XXIV and his excellency Premier Yersinsky know at least that much."

The Secretary of the Treasury said: "What would you all think of Steiner for Defense?"

The Director of the Budget was astonished. "Would he take it?"

Treasury cleared his throat. "As a matter of fact, I've asked him to stop by right about now." He hurled a medicine ball into the budgetary gut.

"Oof!" said the Director. "You bastard. Steiner would be perfect. He runs Standards like a watch." He treacherously fired the medicine ball at the Secretary of Raw Materials, who blandly caught it and slammed it back.

"Here he comes," said the Secretary of Raw Materials. "Steiner! Come and sweat some oleo off!"

Steiner ambled over, a squat man in his fifties, and said: "I don't mind if I do. Where's Willy?"

State said: "The President unmasked him as a traitor. He's probably been executed by now."

Steiner looked grim, and grimmer yet when the Secretary of the Treasury said, dead-pan: "We want to propose you for Defense."

"I'm happy in Standards," Steiner said. "Safer, too. The Man's father took an interest in science, but The Man never comes around. Things are very quiet. Why don't you invite Winch, from the National Art Commission? It wouldn't be much of a change for the worse for him."

"No brains," the Secretary for Raw Materials said briefly. "Heads up!"

Steiner caught the ball and slugged it back at him. "What good are brains?" he asked quietly.

"Close the ranks, gentlemen," State said. "These long shots are too hard on my arms."

The ranks closed and the Cabinet told Steiner what good were brains. He ended by accepting.

The Moon is all Republic. Mars is all Soviet. Titan is all Republic. Ganymede is all Soviet. But Io and Callisto, by the Treaty of Greenwich, are half-and-half Republic and Soviet.

Down the main street of the principal settlement on Io runs an invisible line. On one side of the line, the principal settlement is known as New Pittsburgh. On the other side it is known as Nizhni-Magnitogorsk.

Into a miner's home in New Pittsburgh one day an eight-year-old boy named Grayson staggered, bleeding from the head. His eyes were swollen almost shut.

His father lurched to his feet, knocking over a bottle. He looked stupidly at the bottle, set it upright too late to save much of the alcohol, and then stared fixedly at the boy. "See what you made me do, you little bastard?" he growled, and fetched the boy a clout on his bleeding head that sent him spinning against the wall of the hut. The boy got up slowly and silently—there seemed to be something wrong with his left arm—and glowered at his father.

He said nothing.

"Fighting again," the father said, in a would-be fierce voice. His eyes fell under the peculiar fire in the boy's stare. "Damn fool—"

A woman came in from the kitchen. She was tall and thin. In a flat voice she said to the man: "Get out of here." The man hiccupped and said: "Your brat spilled my bottle. Gimme a dollar."

In the same flat voice: "I have to buy food."

"*I said gimme a dollar!*" The man slapped her face—it did not change—and wrenched a small purse from the string that suspended it around her neck. The boy suddenly was a demon, flying at his father with fists and teeth. It lasted only a second or two. The father kicked him into a corner where he lay, still glaring, wordless and dry-eyed. The mother had not moved; her husband's handmark was still red on her face when he hulked out, clutching the money bag.

Mrs. Grayson at last crouched in the corner with the eight-year-old boy. "Little Tommy," she said softly. "My little Tommy! Did you cross the line again?"

He was blubbering in her arms, hysterically, as she caressed him. At last he was able to say: "I didn't cross the line, Mom. Not this time. It was in school. They said our name was really Krasinsky. God-damn him!" the boy shrieked. "They said his grandfather was named Krasinsky and he moved over the line and changed his name to Grayson! God-damn him! Doing that to us!"

"Now, darling," his mother said, caressing him. "Now, darling." His trembling began to ebb. She said: "Let's get out the spools, Tommy. You mustn't fall behind in school. You owe that to me, don't you, darling?"

"Yes, Mom," he said. He threw his spindly arms around her and kissed her. "Get out the spools. We'll show him. I mean them."

President Folsom XXIV lay on his death-bed, feeling no pain, mostly because his personal physician had pumped him full of morphine. Dr. Barnes sat by the bed holding the presidential wrist and waiting, occasionally nodding off and recovering with a belligerent stare around the room. The four wire-service men didn't care whether he fell asleep or not; they were worriedly discussing the nature and habits of the President's first-born, who would shortly succeed to the highest office in the

Republic.

"A firebrand, they tell me," the A.P. man said unhappily.

"Firebrands I don't mind," the U.P. man said. "He can send out all the inflammatory notes he wants just as long as he isn't a fiend for exercise. I'm not as young as I once was. You boys wouldn't remember the *old* President, Folsom XXII. He used to do point-to-point hiking. He worshipped old F.D.R."

The I.N.S. man said, lowering his voice: "Then he was worshipping the wrong Roosevelt. Teddy was the athlete."

Dr. Barnes started, dropped the presidential wrist and held a mirror to the mouth for a moment. "Gentlemen," he said, "the President is dead."

"Okay," the A.P. man said. "Let's go, boys. I'll send in the flash. U.P., you go cover the College of Electors. I.N.S., get onto the President Elect. Trib, collect some interviews and background—"

The door opened abruptly; a colonel of infantry was standing there, breathing hard, with an automatic rifle at port. "Is he dead?" he asked.

"Yes," the A.P. man said. "If you'll let me past—"

"Nobody leaves the room," the colonel said grimly. "I represent General Slocum, Acting President of the Republic. The College of Electors is acting now to ratify—"

A burst of gunfire caught the colonel in the back; he spun and fell, with a single hoarse cry. More gunfire sounded through the White House. A Secret Serviceman ducked his head through the door: "President's dead? You boys stay put. We'll have this thing cleaned up in an hour—" He vanished.

The doctor sputtered his alarm and the newsmen ignored him with professional poise. The A.P. man asked: "Now who's Slocum? Defense Command?"

I.N.S. said: "I remember him. Three stars. He headed up the Tactical Airborne Force out in Kansas four-five years ago. I think he was retired since then."

A phosphorus grenade crashed through the window and exploded with a globe of yellow flame the size of a basketball; dense clouds of phosphorus pentoxide gushed from it and the sprinkler system switched on, drenching the room.

"Come on!" hacked the A.P. man, and they scrambled from the room and slammed the door. The doctor's coat was burning in two or three places, and he was retching feebly on the corridor floor. They tore his coat off and flung it back into the room.

The U.P. man, swearing horribly, dug a sizzling bit of phosphorus from the back of his hand with a pen-knife and collapsed, sweating, when it was out. The I.N.S. man passed him a flask and he gurgled down half a pint of liquor. "Who flang that brick?" he asked faintly.

"Nobody," the A.P. man said gloomily. "That's the hell of it. None of this is happening. Just the way Taft the Pretender never happened in '03. Just the way the Pentagon Mutiny never happened in '67."

"'68," the U.P. man said faintly. "It didn't happen in '68, not '67."

The A.P. man smashed a fist into the palm of his hand and swore. "*God*-damn," he said. "Some day I'd like to—" He broke off and was bitterly silent.

The U.P. man must have been a little dislocated with shock and quite drunk to talk the way he did. "Me too," he said. "Like to tell the story. Maybe it was '67 not '68. I'm not sure now. Can't write it down so the details get lost and then after a while it didn't happen at all. Revolution'd be good deal. But it takes people t' make revolution. *People*. With eyes 'n ears. 'N memories. We make things not-happen an' we make people not-see an' not-hear. . . ." He slumped back against the corridor wall, nursing his burned hand. The others were watching him, very scared.

Then the A.P. man caught sight of the Secretary of Defense striding down the corridor, flanked by Secret Servicemen. "Mr. Steiner!" he called. "What's the picture?"

Steiner stopped, breathing heavily, and said: "Slocum's barricaded in the Oval Study. They don't want to smash in. He's about the only one left. There were only fifty or so. The Acting President's taken charge at the Study. You want to come along?"

They did, and even hauled the U.P. man after them.

The Acting President, who would be President Folsom XXV as soon as the Electoral College got around to it, had his father's face—the petulant lip, the soft jowl—on a hard young body. He also had an auto-rifle ready to fire from the hip. Most of the Cabinet was present. When the Secretary of Defense arrived, he turned on him. "Steiner," he said nastily, "can you explain why there should be a rebellion against the Republic in your department?"

"Mr. President," Steiner said, "Slocum was retired on my recommendation two years ago. It seems to me that my responsibility ended there and Security should have taken over."

The President Elect's finger left the trigger of the auto-rifle and his lip drew in a little. "Quite so," he said curtly, and, turned to the door. "Slocum!" he shouted. "Come out of there. We can use gas if we want."

The door opened unexpectedly and a tired-looking man with three stars on each shoulder stood there, bare-handed. "All right," he said drearily. "I was fool enough to think something could be done about the regime. But you fat-faced imbeciles are going to go on and on and—"

The stutter of the auto-rifle cut him off. The President Elect's knuckles were white as he clutched the piece's forearm and grip; the torrent of slugs continued to hack and plow the general's body until the magazine was empty. "Burn that," he said curtly, turning his back on it. "Dr. Barnes, come here. I want to know about my father's passing."

The doctor, hoarse and red-eyed from the whiff of phosphorus smoke, spoke with him. The U.P. man had sagged drunkenly into a chair, but the other newsmen noted that Dr. Barnes glanced at them as he spoke, in a confidential murmur.

"Thank you, Doctor," the President Elect said at last, decisively. He gestured to a Secret Serviceman. "Take those traitors away." They went, numbly.

The Secretary of State cleared his throat. "Mr. President," he said, "I take this opportunity to submit the resignations of myself and fellow Cabinet members according to custom."

"That's all right," the President Elect said. "You may as well stay on. I intend to run things myself anyway." He hefted the auto-rifle. "You," he said to the Secretary of Public Opinion. "You have some work to do. Have the memory of my father's—artistic—preoccupations obliterated as soon as possible. I wish the Republic to assume a war-like posture—yes; what is it?"

A trembling messenger said: "Mr. President, I have the honor to inform you that the College of Electors has elected you President of the Republic—unanimously."

Cadet Fourth-Classman Thomas Grayson lay on his bunk and sobbed in an agony of loneliness. The letter from his mother was crumpled in his hand: "—prouder than words can tell of your appointment to the Academy. Darling, I hardly knew my grandfather but I know that you will serve as brilliantly as he did, to the eternal credit of the Republic. You must be brave and strong for my sake—"

He would have given everything he had or ever could hope to have to be back with her, and away from the bullying, sneering fellow-cadets of the Corps. He kissed the letter—and then hastily shoved it under his mattress as he heard footsteps.

He popped to a brace, but it was only his roommate Ferguson. Ferguson was from Earth, and rejoiced in the lighter Lunar gravity which was punishment to Grayson's Io-bred muscles.

"Rest, mister," Ferguson grinned.

"Thought it was night inspection."

"Any minute now. They're down the hall. Lemme tighten your bunk or you'll be in trouble—" Tightening the bunk he pulled out the letter and said, calvishly: "Ah-*hah*! Who is she?—" and opened it.

When the cadet officers reached the room they found Ferguson on the floor being strangled black in the face by spidery little Grayson. It took all three of them to pull him off. Ferguson went to the infirmary and Grayson went to the Commandant's office.

The Commandant glared at the cadet from under the most spectacular pair of eyebrows in the Service. "Cadet Grayson," he said, "explain what occurred."

"Sir, Cadet Ferguson began to read a letter from my mother without my permission."

"That is not accepted by the Corps as grounds for mayhem. Do you have anything further to say?"

"Sir, I lost my temper. All I thought of was that it was an act of disrespect to my mother and somehow to the Corps and the Republic too—that Cadet Ferguson was dishonoring the Corps."

Bushwah, the Commandant thought. *A snow job and a crude one.* He studied the youngster. He had never seen such a brace from an Io-bred fourth-classman. It must be torture to muscles not yet toughened up to even Lunar gravity. Five minutes more and the boy would have to give way, and serve him right for showing off.

He studied Grayson's folder. It was too early to tell about academic work, but the fourth-classman was a bear—or a fool—for extra duty. He had gone out for half a dozen teams and applied for membership in the exacting Math Club *and* Writing Club. The Commandant glanced up; Grayson was still in his extreme brace. The Commandant suddenly had the queer idea that Grayson could hold it until it killed him.

"One hundred hours of pack-drill," he barked, "to be completed before quarter-term. Cadet Grayson, if you succeed in walking off your tours, remember that there is a tradition of fellowship in the Corps which its members are expected to observe. Dismiss."

After Grayson's steel-sharp salute and exit the Commandant dug deeper into the folder. Apparently there was something wrong with the boy's left arm, but it had been passed by the examining team that visited

Io. Most unusual. Most irregular. But nothing could be done about it now.

The President, softer now in body than on his election day, and infinitely more cautious, snapped: "It's all very well to create an incident. But where's the money to come from? Who wants the rest of Io anyway? And what will happen if there's war?"

Treasury said: "The hoarders will supply the money, Mr. President. A system of percentage-bounties for persons who report currency-hoarders, and then enforced purchase of a bond issue."

Raw materials said: "We need that iron, Mr. President. We need it desperately."

State said: "All our evaluations indicate that the Soviet Premier would consider nothing less than armed invasion of his continental borders as occasion for all-out war. The consumer-goods party in the Soviet has gained immensely during the past five years and of course their armaments have suffered. Your shrewd directive to put the Republic in a war-like posture has borne fruit, Mr. President. . . ."

President Folsom XXV studied them narrowly. To him the need for a border incident culminating in a forced purchase of Soviet Io did not seem as pressing as they thought, but they were, after all, specialists. And there was no conceivable way they could benefit from it personally. The only alternative was that they were offering their professional advice and that it would be best to heed it. Still, there was a vague, nagging something. . . .

Nonsense, he decided. The spy dossiers on his Cabinet showed nothing but the usual. One had been blackmailed by an actress after an affair and railroaded her off the Earth. Another had a habit of taking bribes to advance favorite sons in civil and military service. And so on. The Republic could not suffer at their hands; the Republic and the dynasty were impregnable. You simply spied on everybody—including the spies—and ordered summary executions often enough to show that you meant it, and kept the public ignorant: deaf-dumb-blind ignorant. The spy system was simplicity itself; you had only to let things get as tangled and confused as possible until *nobody* knew who was who. The executions were literally no problem, for guilt or innocence made no matter. And mind-control when there were four newspapers, six magazines and three radio and television stations was a job for a handful of clerks.

No; the Cabinet couldn't be getting away with anything. The system was unbeatable.

President Folsom XXV said: "Very well. Have it done."

Mrs. Grayson, widow, of New Pittsburgh, Io, disappeared one night. It was in all the papers and on all the broadcasts. Some time later she was found dragging herself back across the line between Nizhni-Magnitogorsk and New Pittsburgh in sorry shape. She had a terrible tale to tell about what she had suffered at the hands and so forth of the Nizhni-Magnitogorskniks. A diplomatic note from the Republic to the Soviet was answered by another note which was answered by the dispatch of the Republic's First Fleet to Io which was answered by the dispatch of the Soviet's First and Fifth Fleets to Io.

The Republic's First Fleet blew up the customary deserted target hulk, fulminated over a sneak sabotage attack and moved in its destroyers. Battle was joined.

Ensign Thomas Grayson took over the command of his destroyer when its captain was killed on his bridge. An electrified crew saw the strange, brooding youngster perform prodigies of skill and courage, and responded to them. In one week of desultory action the battered destroyer had accounted for seven Soviet destroyers and a cruiser.

As soon as this penetrated to the flagship, Grayson was decorated and given a flotilla. His weird magnetism extended to every officer and man aboard the seven craft. They struck like phantoms, cutting out cruisers and battlewagons in wild unorthodox actions that couldn't have succeeded but did—every time. Grayson was badly wounded twice, but his driving nervous energy carried him through.

He was decorated again and given the battlewagon of an ailing four-striper.

Without orders he touched down on the Soviet side of Io, led out a landing party of marines and bluejackets, cut through two regiments of Soviet infantry, and returned to his battlewagon with prisoners: the top civil and military administrators of Soviet Io.

They discussed him nervously aboard the flagship.

"He has a mystical quality, Admiral. His men would follow him into an atomic furnace. And—and I almost believe he could bring them through safely if he wanted to." The laugh was nervous.

"He doesn't look like much. But when he turns on the charm—watch out!"

"He's—he's a *winner*. Now I wonder what I mean by that?"

"I know what you mean. They turn up every so often. People who can't be stopped. People who have everything. Napoleons. Alexanders.

Stalins. Up from nowhere."

"Suleiman. Hitler. Folsom I. Jenghis Khan."

"Well, let's get it over with."

They tugged at their gold-braided jackets and signalled the honor guard.

Grayson was piped aboard, received another decoration and another speech. This time he made a speech in return.

President Folsom XXV, not knowing what else to do, had summoned his cabinet. "Well?" he rasped at the Secretary of Defense.

Steiner said with a faint shrug: "Mr. President, there is nothing to be done. He has the fleet, he has the broadcasting facilities, he has the people."

"People!" snarled the President. His finger stabbed at a button and the wall panels snapped down to show the Secret Servicemen standing in their niches. The finger shot tremulously out at Steiner. "Kill that traitor!" he raved.

The chief of the detail said uneasily: "Mr. President, we were listening to Grayson before we came on duty. He says he's de facto President now—"

"Kill him! Kill him!"

The chief went doggedly on: "—and we liked what he had to say about the Republic and he said citizens of the Republic shouldn't take orders from you and he'd relieve you—"

The President fell back.

Grayson walked in, wearing his plain ensign's uniform and smiling faintly. Admirals and four-stripers flanked him.

The chief of the detail said: "Mr. Grayson! Are you taking over?"

The man in the ensign's uniform said gravely: "Yes. And just call me 'Grayson,' please. The titles come later. You can go now."

The chief gave a pleased grin and collected his detail. The rather slight, youngish man who had something wrong with one arm was in charge—*complete* charge.

Grayson said: "Mr. Folsom, you are relieved of the presidency. Captain, take him out and—" He finished with a whimsical shrug. A portly four-striper took Folsom by one arm. Like a drugged man the deposed president let himself be led out.

Grayson looked around the table. "Who are you gentlemen?"

They felt his magnetism, like the hum when you pass a power station.

Steiner was the spokesman. "Grayson," he said soberly, "we were Folsom's Cabinet. However, there is more that we have to tell you. Alone, if you will allow it."

"Very well, gentlemen." Admirals and captains backed out, looking concerned.

Steiner said: "Grayson, the story goes back many years. My predecessor, William Malvern, determined to overthrow the regime, holding that it was an affront to the human spirit. There have been many such attempts. All have broken up on the rocks of espionage, terrorism and opinion-control—the three weapons which the regime holds firmly in its hands.

"Malvern tried another approach than espionage versus espionage, terrorism versus terrorism and opinion-control versus opinion-control. He determined to use the basic fact that certain men make history: that there are men born to be mould-breakers. They are the Phillips of Macedon, the Napoleons, Stalins and Hitlers, the Suleimans—the adventurers. Again and again they flash across history, bringing down an ancient empire, turning ordinary soldiers of the line into unkillable demons of battle, uprooting cultures, breathing new life into moribund peoples.

"There are common denominators among all the adventurers. Intelligence, of course. Other things are more mysterious but are always present. They are foreigners. Napoleon the Corsican. Hitler the Austrian. Stalin the Georgian. Phillip the Macedonian. Always there is an Oedipus complex. Always there is physical deficiency. Napoleon's stature. Stalin's withered arm—and yours. Always there is a minority disability, real or fancied.

"This is a shock to you, Grayson, but you must face it. *You were manufactured.*

"Malvern packed the cabinet with the slyest double-dealers he could find and they went to work. Eighty-six infants were planted on the outposts of the Republic in simulated family environments. Your mother was not your mother but one of the most brilliant actresses ever to drop out of sight on Earth. Your intelligence-heredity was so good that we couldn't turn you down for lack of a physical deficiency. We withered your arm with gamma radiation. I hope you will forgive us. There was no other way.

"Of the eighty-six you are the one that worked. Somehow the combination for you was minutely different from all the other combinations, genetically or environmentally, and it worked. That is all we were after.

The mould has been broken, you know now what you are. Let come whatever chaos is to come; the dead hand of the past no longer lies on—"

Grayson went to the door and beckoned; two captains came in. Steiner broke off his speech as Grayson said to them: "These men deny my godhood. Take them out and—" he finished with a whimsical shrug.

"Yes, your divinity," said the captains, without a trace of humor in their voices.

THE ALTAR AT MIDNIGHT

He had quite a rum-blossom on him for a kid, I thought at first. But when he moved closer to the light by the cash register to ask the bartender for a match or something, I saw it wasn't that. Not just the nose. Broken veins on his cheeks, too, and the funny eyes. He must have seen me look, because he slid back away from the light.

The bartender shook my bottle of ale in front of me like a Swiss bell-ringer so it foamed inside the green glass.

"You ready for another, sir?" he asked.

I shook my head. Down the bar, he tried it on the kid—he was drinking scotch and water or something like that—and found out he could push him around. He sold him three scotch and waters in ten minutes.

When he tried for number four, the kid had his courage up and said, "I'll tell *you* when I'm ready for another, Jack." But there wasn't any trouble.

It was almost nine and the place began to fill up. The manager, a real hood type, stationed himself by the door to screen out the high-school kids and give the big hello to conventioneers. The girls came hurrying in, too, with their little makeup cases and their fancy hair piled up and their frozen faces with the perfect mouths drawn on them. One of them stopped to say something to the manager, some excuse about something, and he said: "That's aw ri'; get inna dressing room."

A three-piece band behind the drapes at the back of the stage began to make warm-up noises and there were two bartenders keeping busy. Mostly it was beer—a midweek crowd. I finished my ale and had to wait a couple of minutes before I could get another bottle. The bar filled up from the end near the stage because all the customers wanted a good, close look at the strippers for their fifty-cent bottles of beer. But I noticed that nobody sat down next to the kid, or, if anybody did, he didn't stay long—you go out for some fun and the bartender pushes you around and nobody wants to sit next to you. I picked up my bottle and glass and went down on the stool to his left.

He turned to me right away and said: "What kind of a place is this, anyway?" The broken veins were all over his face, little ones, but so many, so close, that they made his face look something like marbled rubber. The funny look in his eyes was it—the trick contact lenses. But I tried not to stare and not to look away.

"It's okay," I said. "It's a good show if you don't mind a lot of noise from—"

He stuck a cigarette into his mouth and poked the pack at me. "I'm a spacer," he said, interrupting.

I took one of his cigarettes and said: "Oh."

He snapped a lighter for the cigarettes and said: "Venus."

I was noticing that his pack of cigarettes on the bar had some kind of yellow sticker instead of the blue tax stamp.

"Ain't that a crock?" he asked. "You can't smoke and they give you lighters for a souvenir. But it's a good lighter. On Mars last week, they gave us all some cheap pen-and-pencil sets."

"You get something every trip, hah?" I took a good, long drink of ale and he finished his scotch and water.

"Shoot. You call a trip a 'shoot.'"

One of the girls was working her way down the bar. She was going to slide onto the empty stool at his right and give him the business, but she looked at him first and decided not to. She curled around me and asked if I'd buy her a li'l ole drink. I said no and she moved on to the next. I could kind of feel the young fellow quivering. When I looked at him, he stood up. I followed him out of the dump. The manager grinned without thinking and said, "G'night, boys," to us.

The kid stopped in the street and said to me: "You don't have to follow me around, Pappy." He sounded like one wrong word and I would get socked in the teeth.

"Take it easy. I know a place where they won't spit in your eye."

He pulled himself together and made a joke of it. "This I have to see," he said. "Near here?"

"A few blocks."

We started walking. It was a nice night.

"I don't know this city at all," he said. "I'm from Covington, Kentucky. You do your drinking at home there. We don't have places like this." He meant the whole Skid Row area.

"It's not so bad," I said. "I spend a lot of time here."

"Is that a fact? I mean, down home a man your age would likely have a wife and children."

"I do. The hell with them."

He laughed like a real youngster and I figured he couldn't even be twenty-five. He didn't have any trouble with the broken curbstones in spite of his scotch and waters. I asked him about it.

"Sense of balance," he said. "You have to be tops for balance to be a spacer—you spend so much time outside in a suit. People don't know how much. Punctures. And you aren't worth a damn if you lose your point."

"What's that mean?"

"Oh. Well, it's hard to describe. When you're outside and you lose your point, it means you're all mixed up, you don't know which way the can—that's the ship—which way the can is. It's having all that room around you. But if you have a good balance, you feel a little tugging to the ship, or maybe you just *know* which way the ship is without feeling it. Then you have your point and you can get the work done."

"There must be a lot that's hard to describe."

He thought that might be a crack and he clammed up on me.

"You call this Gandytown," I said after a while. "It's where the stove-up old railroad men hang out. This is the place."

It was the second week of the month, before everybody's pension check was all gone. Oswiak's was jumping. The Grandsons of the Pioneers were on the juke singing the *Man from Mars Yodel* and old Paddy Shea was jigging in the middle of the floor. He had a full seidel of beer in his right hand and his empty left sleeve was flapping.

The kid balked at the screen door. "Too damn bright," he said.

I shrugged and went on in and he followed. We sat down at a table. At Oswiak's you can drink at the bar if you want to, but none of the regulars do.

Paddy jigged over and said: "Welcome home, Doc." He's a Liverpool Irishman; they talk like Scots, some say, but they sound almost like Brooklyn to me.

"Hello, Paddy. I brought somebody uglier than you. Now what do you say?"

Paddy jigged around the kid in a half-circle with his sleeve flapping and then flopped into a chair when the record stopped. He took a big drink from the seidel and said: "Can he do this?" Paddy stretched his face into an awful grin that showed his teeth. He has three of them. The kid laughed and asked me: "What the hell did you drag me into here for?"

"Paddy says he'll buy drinks for the house the day anybody uglier than he is comes in."

Oswiak's wife waddled over for the order and the kid asked us what we'd have. I figured I could start drinking, so it was three double scotches.

After the second round, Paddy started blowing about how they took his arm off without any anesthetics except a bottle of gin because the red-ball freight he was tangled up in couldn't wait.

That brought some of the other old gimps over to the table with their stories.

Blackie Bauer had been sitting in a boxcar with his legs sticking through the door when the train started with a jerk. Wham, the door closed. Everybody laughed at Blackie for being that dumb in the first place, and he got mad.

Sam Fireman has palsy. This week he was claiming he used to be a watchmaker before he began to shake. The week before, he'd said he was a brain surgeon. A woman I didn't know, a real old Boxcar Bertha, dragged herself over and began some kind of story about how her sister married a Greek, but she passed out before we found out what happened.

Somebody wanted to know what was wrong with the kid's face—Bauer, I think it was, after he came back to the table.

"Compression and decompression," the kid said. "You're all the time climbing into your suit and out of your suit. Inboard air's thin to start with. You get a few redlines—that's these ruptured blood vessels—and you say the hell with the money; all you'll make is just one more trip. But, God, it's a lot of money for anybody my age! You keep saying that until you can't be anything but a spacer. The eyes are hard-radiation scars."

"You like dot all ofer?" asked Oswiak's wife politely.

"All over, ma'am," the kid told her in a miserable voice. "But I'm going to quit before I get a Bowman Head."

"I don't care," said Maggie Rorty. "I think he's cute."

"Compared with—" Paddy began, but I kicked him under the table.

* * * *

We sang for a while, and then we told gags and recited limericks for a while, and I noticed that the kid and Maggie had wandered into the back room—the one with the latch on the door.

Oswiak's wife asked me, very puzzled: "Doc, w'y dey do dot flyink by planyets?"

"It's the damn govermint," Sam Fireman said.

"Why not?" I said. "They got the Bowman Drive, why the hell shouldn't they use it? Serves 'em right." I had a double scotch and added: "Twenty years of it and they found out a few things they didn't know. Redlines are only one of them. Twenty years more, maybe they'll find out a few more things they didn't know. Maybe by the time there's a bathtub in every American home and an alcoholism clinic in every American town, they'll find out a whole *lot* of things they didn't know. And every American boy will be a pop-eyed, blood-riddled wreck, like our friend here, from riding the Bowman Drive."

"It's the damn govermint," Sam Fireman repeated.

"And what the hell did you mean by that remark about alcoholism?" Paddy said, real sore. "Personally, I can take it or leave it alone."

So we got to talking about that and everybody there turned out to be people who could take it or leave it alone.

It was maybe midnight when the kid showed at the table again, looking kind of dazed. I was drunker than I ought to be by midnight, so I said I was going for a walk. He tagged along and we wound up on a bench at Screwball Square. The soap-boxers were still going strong. Like I said, it was a nice night. After a while, a potbellied old auntie who didn't give a damn about the face sat down and tried to talk the kid into going to see some etchings. The kid didn't get it and I led him over to hear the soap-boxers before there was trouble.

One of the orators was a mush-mouthed evangelist. "And, oh, my friends," he said, "when I looked through the porthole of the spaceship and beheld the wonder of the Firmament—"

"You're a stinkin' Yankee liar!" the kid yelled at him. "You say one damn more word about can-shootin' and I'll ram your spaceship down your lyin' throat! Wheah's your redlines if you're such a hot spacer?"

The crowd didn't know what he was talking about, but "wheah's your redlines" sounded good to them, so they heckled mush-mouth off his box with it.

I got the kid to a bench. The liquor was working in him all of a sudden. He simmered down after a while and asked: "Doc, should I've given Miz Rorty some money? I asked her afterward and she said she'd admire to have something to remember me by, so I gave her my lighter. She seem' to be real pleased with it. But I was wondering if maybe I embarrassed her by asking her right out. Like I tol' you, back in Covington, Kentucky, we don't have places like that. Or maybe we did and I just didn't know about them. But what do you think I should've done about Miz Rorty?"

"Just what you did," I told him. "If they want money, they ask you for it first. Where you staying?"

"Y.M.C.A.," he said, almost asleep. "Back in Covington, Kentucky,

I was a member of the Y and I kept up my membership. They have to let me in because I'm a member. Spacers have all kinds of trouble, Doc. Woman trouble. Hotel trouble. Fam'ly trouble. Religious trouble. I was raised a Southern Baptist, but wheah's Heaven, anyway? I ask' Doctor Chitwood las' time home before the redlines got so thick—Doc, you aren't a minister of the Gospel, are you? I hope I di'n' say anything to offend you."

"No offense, son," I said. "No offense."

I walked him to the avenue and waited for a fleet cab. It was almost five minutes. The independents that roll drunks dent the fenders of fleet cabs if they show up in Skid Row and then the fleet drivers have to make reports on their own time to the company. It keeps them away. But I got one and dumped the kid in.

"The Y Hotel," I told the driver. "Here's five. Help him in when you get there."

When I walked through Screwball Square again, some college kids were yelling "wheah's your redlines" at old Charlie, the last of the Wobblies.

Old Charlie kept roaring: "The hell with your breadlines! I'm talking about atomic bombs. *Right—up—there!*" And he pointed at the Moon.

It was a nice night, but the liquor was dying in me.

There was a joint around the corner, so I went in and had a drink to carry me to the club; I had a bottle there. I got into the first cab that came.

"Athletic Club," I said.

"Inna dawghouse, harh?" the driver said, and he gave me a big personality smile.

I didn't say anything and he started the car.

He was right, of course. I was in everybody's doghouse. Some day I'd scare the hell out of Tom and Lise by going home and showing them what their daddy looked like.

Down at the Institute, I was in the doghouse.

"Oh, dear," everybody at the Institute said to everybody, "I'm sure I don't know what ails the man. A lovely wife and two lovely grown children and she had to tell him 'either you go or I go.' And *drinking*! And this is rather subtle, but it's a well-known fact that neurotics seek out low company to compensate for their guilt-feelings. The *places* he frequents. Doctor Francis Bowman, the man who made space-flight a reality. The man who put the Bomb Base on the Moon! Really, I'm sure I don't know what ails him."

The hell with them all.

THE MARCHING MORONS

Some things had not changed. A potter's wheel was still a potter's wheel and clay was still clay. Efim Hawkins had built his shop near Goose Lake, which had a narrow band of good fat clay and a narrow beach of white sand. He fired three bottle-nosed kilns with willow charcoal from the wood lot. The wood lot was also useful for long walks while the kilns were cooling; if he let himself stay within sight of them, he would open them prematurely, impatient to see how some new shape or glaze had come through the fire, and — ping! — the new shape or glaze would be good for nothing but the shard pile back of his slip tanks.

A business conference was in full swing in his shop, a modest cube of brick, tile-roofed, as the Chicago-Los Angeles "rocket" thundered over-head — very noisy, very swept back, very fiery jets, shaped as sleekly swift-looking as an airborne barracuda. The buyer from Marshall Fields was turning over a black-glazed one-liter carafe, nodding approval with his massive, handsome head. "This is real pretty," he told Hawkins and his own secretary, Gomez-Laplace. "This has got lots of what ya call real est'etic principles. Yeah, it is real pretty."

"How much?" the secretary asked the potter.

"Seven-fifty in dozen lots," said Hawkins. "I ran up fifteen dozen last month."

"They are real est'etic," repeated the buyer from Fields. "I will take them all."

"I don't think we can do that, doctor," said the secretary. "They'd cost us $1,350. That would leave only $532 in our quarter's budget. And we still have to run down to East Liverpool to pick up some cheap dinner sets."

"Dinner sets?" asked the buyer, his big face full of wonder.

"Dinner sets. The department's been out of them for two months now. Mr. Garvy-Seabright got pretty nasty about it yesterday. Remember?"

"Garvy-Seabright, that meat-headed bluenose," the buyer said contemptuously. "He don't know nothin' about est'etics. Why for don't he lemme run my own department?" His eye fell on a stray copy of Whambozambo Comix and he sat down with it. An occasional deep chuckle or grunt of surprise escaped him as he turned the pages.

Uninterrupted, the potter and the buyer's secretary quickly closed a deal for two dozen of the liter carafes.

"I wish we could take more," said the secretary, "but you heard what

I told him. We've had to turn away customers for ordinary dinnerware because he shot the last quarter's budget on some Mexican piggy banks some equally enthusiastic importer stuck him with. The fifth floor is packed solid with them."

"I'll bet they look mighty est'etic."

"They're painted with purple cacti." The potter shuddered and caressed the glaze of the sample carafe.

The buyer looked up and rumbled, "Ain't you dummies through yakkin' yet? What good's a seckertary for if'n he don't take the burden of detail off'n my back, harh?"

"We're all through, doctor. Are you ready to go?"

The buyer grunted peevishly, dropped Whambozambo Comix on the floor and led the way out of the building and down the log corduroy road to the highway. His car was waiting on the concrete. It was, like all contemporary cars, too low slung to get over the logs. He climbed down into the car and started the motor with a tremendous sparkle and roar.

"Gomez-Laplace," called out the potter under cover of the noise, "did anything come of the radiation program they were working on the last time I was on duty at the Pole?"

"The same old fallacy," said the secretary gloomily. "It stopped us on mutation, it stopped us on culling, it stopped us on segregation, and now it's stopped us on hypnosis."

"Well, I'm scheduled back to the grind in nine days. Time for another firing right now. I've got a new luster to try. . ."

"I'll miss you. I shall be 'vacationing' — running the drafting room of the New Century Engineering Corporation in Denver. They're going to put up a two-hundred-story office building, and naturally somebody's got to be on hand."

"Naturally," said Hawkins with a sour smile.

There was an ear-piercingly sweet blast as the buyer leaned on the horn button. Also, a yard-tall jet of what looked like flame spurted up from the car's radiator cap; the car's power plant was a gas turbine and had no radiator. "I'm coming, doctor," said the secretary dispiritedly. He climbed down into the car and it whooshed off with much flame and noise. The potter, depressed, wandered back up the corduroy road and contemplated his cooling kilns. The rustling wind in the boughs was obscuring the creak and mutter of the shrinking refractory brick. Hawkins wondered about the number two kiln — a reduction fire on a load of lusterware mugs. Had the clay chinking excluded the air? Had it been a properly smoky blaze? Would it do any harm if he just took one close —? Common sense took Hawkins by the scruff of the neck and yanked him over to the tool shed. He got out his pick and resolutely set off on a prospecting jaunt to a hummocky field that might yield some oxides. He was especially low on coppers. The long walk left him sweating hard, with his lust for a peek into the kiln quiet in his breast. He swung his pick almost at random into one of the hummocks; it clanged on a stone which he excavated. A largely obliterated inscription said:

ERSITY OF CHIC
OGICAL LABO
ELOVED MEMORY OF
KILLED IN ACT

The potter swore mildly. He had hoped the field would turn out to be a cemetery, preferably a once-fashionable cemetery full of once-massive bronze caskets moldered into oxides of tin and copper. Well, hell, maybe there was some around anyway. He headed lackadaisically for the second largest hillock and sliced into it with his pick. There was a stone to undercut and topple into a trench, and then the potter was very glad he'd stuck at it. His nostrils were filled with the bitter smell and the dirt was tinged with the exciting blue of copper salts. The pick went clang! Hawkins, puffing, pried up a stainless steel plate that was quite badly stained and was also marked with incised letters. It seemed to have pulled loose from rotting bronze; there were rivets on the back that brought up flakes of green patina. The potter wiped off the surface dirt with his sleeve, turned it to catch the sunlight obliquely and read:

HONEST JOHN BARLOW

Honest John, famed in university annals, represents a challenge which medical science has not yet answered: revival of a human being accidentally thrown into a state of suspended animation. In 1988 Mr. Barlow, a leading Evanston real estate dealer, visited his dentist for treatment of an impacted wisdom tooth. His dentist requested and received permission to use the experimental anesthetic Cycloparadimethanol–B–7, developed at the University. After administration of the anesthetic, the dentist resorted to his drill. By freakish mischance, a short circuit in his machine delivered 220 volts of 60-cycle current into the patient. (In a damage suit instituted by Mrs. Barlow against the dentist, the University and the makers of the drill, a jury found for the defendants.) Mr. Barlow never got up from the dentist's chair and was assumed to have died of poisoning, electrocution or both. Morticians preparing him for embalming discovered, however, that their subject was — though certainly not living — just as certainly not dead. The University was notified and a series of exhaustive tests was begun, including attempts to duplicate the trance state on volunteers. After a bad run of seven cases which ended fatally, the attempts were abandoned. Honest John was long an exhibit at the University museum and livened many a football game as mascot of the University's Blue Crushers. The bounds of taste were overstepped, however, when a pledge to Sigma Delta Chi was ordered in '03 to "kidnap" Honest John from his loosely guarded glass museum case and introduce him into the Rachel Swanson Memorial Girls' Gymnasium shower room. On May 22, 2003, the University Board of Regents issued the following order: "By unanimous vote, it is directed that the remains of Honest John Barlow be removed from the University museum and conveyed to the University's Lieutenant James Scott III Memorial Biological Laboratories and there be securely locked in a specially prepared vault. It is further directed that all possible measures for the preservation of these remains be taken by the Laboratory administration and that access to these remains be denied to all persons except qualified scholars authorized in writing by the Board. The Board reluctantly takes this action in view of recent notices and plwtographs in the nation's press which, to say the least, reflect but small credit upon the University.

It was far from his field, but Hawkins understood what had happened — an early and accidental blundering onto the bare bones of the Levantman shock anesthesia, which had since been replaced by other methods. To bring subjects out of Levantman shock, you let them have a squirt of simple saline in the trigeminal nerve. Interesting. And now about that bronze —

He heaved the pick into the rotting green salts, expecting no resistance, and almost fractured his wrist. Something down there was solid. He began to flake off the oxides. A half hour of work brought him down to phosphor bronze, a huge casting of the almost incorruptible metal. It had weakened structurally over the centuries; he could fit the point of his pick under a corroded boss and pry off great creaking and grumbling striae of the stuff. Hawkins wished he had an archaeologist with him but didn't dream of returning to his shop and caffing one to take over the find. He was an all-around man: by choice, and in his free time, an artist in clay and glaze; by necessity, an automotive, electronics and atomic engineer who could also swing a project in traffic control, individual and group psychology, architecture or tool design. He didn't yell for a specialist every time something out of his line came up; there were so few with so much to do. He trenched around his find, discovering that it was a great brick-shaped bronze mass with an excitingly hollow sound. A long strip of moldering metal from one of the long vertical faces pulled away, exposing red rust that went whoosh and was sucked into the interior of the mass. It had been de-aired, thought Hawkins, and there must have been an inner jacket of glass which had crystallized through the centuries and quietly crumbled at the first clang of his pick. He didn't know what a vacuum would do to a subject of Levantman shock, but he had hopes, nor did he quite understand what a real estate dealer was, but it might have something to do with pottery. And anything might have a bearing on Topic Number One. He flung his pick out of the trench, climbed out and set off at a dog-trot for his shop. A little rummaging turned up a hypo and there was a plastic container of salt in the kitchen.

Back at his dig, he chipped for another half hour to expose the juncture of lid and body. The hinges were hopeless; he smashed them off. Hawkins extended the telescopic handle of the pick for the best leverage, fitted its point into a deep pit, set its built-in fulcrum, and heaved. Five more heaves and he could see, inside the vault, what looked like a dusty marble statue. Ten more and he could see that it was the naked body of Honest John Barlow, Evanston real estate dealer, uncorrupted by time. The potter found the apex of the trigeminal nerve with his needle's point and gave him 60 cc. In an hour Barlow's chest began to pump. In another hour, he rasped, "Did it work?"

"Did it!" muttered Hawkins.

Barlow opened his eyes and stirred, looked down, turned his hands before his eyes —

"I'll sue!" he screamed. "My clothes! My fingernails!" A horrid suspicion came over his face and he clapped his hands to his hairless scalp. "My hair!" he wailed. "I'll sue you for every penny you've got! That release won't mean a damned thing in court — I didn't sign away my hair and clothes and fingernails!"

"They'll grow back," said Hawkins casually. "Also your epidermis. Those parts of you weren't alive, you know, so they weren't preserved like the rest of you. I'm afraid the clothes are gone, though."

"What is this — the University hospital?" demanded Barlow. "I want a phone. No, you phone. Tell my wife I'm all right and tell Sam Zimmerman — he's my lawyer — to get over here right away. Greenleaf 7-4022. Ow!" He had tried to sit up, and a portion of his pink skin rubbed against the inner surface of the casket, which was powdered by the ancient crystallized glass. "What the hell did you guys do, boil me alive? Oh, you're going to pay for this!"

"You're all right," said Hawkins, wishing now he had a reference book to clear up several obscure terms. "Your epidermis will start growing immediately. You're not in the hospital. Look here." He handed Barlow the stainless steel plate that had labeled the casket. After a suspicious glance, the man started to read. Finishing, he laid the plate carefully on the edge of the vault and was silent for a spell. "Poor Verna," he said at last. "It doesn't say whether she was stuck with the court costs. Do you happen to know —"

"No," said the potter. "All I know is what was on the plate, and how to revive you. The dentist accidentally gave you a dose of what we call Levantman shock anesthesia. We haven't used it for centuries; it was powerful, but too dangerous."

"Centuries …" brooded the man. "Centuries … I'll bet Sam swindled her out of her eyeteeth. Poor Verna. How long ago was it? What year is this?"

Hawkins shrugged. "We call it 7–B–936. That's no help to you. It takes a long time for these metals to oxidize."

"Like that movie," Barlow muttered. "Who would have thought it? Poor Verna!" He blubbered and sniffled, reminding Hawkins powerfully of the fact that he had been found under a flat rock.

Almost angrily, the potter demanded, "How many children did you have?"

"None yet," sniffed Barlow. "My first wife didn't want them. But Verna wants one — wanted one — but we're going to wait until — we were going to wait until —"

"Of course," said the potter, feeling a savage desire to tell him off, blast him to hell and gone for his work. But he choked it down. There was The Problem to think of; there was always The Problem to think of, and this poor blubberer might unexpectedly supply a clue. Hawkins would have to pass him on. "Come along," Hawkins said. "My time is short."

Barlow looked up, outraged. "How can you be so unfeeling? I'm a human being like —"

The Los Angeles-Chicago "rocket" thundered overhead and Barlow broke off in mid-complaint. "Beautiful!" he breathed, following it with his eyes. "Beautiful!" He climbed out of the vault, too interested to be pained by its roughness against his infantile skin. "After all," he said briskly, "this should have its sunny side. I never was much for reading, but this is just like one of those stories. And I ought to make some money out of it, shouldn't I?" He gave Hawkins a shrewd glance.

"You want money?" asked the potter. "Here." He handed over a fist-ful of change and bills. "You'd better put my shoes on. It'll be about a quarter mile. Oh, and you're — uh, modest? — yes, that was the word. Here."

Hawkins gave him his pants, but Barlow was excitedly counting the money. "Eighty-five, eighty-six — and it's dollars, too! I thought it'd be credits or whatever they call them. 'E Pluribus Unum' and 'Liberty' — just different faces. Say, is there a catch to this? Are these real, genuine, honest twenty-two-cent dollars like we had or just wallpaper?"

"They're quite all right, I assure you," said the potter. "I wish you'd come along. I'm in a hurry."

The man babbled as they stumped toward the shop. "Where are we going — The Council of Scientists, the World Coordinator or something like that?"

"Who? Oh, no. We call them 'President' and 'Congress.' No, that wouldn't do any good at all. I'm just taking you to see some people."

"I ought to make plenty out of this. Plenty! I could write books. Get some smart young fellow to put it into words for me and I'll bet I could turn out a best seller. What's the setup on things like that?"

"It's about like that. Smart young fellows. But there aren't any best sellers any more. People don't read much nowadays. We'll find some-thing equally profitable for you to do." Back in the shop, Hawkins gave Barlow a suit of clothes, deposited him in the waiting room and called Central in Chicago. "Take him away," he pleaded. "I have time for one more firing and he blathers and blathers. I haven't told him anything. Perhaps we should just turn him loose and let him find his own level, but there's a chance —"

"The Problem," agreed Central. "Yes, there's a chance." The pot-ter delighted Barlow by making him a cup of coffee with a cube that not only dissolved in cold water but heated the water to boiling point. Killing time, Hawkins chatted about the "rocket" Barlow had admired and had to haul himself up short; he had almost told the real estate man what its top speed really was — almost, indeed, revealed that it was not a rocket. He regretted, too, that he had so casually handed Barlow a couple of hundred dollars. The man seemed obsessed with fear that they were worthless since Hawkins refused to take a note or I.O.U. or even a definite promise of repayment. But Hawkins couldn't go into details, and was very glad when a stranger arrived from Central.

"Tinny-Peete, from Algeciras," the stranger told him swiftly as the two of them met at the door. "Psychist for Poprob. Polassigned special overtake Barlow."

"Thank Heaven," said Hawkins. "Barlow," he told the man from the past, "this is Tinny-Peete. He's going to take care of you and help you make lots of money." The psychist stayed for a cup of the coffee whose preparation had delighted Barlow, and then conducted the real estate man down the corduroy road to his car, leaving the potter to speculate on whether he could at last crack his kilns. Hawkins, abruptly dismissing Barlow and The Problem, happily picked the chinking from around the door of the number two kiln, prying it open a trifle. A blast of heat and the heady, smoky scent of the reduction fire delighted him. He peered and saw a corner of a shelf glowing cherry red, becoming obscured by wavering black areas as it lost heat through the opened door. He slipped a charred wood paddle under a mug on the shelf and pulled it out as a sample, the hairs on the back of his hand curling and scorching. The mug crackled and pinged and Hawkins sighed happily. The bismuth resinate luster had fired to perfection, a haunting film of silvery-black metal with strange bluish lights in it as it turned before the eyes, and the Problem of Population seemed very far away to Hawkins then. Barlow and Tinny-Peete arrived at the concrete highway where the psychist's car was parked in a safety bay.

"What-a-boat!" gasped the man from the past.

"Boat? No, that's my car."

Barlow surveyed it with awe. Swept-back lines, deep-drawn compound curves, kilograms of chrome. He ran his hands over the door — or was it the door? — in a futile search for a handle, and asked respectfully, "How fast does it go?"

The psychist gave him a keen look and said slowly, "Two hundred and fifty. You can tell by the speedometer."

"Wow! My old Chevvy could hit a hundred on a straightaway, but you're out of my class, mister!" Tinny-Peete somehow got a huge, low door open and Barlow descended three steps into immense cushions, floundering over to the right. He was too fascinated to pay serious attention to his flayed dermis. The dashboard was a lovely wilderness of dials, plugs, indicators, lights, scales and switches. The psychist climbed down into the driver's seat and did something with his feet. The motor started like lighting a blowtorch as big as a silo. Wallowing around in the cushions, Barlow saw through a rearview mirror a tremendous exhaust filled with brilliant white sparkles.

"Do you like it?" yelled the psychist.

"It's terrific!" Barlow yelled back. "It's —"

He was shut up as the car pulled out from the bay into the road with a great voo-ooo-ooom! A gale roared past Barlow's head, though the windows seemed to be closed; the impression of speed was terrific. He located the speedometer on the dashboard and saw it climb past 90, 100, 150, 200.

"Fast enough for me," yelled the psychist, noting that Barlow's face fell in response. "Radio?" He passed over a surprisingly light object like a football helmet, with no trailing wires, and pointed to a row of buttons. Barlow put on the helmet, glad to have the roar of air stilled, and pushed a pushbutton. It lit up satisfyingly, and Barlow settled back even farther for a sample of the brave new world's supermodern taste in ingenious entertainment.

"TAKE IT AND STICK IT!" a voice roared in his ears.

He snatched off the helmet and gave the psychist an injured look. Tinny-Peete grinned and turned a dial associated with the pushbutton layout. The man from the past donned the helmet again and found the voice had lowered to normal.

"The show of shows! The supershow! The super-duper show! The quiz of quizzes! *Take It and Stick It!*" There were shrieks of laughter in the background. "Here we got the contes-tants all ready to go. You know how we work it. I hand a conte-stant a triangle-shaped cutout and like that down the line. Now we got these here boards, they got cutout places the same shape as the triangles and things, only they're all different shapes, and the first contes-tant that sticks the cutouts into the boards, he wins. "Now I'm gonna innaview the first contes-tant. Right here, honey. What's your name?"

"Name? Uh —"

"Hoddaya like that, folks? She don't remember her name! Hah? Would you buy that for a quarter?"

The question was spoken with arch significance, and the audience shrieked, howled and whistled its appreciation. It was dull listening when you didn't know the punch lines and catch lines. Barlow pushed another button, with his free hand ready at the volume control.

" — latest from Washington. It's about Senator Hull-Mendoza. He is still attacking the Bureau of Fisheries. The North California Syndicalist says he got affydavits that John Kingsley-Schultz is a bluenose from way back. He didn't publistat the affydavits, but he says they say that Kingsley-Schultz was saw at bluenose meetings in Oregon State College and later at Florida University. Kingsley-Schultz says he gotta confess he did major in fly casting at Oregon and got his Ph.D. in game-fish at Florida.

"And here is a quote from Kingsley-Schultz: 'Hull-Mendoza don't know what he's talking about. He should drop dead.' Unquote. Hull-

Mendoza says he won't publistat the affydavits to pertect his sources. He says they was sworn by three former employes of the Bureau which was fired for in-competence and in-com-pat-ibility by Kingsley-Schultz.

"Elsewhere they was the usual run of traffic accidents. A three-way pileup of cars on Route 66 going outta Chicago took twelve lives. The Chicago-Los Angeles morning rocket crashed and exploded in the Mo-have-Mo-javvy-whatever-you-call-it Desert. All the 94 people aboard got killed. A Civil Aeronautics Authority investigator on the scene says that the pilot was buzzing herds of sheep and didn't pull out in time.

"Hey! Here's a hot one from New York! A diesel tug run wild in the harbor while the crew was below and shoved in the port bow of the luck-shury liner S. S. Placentia. It says the ship filled and sank taking the lives of an es-ti-mated 180 passengers and 50 crew members. Six divers was sent down to study the wreckage, but they died, too, when their suits turned out to be fulla little holes.

"And here is a bulletin I just got from Denver. It seems —"

Barlow took off the headset uncomprehendingly. "He seemed so callous," he yelled at the driver. "I was listening to a newscast —"

Tinny-Peete shook his head and pointed at his ears. The roar of air was deafening. Barlow frowned baffledly and stared out of the window. A glowing sign said: MOOGS! WOULD YOU BUY IT FOR A QUARTER? He didn't know what Moogs was or were; the illustration showed an incredibly proportioned girl, 99.9 percent naked, writhing passionately in animated full color. The roadside jingle was still with him, but with a new feature. Radar or something spotted the car and alerted the lines of the jingle. Each in turn sped along a roadside track, even with the car, so it could be read before the next line was alerted.

IF THERE'S A GIRL YOU WANT TO GET
DEFLOCCULIZE UNROMANTIC SWEAT.
"A*R*M*P*I*T*T*O"

Another animated job, in two panels, the familiar "Before and After." The first said, "Just Any Cigar?" and was illustrated with a two-person domestic tragedy of a wife holding her nose while her coarse and red-faced husband puffed a slimy-looking rope. The second panel glowed, "Or a VUELTA ABAJO?" and was illustrated with — Barlow blushed and looked at his feet until they had passed the sign.

"Coming into Chicago!" bawled Tinny-Peete. Other cars were showing up, all of them dreamboats. Watching them, Barlow began to wonder if he knew what a kilometer was, exactly. They seemed to be traveling so slowly, if you ignored the roaring air past your ears and didn't let the speedy lines of the dreamboats fool you. He would have sworn they were really crawling along at twenty-five, with occasional spurts up to thirty. How much was a kilometer, anyway? The city loomed ahead, and it was just what it ought to be: towering skyscrapers, overhead ramps, landing platforms for helicopters —

He clutched at the cushions. Those two copters. They were going to — they were going to — they —

He didn't see what happened because their apparent collision courses took them behind a giant building. Screamingly sweet blasts of sound surrounded them as they stopped for a red light.

"What the hell is going on here?" said Barlow in a shrill, frightened voice, because the braking time was just about zero, and he wasn't hurled against the dashboard. "Who's kidding who?"

"Why, what's the matter?" demanded the driver.

The light changed to green and he started the pickup. Barlow stiffened as he realized that the rush of air past his ears began just a brief, unreal split second before the car was actually moving. He grabbed for the door handle on his side. The city grew on them slowly: scattered buildings, denser buildings, taller buildings, and a red light ahead. The car rolled to a stop in zero braking time, the rush of air cut off an instant after it stopped, and Barlow was out of the car and running frenziedly down a sidewalk one instant after that.

They'll track me down, he thought, panting. *It's a secret police thing. They'll get you — mind-reading machines, television eyes everywhere, afraid you'll tell their slaves about freedom and stuff. They don't let anybody cross them, like that story I once read.* Winded, he slowed to a walk and congratulated himself that he had guts enough not to turn around. That was what they always watched for. Walking, he was just another business-suited back among hundreds. He would be safe, he would be safe —

A hand gripped his shoulder and words tumbled from a large, coarse, handsome face thrust close to his: "Wassamatta bumpinninna people likeya owna sidewalk gotta miner slamya jima mushya bassar!" It was neither the mad potter nor the mad driver.

"Excuse me," said Barlow. "What did you say?"

"Oh, yeah?" yelled the stranger dangerously, and waited for an answer.

Barlow, with the feeling that he had somehow been suckered into the short end of an intricate land-title deal, heard himself reply belligerently, "Yeah!"

The stranger let go of his shoulder and snarled, "Oh, yeah?"

"Yeah!" said Barlow, yanking his jacket back into shape.

"Aaah!" snarled the stranger, with more contempt and disgust than ferocity. He added an obscenity current in Barlow's time, a standard but physiologically impossible directive, and strutted off hulking his shoulders and balling his fists.

Barlow walked on, trembling. Evidently he had handled it well enough. He stopped at a red light while the long, low dreamboats roared before him and pedestrians in the sidewalk flow with him threaded their ways through the stream of cars. Brakes screamed, fenders clanged and dented, hoarse cries flew back and forth between drivers and walkers.

He leaped backward frantically as one car swerved over an arc of sidewalk to miss another. The signal changed to green; the cars kept on coming for about thirty seconds and then dwindled to an occasional light runner. Barlow crossed warily and leaned against a vending machine, blowing big breaths.

Look natural, he told himself. Do something normal. Buy something from the machine. He fumbled out some change, got a newspaper for a dime, a handkerchief for a quarter and a candy bar for another quarter. The faint chocolate smell made him ravenous suddenly. He clawed at the glassy wrapper printed "Crigglies" quite futilely for a few seconds, and then it divided neatly by itself. The bar made three good bites, and he bought two more and gobbled them down. Thirsty, he drew a carbonated orange drink in another one of the glassy wrappers from the machine for another dime. When he fumbled with it, it divided neatly and spilled all over his knees.

Barlow decided he had been there long enough and walked on. The shop windows were — shop windows. People still wore and bought clothes, still smoked and bought tobacco, still ate and bought food. And they still went to the movies, he saw with pleased surprise as he passed and then returned to a glittering place whose sign said it was THE BIJOU. The place seemed to be showing a triple feature, *Babies Are Terrible*, *Don't Have Children*, and *The Canali Kid*.

It was irresistible; he paid a dollar and went in. He caught the tail end of *The Canali Kid* in three-dimensional, full-color, full-scent production. It appeared to be an interplanetary saga winding up with a chase scene and a reconciliation between estranged hero and heroine. *Babies Are Terrible* and *Don't Have Children* were fantastic arguments against parenthood — the grotesquely exaggerated dangers of painfully graphic childbirth, vicious children, old parents beaten and starved by their sadistic offspring. The audience, Barlow astoundedly noted, was placidly chomping sweets and showing no particular signs of revulsion.

The Coming Attractions drove him into the lobby. The fanfares were shattering, the blazing colors blinding, and the added scents stomach-heaving. When his eyes again became accustomed to the moderate lighting of the lobby, he groped his way to a bench and opened the newspaper he had bought.

It turned out to be *The Racing Sheet*, which afflicted him with a crushing sense of loss. The familiar boxed index in the lower-left-hand corner of the front page showed almost unbearably that Churchill Downs and Empire City were still in business.

Blinking back tears, he turned to the Past Performance at Churchill. They weren't using abbreviations any more, and the pages because of that were single-column instead of double. But it was all the same — or was it?

He squinted at the first race, a three-quarter-mile maiden claimer for thirteen hundred dollars. Incredibly, the track record was two minutes, ten and three-fifths seconds. Any beetle in his time could have knocked off the three-quarter in one-fifteen. It was the same for the other distances, much worse for route events. What the hell had happened to everything?

He studied the form of a five-year-old brown mare in the second and couldn't make head or tail of it. She'd won and lost and placed and showed and lost and placed without rhyme or reason. She looked like a front runner for a couple of races and then she looked like a no-good pig and then she looked like a mudder but the next time it rained she wasn't and then she was a stayer and then she was a pig again. In a good five-thousand-dollar allowances event, too! Barlow looked at the other entries and it slowly dawned on him that they were all like the five-year-old brown mare. Not a single damned horse running had even the slightest trace of class.

Somebody sat down beside him and said, "That's the story."

Barlow whirled to his feet and saw it was Tinny-Peete, his driver.

"I was in doubts about telling you," said the psychist, "but I see you have some growing suspicions of the truth. Please don't get excited. It's all right, I tell you."

"So you've got me," said Barlow.

"Got you?"

"Don't pretend. I can put two and two together. You're the secret police. You and the rest of the aristocrats live in luxury on the sweat of these oppressed slaves. You're afraid of me because you have to keep them ignorant."

There was a bellow of bright laughter from the psychist that got them blank looks from other patrons of the lobby. The laughter didn't sound at all sinister.

"Let's get out of here," said Tinny-Peete, still chuckling. "You couldn't possibly have it more wrong." He engaged Barlow's arm and led him to the street. "The actual truth is that the millions of workers live in luxury on the sweat of the handful of aristocrats. I shall probably die before my time of overwork unless —" He gave Barlow a speculative look. "You may be able to help us."

"I know that gag," sneered Barlow. "I made money in my time and to make money you have to get people on your side. Go ahead and shoot me if you want, but you're not going to make a fool out of me."

"You nasty little ingrate!" snapped the psychist, with a kaleidoscopic change of mood. "This damned mess is all your fault and the fault of people like you! Now come along and no more of your nonsense." He yanked Barlow into an office building lobby and an elevator that, disconcertingly, went whoosh loudly as it rose.

The real estate man's knees were wobbly as the psychist pushed him from the elevator, down a corridor and into an office.

A hawk-faced man rose from a plain chair as the door closed behind them. After an angry look at Barlow, he asked the psychist, "Was I called from the Pole to inspect this — this — ?"

"Unget updandered. I've deeprobed etfind quasichance exhim Poprobattackline," said the psychist soothingly.

"Doubt," grunted the hawk-faced man.

"Try," suggested Tinny-Peete.

"Very well. Mr. Barlow, I understand you and your lamented had no children."

"What of it?"

"This of it. You were a blind, selfish stupid ass to tolerate economic and social conditions which penalized childbearing by the prudent and foresighted. You made us what we are today, and I want you to know that we are far from satisfied. Damn-fool rockets! Damn-fool automobiles! Damn-fool cities with overhead ramps!"

"As far as I can see," said Barlow, "you're running down the best features of your time. Are you crazy?"

"The rockets aren't rockets. They're turbojets — good turbojets, but the fancy shell around them makes for a bad drag. The automobiles have a top speed of one hundred kilometers per hour — a kilometer is, if I recall my paleolinguistics, three-fifths of a mile — and the speedometers are all rigged accordingly so the drivers will think they're going two hundred and fifty. The cities are ridiculous, expensive, unsanitary, wasteful conglomerations of people who'd be better off and more productive if they were spread over the countryside.

"We need the rockets and trick speedometers and cities because, while you and your kind were being prudent and foresighted and not having children, the migrant workers, slum dwellers and tenant farmers were shiftlessly and shortsightedly having children — breeding, breeding. My God, how they bred!"

"Wait a minute," objected Barlow. "There were lots of people in our crowd who had two or three children."

"The attrition of accidents, illness, wars and such took care of that. Your intelligence was bred out. It is gone. Children that should have been born never were. The just-average, they'll-get-along majority took over the population. The average IQ now is 45."

"But that's far in the future —"

"So are you," grunted the hawk-faced man sourly.

"But who are you people?"

"Just people — real people. Some generations ago, the geneticists realized at last that nobody was going to pay any attention to what they said, so they abandoned words for deeds. Specifically, they formed and recruited for a closed corporation intended to maintain and improve the breed. We are their descendants, about three million of us. There are five billion of the others, so we are their slaves.

"During the past couple of years I've designed a skyscraper, kept Billings Memorial Hospital here in Chicago running, headed off war with Mexico and directed traffic at LaGuardia Field in New York."

"I don't understand! Why don't you let them go to hell in their own way?"

The man grimaced. "We tried it once for three months. We holed up at the South Pole and waited. They didn't notice it. Some drafting room people were missing, some chief nurses didn't show up, minor government people on the nonpolicy level couldn't be located. It didn't seem to matter. In a week there was hunger. In two weeks there were famine and plague, in three weeks war and anarchy. We called off the experiment; it took us most of the next generation to get things squared away again."

"But why didn't you let them kill each other off?"

"Five billion corpses mean about five hundred million tons of rotting flesh."

Barlow had another idea. "Why don't you sterilize them?"

"Two and one-half billion operations is a lot of operations. Because they breed continuously, the job would never be done."

"I see. Like the marching Chinese!"

"Who the devil are they?"

"It was a — uh — paradox of my time. Somebody figured out that if all the Chinese in the world were to line up four abreast, I think it was, and start marching past a given point, they'd never stop because of the babies that would be born and grow up before they passed the point."

"That's right. Only instead of 'a given point,' make it 'the largest conceivable number of operating rooms that we could build and staff.' There could never be enough."

"Say!" said Barlow. "Those movies about babies — was that your propaganda?"

"It was. It doesn't seem to mean a thing to them. We have abandoned the idea of attempting propaganda contrary to a biological drive."

"So if you work with a biological drive — ?"

"I know of none which is consistent with inhibition of fertility."

Barlow's face went poker blank, the result of years of careful discipline. "You don't, huh? You're the great brains and you can't think of any?"

"Why, no," said the psychist innocently. "Can you?"

"That depends. I sold ten thousand acres of Siberian tundra — through a dummy firm, of course — after the partition of Russia. The buyers thought they were getting improved building lots on the outskirts of Kiev. I'd say that was a lot tougher than this job."

"How so?" asked the hawk-faced man.

"Those were normal, suspicious customers and these are morons, born suckers. You just figure out a con they'll fall for; they won't know enough to do any smart checking."

The psychist and the hawk-faced man had also had training; they kept themselves from looking with sudden hope at each other. "You seem to have something in mind," said the psychist.

Barlow's poker face went blanker still. "Maybe I have. I haven't heard any offer yet."

"There's the satisfaction of knowing that you've prevented Earth's resources from being so plundered," the hawk-faced man pointed out, "that the race will soon become extinct."

"I don't know that," Barlow said bluntly. "All I have is your word."

"If you really have a method, I don't think any price would be too great," the psychist offered.

"Money," said Barlow.

"All you want."

"More than you want," the hawk-faced man corrected.

"Prestige," added Barlow. "Plenty of publicity. My picture and my name in the papers and over TV every day, statues to me, parks and cities and streets and other things named after me. A whole chapter in the history books."

The psychist made a facial sign to the hawk-faced man that meant, "Oh, brother!"

The hawk-faced man signaled back, "Steady, boy!"

"It's not too much to ask," the psychist agreed. Barlow, sensing a seller's market, said, "Power!"

"Power?" the hawk-faced man repeated puzzledly. "Your own hydro station or nuclear pile?"

"I mean a world dictatorship with me as dictator!"

"Well, now —" said the psychist, but the hawk-faced man interrupted, "It would take a special emergency act of Congress but the situation warrants it. I think that can be guaranteed."

"Could you give us some indication of your plan?" the psychist asked.

"Ever hear of lemmings?"

"No."

"They are — were, I guess, since you haven't heard of them — little animals in Norway, and every few years they'd swarm to the coast and swim out to sea until they drowned. I figure on putting some lemming urge into the population."

"How?"

"I'll save that till I get the right signatures on the deal."

The hawk-faced man said, "I'd like to work with you on it, Barlow. My name's Ryan-Ngana."

He put out his hand. Barlow looked closely at the hand, then at the man's face.

"Ryan what?"

"Ngana."

"That sounds like an African name."

"It is. My mother's father was a Watusi."

Barlow didn't take the hand.

"I thought you looked pretty dark. I don't want to hurt your feelings, but I don't think I'd be at my best working with you. There must be somebody else just as well qualified, I'm sure."

The psychist made a facial sign to Ryan-Ngana that meant, "Steady yourself, boy!"

"Very well," Ryan-Ngana told Barlow. "We'll see what arrangement can be made."

"It's not that I'm prejudiced, you understand. Some of my best friends —"

"Mr. Barlow, don't give it another thought. Anybody who could pick on the lemming analogy is going to be useful to us."

And so he would, thought Ryan-Ngana, alone in the office after Tinny-Peete had taken Barlow up to the helicopter stage. So he would. Poprob had exhausted every rational attempt and the new Poprobat-tacklines would have to be irrational or subrational. This creature from the past with his lemming legends and his improved building lots would be a fountain of precious vicious self-interest. Ryan-Ngana sighed and stretched. He had to go and run the San Francisco subway. Summoned early from the Pole to study Barlow, he'd left unfinished a nice little theorem. Between interruptions, he was slowly constructing an n-dimensional geometry whose foundations and superstructure owed no debt whatsoever to intuition.

Upstairs, waiting for a helicopter, Barlow was explaining to Tinny-Peete that he had nothing against Negroes, and Tinny-Peete wished he had some of Ryan-Ngana's imperturbability and humor for the ordeal. The helicopter took them to International Airport where, TinnyPeete explained, Barlow would leave for the Pole. The man from the past wasn't sure he'd like a dreary waste of ice and cold.

"It's all tight," said the psychist. "A civilized layout. Warm, pleasant. You'll be able to work more efficiently there. All the facts at your fingertips, a good secretary —"

"I'll need a pretty big staff," said Barlow, who had learned from thousands of deals never to take the first offer.

"I meant a private, confidential one," said Tinny-Peete readily, "but you can have as many as you want. You'll naturally have top-primary-top-priority if you really have a workable plan."

"Let's not forget this dictatorship angle," said Barlow.

He didn't know that the psychist would just as readily have promised him deification to get him happily on the "rocket" for the Pole. Tinny-Peete had no wish to be torn limb from limb; he knew very well that it would end that way if the population learned from this anachronism that there was a small elite which considered itself head, shoulders, trunk and groin above the rest. The fact that this assumption was perfectly true and the fact that the elite was condemned by its superiority to a life of the most grinding toil would not be considered; the difference would.

The psychist finally put Barlow aboard the "rocket" with some thirty people — real people — headed for the Pole. Barlow was airsick all the way because of a posthypnotic suggestion Tinny-Peete had planted in him. One idea was to make him as averse as possible to a return trip, and another idea was to spare the other passengers from his aggressive, talkative company.

Barlow during the first day at the Pole was reminded of his first day in the Army. It was the same now-where-the-hell-are-we-going-to-put-you? business until he took a firm line with them. Then instead of acting like supply sergeants they acted like hotel clerks. It was a wonderful, wonderfully calculated buildup, and one that he failed to suspect. After all, in his time a visitor from the past would have been lionized. At day's end he reclined in a snug underground billet with the sixty-mile gales roaring yards overhead and tried to put two and two together. It was like old times, he thought — like a coup in real estate where you had the competition by the throat, like a fifty-percent rent boost when you knew damned well there was no place for the tenants to move, like smiling when you read over the breakfast orange juice that the city council had decided to build a school on the ground you had acquired by a deal with the city council.

And it was simple. He would just sell tundra building lots to eagerly suicidal lemmings, and that was absolutely all there was to solving The Problem that had these double-domes spinning. They'd have to work out most of the details, naturally, but what the hell, that was what subordinates were for. He'd need specialists in advertising, engineering, communications — did they know anything about hypnotism? That might be helpful. If not, there'd have to be a lot of bribery done, but he'd make sure — damned sure — there were unlimited funds. Just selling building lots to lemmings.

He wished, as he fell asleep, that poor Verna could have been in on this. It was his biggest, most stupendous deal. Verna — that sharp shyster Sam Immerman must have swindled her.

It began the next day with people coming to visit him. He knew the approach. They merely wanted to be helpful to their illustrious visitor from the past, and would he help fill them in about his era, which unfortunately was somewhat obscure historically, and what did he think could be done about The Problem? He told them he was too old to be roped any more, and they wouldn't get any information out of him until he got a letter of intent from at least the Polar President and a session of the Polar Congress empowered to make him dictator.

He got the letter and the session. He presented his program, was asked whether his conscience didn't revolt at its callousness, explained succinctly that a deal was a deal and anybody who wasn't smart enough to protect himself didn't deserve protection — "Caveat emptor," he threw in for scholarship, and had to translate it to "Let the buyer beware." He didn't, he stated, give a damn about either the morons or their intelligent slaves; he'd told them his price and that was all he was interested in. Would they meet it or wouldn't they?

The Polar President offered to resign in his favor, with certain temporary emergency powers that the Polar Congress would vote him if he thought them necessary. Barlow demanded the title of World Dictator, complete control of world finances, salary to be decided by himself, and the publicity campaign and historical writeup to begin at once.

"As for the emergency powers," he added, "they are neither to be temporary nor limited."

Somebody wanted the floor to discuss the matter, with the declared hope that perhaps Barlow would modify his demands.

"You've got the proposition," Barlow said. "I'm not knocking off even ten percent."

"But what if the Congress refuses, sir?" the President asked.

"Then you can stay up here at the Pole and try to work it out yourselves. I'll get what I want from the morons. A shrewd operator like me doesn't have to compromise; I haven't got a single competitor in this whole cockeyed moronic era."

Congress waived debate and voted by show of hands. Barlow won — unanimously.

"You don't know how close you came to losing me," he said in his first official address to the joint Houses. "I'm not the boy to haggle; either I get what I ask, or I go elsewhere. The first thing I want is to see designs for a new palace for me — nothing un-ostentatious, either — and your best painters and sculptors to start working on my portraits and statues. Meanwhile, I'll get my staff together." He dismissed the Polar President and the Polar Congress, telling them that he'd let them know when the next meeting would be.

A week later, the program started with North America the first target. Mrs. Garvy was resting after dinner before the ordeal of turning on the dishwasher. The TV, of course, was on, and it said, "Oooh!" — long, shuddery and ecstatic, the cue for the Parfum Assault Criminale spot commercial.

"Girls," said the announcer hoarsely, "do you want your man? It's easy to get him — easy as a trip to Venus."

"Huh?" said Mrs. Garvy.

"Wassamatter?" snorted her husband, starting out of a doze.

"Ja hear that?"

"Wha'?"

"He said 'easy like a trip to Venus.'"

"So?"

"Well, I thought ya couldn't get to Venus. I thought they just had that one rocket thing that crashed on the Moon."

"Aah, women don't keep up with the news," said Garvy righteously, subsiding again.

"Oh," said his wife uncertainly.

And the next day, on *Henry's Other Mistress*, there was a new character who had just breezed in: Buzz Rentshaw, Master Rocket Pilot of the Venus run. On *Henry's Other Mistress*, "the broadcast drama about you and your neighbors, folksy people, ordinary people, real people!" Mrs. Garvy listened with amazement over a cooling cup of coffee as Buzz made hay of her hazy convictions.

MONA: Darling, it's so good to see you again!

BUZZ: You don't know how I've missed you on that dreary Venus run.

SOUND: Venetian blind run down, key turned in lock.

MONA: Was it very dull, dearest?

BUZZ: Let's not talk about my humdrum job, darling. Let's talk about us.

SOUND: Creaking bed.

Well, the program was back to normal at last.

That evening, Mrs. Garvy tried to ask again whether her husband was sure about those rockets, but he was dozing right through *Take It and Stick It*, so she watched the screen and forgot the puzzle. She was still rocking with laughter at the gag line, "Would you buy it for a quarter?" when the commercial went on for the detergent powder she always faithfully loaded her dishwasher with on the first of every month. The announcer displayed mountains of suds from a tiny piece of the stuff and coyly added, "Of course, Cleano don't lay around for you to pick up like the soap root on Venus, but it's pretty cheap and it's almost pretty near just as good. So for us plain folks who ain't lucky enough to live up there on Venus, Cleano is the real cleaning stuff!" Then the chorus went into their "Cleano-is-the-stuff" jingle, but Mrs. Garvy didn't hear it. She was a stubborn woman, but it occurred to her that she was very sick indeed. She didn't want to worry her husband.

The next day she quietly made an appointment with her family freud. In the waiting room she picked up a fresh new copy of *Readers Pablum* and put it down with a faint palpitation. The lead article, according to the table of contents on the cover, was titled "The Most Memorable Venusian I Ever Met."

"The freud will see you now," said the nurse, and Mrs. Garvy tottered into his office. His traditional glasses and whiskers were reassuring.

She choked out the ritual, "Freud, forgive me, for I have neuroses."

He chanted the antiphonal, "Tut, my dear girl, what seems to be the trouble?"

"I got like a hole in the head," she quavered. "I seem to forget all kinds of things. Things like everybody seems to know and I don't."

"Well, that happens to everybody occasionally, my dear. I suggest a vacation on Venus."

The freud stared, openmouthed, at the empty chair.

His nurse came in and demanded, "Hey, you see how she scrammed? What was the matter with her?"

He took off his glasses and whiskers meditatively. "You can search me. I told her she should maybe try a vacation on Venus." A momentary bafflement came into his face, and he dug through his desk drawers until he found a copy of the four-color, profusely illustrated journal of his profession. It had come that morning, and he had lip-read it, though looking mostly at the pictures. He leafed to the article "Advantages of the Planet Venus in Rest Cures."

"It's right there," he said.

The nurse looked.

"It sure is," she agreed. "Why shouldn't it be?"

"The trouble with these here neurotics," decided the freud, "is that they all the time got to fight reality. Show in the next twitch."

He put on his glasses and whiskers again and forgot Mrs. Garvy and her strange behavior.

"Freud, forgive me, for I have neuroses."

"Tut, my dear girl, what seems to be the trouble?"

* * * *

Like many cures of mental disorders, Mrs. Garvy's was achieved largely by self-treatment. She disciplined herself sternly out of the crazy notion that there had been only one rocket ship and that one a failure. She could join without wincing, eventually, in any conversation on the desirability of Venus as a place to retire, on its fabulous floral profusion.

Finally she went to Venus. All her friends were trying to book passage with the Evening Star Travel and Real Estate Corporation, but naturally the demand was crushing. She considered herself lucky to get a seat at last for the two-week summer cruise.

The spaceship took off from a place called Los Alamos, New Mexico. It looked just like all the spaceships on television and in the picture magazines but was more comfortable than you would expect. Mrs. Garvy was delighted with the fifty or so fellow-passengers assembled before takeoff. They were from all over the country, and she had a distinct impression that they were on the brainy side. The captain, a tall, hawk-faced, impressive fellow named Ryan Something-or-other, welcomed them aboard and trusted that their trip would be a memorable one. He regretted that there would be nothing to see because, "due to the meteorite season," the ports would be dogged down.

It was disappointing, yet reassuring that the line was taking no chances. There was the expected momentary discomfort at takeoff and then two monotonous days of droning travel through space to be whiled away in the lounge at cards or craps. The landing was a routine bump and the voyagers were issued tablets to swallow to immunize them against any minor ailments. When the tablets took effect, the lock was opened, and Venus was theirs. It looked much like a tropical island on Earth, except for a blanket of cloud overhead. But it had a heady, otherworldly quality that was intoxicating and glamorous. The ten days of the vacation were suffused with a hazy magic. The soap root, as advertised, was free and sudsy. The fruits, mostly tropical varieties transplanted from Earth, were delightful. The simple shelters provided by the travel company were more than adequate for the balmy days and nights. It was with sincere regret that the voyagers filed again into the ship and swallowed more tablets doled out to counteract and sterilize any Venus illnesses they might unwittingly communicate to Earth.

Vacationing was one thing. Power politics was another.

At the Pole, a small man was in a soundproof room, his face deathly pale and his body limp in a straight chair. In the American Senate Chamber, Senator Hull-Mendoza (Synd., N. Cal.) was saying, "Mr. President and gentlemen, I would be remiss in my duty as a legislature if'n I didn't bring to the attention of the au-gust body I see here a perilous situation which is fraught with peril. As is well known to members of this au-gust body, the perfection of space flight has brought with it a situation I can only describe as fraught with peril. Mr. President and gentlemen, now that swift American rockets now traverse the trackless void of space between this planet and our nearest planetarial neighbor in space — and, gentlemen, I refer to Venus, the star of dawn, the brightest jewel in fair Vulcan's diadome — now, I say, I want to inquire what steps are being taken to colonize Venus with a vanguard of patriotic citizens like those minutemen of yore.

"Mr. President and gentlemen! There are in this world nations, envious nations — I do not name Mexico — who by fair means or foul may seek to wrest from Columbia's grasp the torch of freedom of space; nations whose low living standards and innate depravity give them an unfair advantage over the citizens of our fair republic.

"This is my program: I suggest that a city of more than 100,000 population be selected by lot. The citizens of the fortunate city are to be awarded choice lands on Venus free and clear, to have and to hold and convey to their descendants. And the national government shall provide free transportation to Venus for these citizens. And this program shall continue, city by city, until there has been deposited on Venus a sufficient vanguard of citizens to protect our manifest rights in that planet.

"Objections will be raised, for carping critics we have always with us. They will say there isn't enough steel. They will call it a cheap giveaway. I say there is enough steel for one city's population to be transferred to Venus, and that is all that is needed. For when the time comes for the second city to be transferred, the first, emptied city can be wrecked for the needed steel! And is it a giveaway? Yes! It is the most glorious giveaway in the history of mankind! Mr. President and gentlemen, there is no time to waste — Venus must be American!"

Black-Kupperman, at the Pole, opened his eyes and said feebly, "The style was a little uneven. Do you think anybody'll notice?"

"You did fine, boy; just fine," Barlow reassured him.

Hull-Mendoza's bill became law. Drafting machines at the South Pole were busy around the clock and the Pittsburgh steel mills spewed millions of plates into the Los Alamos spaceport of the Evening Star Travel and Real Estate Corporation. It was going to be Los Angeles, for logistic reasons, and the three most accomplished psychokineticists went to Washington and mingled in the crowd at the drawing to make certain that the Los Angeles capsule slithered into the fingers of the blindfolded Senator. Los Angeles loved the idea and a forest of spaceships began to blossom in the desert. They weren't very good spaceships, but they didn't have to be. A team at the Pole worked at Barlow's direction on a mail setup. There would have to be letters to and from Venus to keep the slightest taint of suspicion from arising. Luckily Barlow remembered that the problem had been solved once before — by Hitler. Relatives of persons incinerated in the furnaces of Lublin or Majdanek continued to get cheery postal cards. The Los Angeles flight went off on schedule, under tremendous press, newsreel and television coverage. The world cheered the gallant Angelenos who were setting off on their patriotic voyage to the land of milk and honey. The forest of spaceships thundered up, and up, and out of sight without untoward incident. Billions envied the Angelenos, cramped and on short rations though they were. Wreckers from San Francisco, whose capsule came up second, moved immediately into the city of the angels for the scrap steel their own flight would require. Senator Hull-Mendoza's constituents could do no less. The president of Mexico, hypnotically alarmed at this extension of yanqui imperialismo beyond the stratosphere, launched his own Venus-colony program. Across the water it was England versus Ireland, France versus Germany, China versus Russia, India versus Indonesia. Ancient hatreds grew into the flames that were rocket ships assailing the air by hundreds daily.

Dear Ed, how are you? Sam and I are fine and hope you are fine. Is it nice up there like they say with food and close grone on trees? I drove by Springfield yesterday and it sure looked funny all the buildings down but of coarse it is worth it we have to keep the greasers in their place. Do you have any trouble with them on Venus? Drop me a line some time. Your loving sister, Alma.

Dear Alma, I am fine and hope you are fine. It is a fine place here fine climate and easy living. The doctor told me today that I seem to be ten years younger. He thinks there is something in the air here keeps people young. We do not have much trouble with the greasers here they keep to theirselves it is just a question of us outnumbering them and staking out the best places for the Americans. In South Bay I know a nice little island that I have been saving for you and Sam with lots of blanket trees and ham bushes. Hoping to see you and Sam soon, your loving brother, Ed.

Sam and Alma were on their way shortly. Poprob got a dividend in every nation after the emigration had passed the halfway mark. The lonesome stay-at-homes were unable to bear the melancholy of a low population density; their conditioning had been to swarms of their kin. After that point it was possible to foist off the crudest stripped-down accommodations on would-be emigrants; they didn't care. Black-Kupperman did a final job on President Hull-Mendoza, the last job that genius of hypnotics would ever do on any moron, important or otherwise. Hull-Mendoza, panic stricken by his presidency over an emptying nation, joined his constituents. The Independence, aboard which traveled the national government of America, was the most elaborate of all the spaceships — bigger, more comfortable, with a lounge that was handsome, though cramped, and cloakrooms for Senators and Representatives. It went, however, to the same place as the others and Black-Kupperman killed himself, leaving a note that stated he "couldn't live with my conscience." The day after the American President departed, Barlow flew into a rage. Across his specially built desk were supposed to flow all Poprob high-level documents, and this thing — this outrageous thing — called Poprobterm apparently had got into the executive stage before he had even had a glimpse of it! He buzzed for Rogge-Smith, his statistician. Rogge-Smith seemed to be at the bottom of it. Poprobterm seemed to be about first and second and third derivatives, whatever they were. Barlow had a deep distrust of anything more complex than what he called an "average."

While Rogge-Smith was still at the door, Barlow snapped, "What's the meaning of this? Why haven't I been consulted? How far have you people got and why have you been working on something I haven't authorized?"

"Didn't want to bother you, Chief," said Rogge-Smith. "It was really a technical matter, kind of a final cleanup. Want to come and see the work?"

Mollified, Barlow followed his statistician down the corridor. "You still shouldn't have gone ahead without my okay," he grumbled. "Where the hell would you people have been without me?"

"That's right, Chief. We couldn't have swung it ourselves; our minds just don't work that way. And all that stuff you knew from Hitler — it wouldn't have occurred to us. Like poor Black-Kupperman."

They were in a fair-sized machine shop at the end of a slight upward incline. It was cold. Rogge-Smith pushed a button that started a motor, and a flood of arctic light poured in as the roof parted slowly. It showed a small spaceship with the door open. Barlow gaped as Rogge-Smith took him by the elbow and his other boys appeared: Swenson-Swenson, the engineer; Tsutsugimushi-Duncan, his propellants man; Kalb-French, advertising.

"In you go, Chief," said Tsutsugimushi-Duncan. "This is Poprobterm."

"But I'm the World Dictator!"

"You bet, Chief. You'll be in history, all right — but this is necessary, I'm afraid."

The door was closed. Acceleration slammed Barlow cruelly to the metal floor. Something broke, and warm, wet stuff, salty tasting, ran from his mouth to his chin. Arctic sunlight through a port suddenly became a fierce lancet stabbing at his eyes; he was out of the atmosphere.

Lying twisted and broken under the acceleration, Barlow realized that some things had not changed, that Jack Ketch was never asked to dinner however many shillings you paid him to do your dirty work, that murder will out, that crime pays only temporarily.

The last thing he learned was that death is the end of pain.

THE LITTLE BLACK BAG

Old Dr. Full felt the winter in his bones as he limped down the alley. It was the alley and the back door he had chosen rather than the sidewalk and the front door because of the brown paper bag under his arm. He knew perfectly well that the flat-faced, stringy-haired women of his street and their gap-toothed, sour-smelling husbands did not notice if he brought a bottle of cheap wine to his room. They all but lived on the stuff themselves, varied with whiskey when pay checks were boosted by overtime. But Dr. Full, unlike them, was ashamed. A complicated disaster occurred as he limped down the littered alley. One of the neighborhood dogs — a mean little black one he knew and hated, with its teeth always bared and always snarling with menace — hurled at his legs through a hole in the board fence that lined his path. Dr. Full flinched, then swung his leg in what was to have been a satisfying kick to the animal's gaunt ribs. But the winter in his bones weighed down the leg. His foot failed to clear a half-buried brick, and he sat down abruptly, cursing. When he smelled unbottled wine and realized his brown paper package had slipped from under his arm and smashed, his curses died on his lips. The snarling black dog was circling him at a yard's distance, tensely stalking, but he ignored it in the greater disaster.

With stiff fingers as he sat on the filth of the alley, Dr. Full unfolded the brown paper bag's top, which had been crimped over, grocer-wise. The early autumnal dusk had come; he could not see plainly what was left. He lifted out the jug-handled top of his half gallon, and some fragments, and then the bottom of the bottle. Dr. Full was far too occupied to exult as he noted that there was a good pint left. He had a problem, and emotions could be deferred until the fitting time.

The dog closed in, its snarl rising in pitch. He set down the bottom of the bottle and pelted the dog with the curved triangular glass fragments of its top. One of them connected, and the dog ducked back through the fence, howling. Dr. Full then placed a razor-like edge of the half-gallon bottle's foundation to his lips and drank from it as though it were a giant's cup. Twice he had to put it down to rest his arms, but in one minute he had swallowed the pint of wine.

He thought of rising to his feet and walking through the alley to his room, but a flood of well-being drowned the notion. It was, after all, inexpressibly pleasant to sit there and feel the frost-hardened mud of the alley turn soft, or seem to, and to feel the winter evaporating from his bones under a warmth which spread from his stomach through his limbs.

A three-year-old girl in a cut-down winter coat squeezed through the same hole in the board fence from which the black dog had sprung its ambush. Gravely she toddled up to Dr. Full and inspected him with her dirty forefinger in her mouth. Dr. Full's happiness had been providentially made complete; he had been supplied with an audience.

"Ah, my dear," he said hoarsely. And then: "Preposserous accusation. 'If that's what you call evidence,' I should have told them, 'you better stick to your doctoring.' I should have told them: 'I was here before your County Medical Society. And the License Commissioner never proved a thing on me. So, gennulmen, doesn't it stand to reason? I appeal to you as fellow memmers of a great profession —'"

The little girl, bored, moved away, picking up one of the triangular pieces of glass to play with as she left. Dr. Full forgot her immediately, and continued to himself earnestly: "But so help me, they *couldn't* prove a thing. Hasn't a man got any *rights?*" He brooded over the question, of whose answer he was so sure, but on which the Committee on Ethics of the County Medical Society had been equally certain. The winter was creeping into his bones again, and he had no money and no more wine.

Dr. Full pretended to himself that there was a bottle of whiskey somewhere in the fearful litter of his room. It was an old and cruel trick he played on himself when he simply had to be galvanized into getting up and going home. He might freeze there in the alley. In his room he would be bitten by bugs and would cough at the moldy reek from his sink, but he would not freeze and be cheated of the hundreds of bottles of wine that he still might drink, the thousands of hours of glowing content he still might feel. He thought about that bottle of whiskey — was it back of a mounded heap of medical journals? No; he had looked there last time. Was it under the sink, shoved well to the rear, behind the rusty drain? The cruel trick began to play itself out again. Yes, he told himself with mounting excitement, yes, it might be! Your memory isn't so good nowadays, he told himself with rueful good-fellowship. You know perfectly well you might have bought a bottle of whiskey and shoved it behind the sink drain for a moment just like this.

The amber bottle, the crisp snap of the sealing as he cut it, the pleasurable exertion of starting the screw cap on its threads, and then the refreshing tangs in his throat, the warmth in his stomach, the dark, dull happy oblivion of drunkenness — they became real to him. You *could* have, you know! You *could* have! he told himself. With the blessed conviction growing in his mind — It *could* have happened, you know! It *could* have! — he struggled to his right knee. As he did, he heard a yelp behind him, and curiously craned his neck around while resting. It was the little girl, who had cut her hand quite badly on her toy, the piece of glass. Dr. Full could see the rilling bright blood down her coat, pooling at her feet.

He almost felt inclined to defer the image of the amber bottle for her, but not seriously. He knew that it was there, shoved well to the rear under the sink, behind the rusty drain where he had hidden it. He would have a drink and then magnanimously return to help the child. Dr. Full got to his other knee and then his feet, and proceeded at a rapid totter down the littered alley toward his room, where he would hunt with calm optimism at first for the bottle that was not there, then with anxiety, and then with frantic violence. He would hurl books and dishes about before he was done looking for the amber bottle of whiskey, and finally would beat his swollen knuckles against the brick wall until old scars on them opened and his thick old blood oozed over his hands. Last of all, he would sit down somewhere on the floor, whimpering, and would plunge into the abyss of purgative nightmare that was his sleep.

After twenty generations of shilly-shallying and "we'll cross that bridge when we come to it," genus homo had bred himself into an impasse. Dogged biometricians had pointed out with irrefutable logic that mental subnormals were outbreeding mental normals and supernormals, and that the process was occurring on an exponential curve. Every fact that could be mustered in the argument proved the biometricians' case, and led inevitably to the conclusion that genus homo was going to wind up in a preposterous jam quite soon. If you think that had any effect on breeding practices, you do not know genus homo.

There was, of course, a sort of masking effect produced by that other exponential function, the accumulation of technological devices. A moron trained to punch an adding machine seems to be a more skillful computer than a medieval mathematician trained to count on his fingers. A moron trained to operate the twenty-first century equivalent of a linotype seems to be a better typographer than a Renaissance printer limited to a few fonts of movable type. This is also true of medical practice.

It was a complicated affair of many factors. The supernormals "improved the product" at greater speed than the subnormals degraded it, but in smaller quantity because elaborate training of their children was practiced on a custom-made basis. The fetish of higher education had some weird avatars by the twentieth generation: "colleges" where not a member of the student body could read words of three syllables; "universities" where such degrees as "Bachelor of Typewriting," "Master of Shorthand" and "Doctor of Philosophy (Card Filing)" were conferred with the traditional pomp. The handful of supernormals used such devices in order that the vast majority might keep some semblance of a social order going.

Some day the supernormals would mercilessly cross the bridge; at the twentieth generation they were standing irresolutely at its approaches wondering what had hit them. And the ghosts of twenty generations of biometricians chuckled malignantly.

It is a certain Doctor of Medicine of this twentieth generation that we are concerned with. His name was Hemingway — John Hemingway, B.Sc., M.D. He was a general practitioner, and did not hold with running to specialists with every trifling ailment. He often said as much, in approximately these words: "Now, uh, what I mean is you got a good old G.P. See what I mean? Well, uh, now a good old G.P. don't claim he knows all about lungs and glands and them things, get me? But you got a G.P., you got, uh, you got a, well, you got a . . . *all-around man!* That's what you got when you got a G.P — you got a all-around man."

But from this, do not imagine that Dr. Hemingway was a poor doctor. He could remove tonsils or appendixes, assist at practically any confinement and deliver a living, uninjured infant, correctly diagnose hundreds of ailments, and prescribe and administer the correct medication or treatment for each. There was, in fact, only one thing he could not do in the medical line, and that was, violate the ancient canons of medical ethics. And Dr. Hemingway knew better than to try.

Dr. Hemingway and a few friends were chatting one evening when the event occurred that precipitates him into our story. He had been through a hard day at the clinic, and he wished his physicist friend Walter Gillis, B.Sc., M.Sc., Ph.D., would shut up so he could tell everybody about it. But Gillis kept rambling on, in his stilted fashion: "You got to hand it to old Mike; he don't have what we call the scientific method, but you got to hand it to him. There this poor little dope is, puttering around with some glassware and I come up and I ask him, kidding of course, 'How's about a time-travel machine, Mike?'"

Dr. Gillis was not aware of it, but "Mike" had an I.Q. six times his own, and was — to be blunt — his keeper. "Mike" rode herd on the pseudo-physicists in the pseudo-laboratory, in the guise of a bottle-washer. It was a social waste — but as has been mentioned before, the supernormals were still standing at the approaches to a bridge. Their irresolution led to many such preposterous situations. And it happens that

"Mike," having grown frantically bored with his task, was malevolent enough to — but let Dr. Gillis tell it:

"So he gives me these here tube numbers and says, 'Series circuit. Now stop bothering me. Build your time machine, sit down at it and turn on the switch. That's all I ask, Dr. Gillis — that's all I ask.'"

"Say," marveled a brittle and lovely blonde guest, "you remember real good, don't you, doc?" She gave him a melting smile.

"Heck," said Gillis modestly, "I always remember good. It's what you call an inherent facility. And besides I told it quick to my secretary, so she wrote it down. I don't read so good, but I sure remember good, all right. Now, where was I?"

Everybody thought hard, and there were various suggestions:

"Something about bottles, doc?"

"You was starting a fight. You said 'time somebody was traveling.'"

"Yeah — you called somebody a swish. Who did you call a swish?"

"Not swish — *switch*."

Dr. Gillis's noble brow grooved with thought, and he declared: "Switch is right. It was about time travel. What we call travel through time. So I took the tube numbers he gave me and I put them into the circuit-builder; I set it for 'series' and there it is — my time-traveling machine. It travels things through time real good." He displayed a box.

"What's in the box?" asked the lovely blonde.

Dr. Hemingway told her: "Time travel. It travels things through time."

"Look," said Gillis, the physicist. He took Dr. Hemingway's little black bag and put it on the box. He turned on the switch and the little black bag vanished.

"Say," said Dr. Hemingway, "that was, uh, swell. Now bring it back."

"Huh?"

"Bring back my little black bag."

"Well," said Dr. Gillis, "they don't come back. I tried it backwards and they don't come back. I guess maybe that dummy Mike give me a bum steer."

There was wholesale condemnation of "Mike" but Dr. Hemingway took no part in it. He was nagged by a vague feeling that there was something he would have to do. He reasoned: "I am a doctor and a doctor has got to have a little black bag. I ain't got a little black bag — so ain't I a doctor no more?" He decided that this was absurd. He *knew* he was a doctor. So it must be the bag's fault for not being there. It was no good, and he would get another one tomorrow from that dummy Al, at the clinic. Al could find things good, but he was a dummy — never liked to talk sociable to you.

So the next day Dr. Hemingway remembered to get another little black bag from his keeper — another little black bag with which he could perform tonsillectomies, appendectomies and the most difficult confinements, and with which he could diagnose and cure his kind until the day when the supernormals could bring themselves to cross that bridge. Al was kinda nasty about the missing little black bag, but Dr. Hemingway didn't exactly remember what had happened, so no tracer was sent out, so —

Old Dr. Full awoke from the horrors of the night to the horrors of the day. His gummy eyelashes pulled apart convulsively. He was propped against a corner of his room, and something was making a little drumming noise. He felt very cold and cramped. As his eyes focused on his lower body, he croaked out a laugh. The drumming noise was being made by his left heel, agitated by fine tremors against the bare floor. It was going to be the D.T.'s again, he decided dispassionately. He wiped his mouth with his bloody knuckles, and the fine tremor coarsened; the snare-drum beat became louder and slower. He was getting a break this fine morning, he decided sardonically. You didn't get the horrors until you had been tightened like a violin string, just to the breaking point. He had a reprieve, if a reprieve into his old body with the blazing, endless headache just back of the eyes and the screaming stiffness in the joints were anything to be thankful for.

There was something or other about a kid, he thought vaguely. He was going to doctor some kid. His eyes rested on a little black bag in the center of the room, and he forgot about the kid. "I could have sworn," said Dr. Full, "I hocked that two years ago!" He hitched over and reached the bag, and then realized it was some stranger's kit, arriving here he did not know how. He tentatively touched the lock and it snapped open and lay flat, rows and rows of instruments and medications tucked into loops in its four walls. It seemed vastly larger open than closed. He didn't see how it could possibly fold up into that compact size again, but decided it was some stunt of the instrument makers. Since his time — that made it worth more at the hock shop, he thought with satisfaction.

Just for old times' sake, he let his eyes and fingers rove over the instruments before he snapped the bag shut and headed for Uncle's. More than a few were a little hard to recognize — exactly, that is. You could see the things with blades for cutting, the forceps for holding and pulling, the retractors for holding fast, the needles and gut for suturing, the hypos — a fleeting thought crossed his mind that he could peddle the hypos separately to drug addicts.

Let's go, he decided, and tried to fold up the case. It didn't fold until he happened to touch the lock, and then it folded all at once into a little black bag. Sure have forged ahead, he thought, almost able to forget that what he was primarily interested in was its pawn value.

With a definite objective, it was not too hard for him to get to his feet. He decided to go down the front steps, out the front door and down the sidewalk. But first —

He snapped the bag open again on his kitchen table, and pored through the medication tubes. "Anything to sock the autonomic nervous system good and hard," he mumbled. The tubes were numbered, and there was a plastic card which seemed to list them. The left margin of the card was a run-down of the systems — vascular, muscular, nervous. He followed the last entry across to the right. There were columns for "stimulant," "depressant," and so on. Under "nervous system" and "depressant" he found the number 17, and shakily located the little glass tube which bore it. It was full of pretty blue pills and he took one.

It was like being struck by a thunderbolt.

Dr. Full had so long lacked any sense of well-being except the brief glow of alcohol that he had forgotten its very nature. He was panic-stricken for a long moment at the sensation that spread through him slowly, finally tingling in his fingertips. He straightened up, his pains gone and his leg tremor stilled.

That was great, he thought. He'd be able to *run* to the hock shop, pawn the little black bag and get some booze. He started down the stairs. Not even the street, bright with mid-morning sun, into which he emerged made him quail. The little black bag in his left hand had a satisfying, authoritative weight. He was walking erect, he noted, and not in the somewhat furtive crouch that had grown on him in recent years. A little self-respect, he told himself, that's what I need. Just because a man's down doesn't mean —

"Docta, please-a come wit'!" somebody yelled at him, tugging his arm. "Da litt-la girl, she's-a burn' up!" It was one of the slum's innumerable flat-faced, stringy-haired women, in a slovenly wrapper.

"Ah, I happen to be retired from practice —" he began hoarsely, but she would not be put off.

"In by here, Docta!" she urged, tugging him to a doorway. "You come look-a da litt-la girl. I got two dolla, you come look!" That put a different complexion on the matter. He allowed himself to be towed through the doorway into a mussy, cabbage-smelling flat. He knew the woman now, or rather knew who she must be — a new arrival who had moved in the other night. These people moved at night, in motorcades of battered cars supplied by friends and relations, with furniture lashed to the tops, swearing and drinking until the small hours. It explained why she had stopped him: she did not yet know he was old Dr. Full, a drunken reprobate whom nobody would trust. The little black bag had been his guarantee, outweighing his whiskery face and stained black suit.

He was looking down on a three-year-old girl who had, he rather suspected, just been placed in the mathematical center of a freshly changed double bed. God knew what sour and dirty mattress she usually slept on. He seemed to recognize her as he noted a crusted bandage on her right hand. Two dollars, he thought — An ugly flush had spread up her pipe-stem arm. He poked a finger into the socket of her elbow, and felt little spheres like marbles under the skin and ligaments roll apart. The child began to squall thinly; beside him, the woman gasped and began to weep herself.

"Out," he gestured briskly at her, and she thudded away, still sobbing.

Two dollars, he thought — Give her some mumbo jumbo, take the money and tell her to go to a clinic. Strep, I guess, from that stinking alley. It's a wonder any of them grow up. He put down the little black bag and forgetfully fumbled for his key, then remembered and touched the lock. It flew open, and he selected a bandage shears, with a blunt wafer for the lower jaw. He fitted the lower jaw under the bandage, trying not to hurt the kid by its pressure on the infection, and began to cut. It was amazing how easily and swiftly the shining shears snipped through the crusty rag around the wound. He hardly seemed to be driving the shears with fingers at all. It almost seemed as though the shears were driving his fingers instead as they scissored a clean, light line through the bandage.

Certainly have forged ahead since my time, he thought — sharper than a microtome knife. He replaced the shears in their loop on the extraordinarily big board that the little black bag turned into when it unfolded, and leaned over the wound. He whistled at the ugly gash, and the violent infection which had taken immediate root in the sickly child's thin body. Now what can you do with a thing like that? He pawed over the contents of the little black bag, nervously. If he lanced it and let some of the pus out, the old woman would think he'd done something for her and he'd get the two dollars. But at the clinic they'd want to know who did it and if they got sore enough they might send a cop around. Maybe there was something in the kit —

He ran down the left edge of the card to "lymphatic" and read across to the column under "infection." It didn't sound right at all to him; he checked again, but it still said that. In the square to which the line and column led were the symbols: "IV-g-3cc." He couldn't find any bottles marked with Roman numerals, and then noticed that that was how the hypodermic needles were designated. He lifted number IV from its loop, noting that it was fitted with a needle already and even seemed to be charged. What a way to carry those things around! So — three cc. of whatever was in hypo number IV ought to do something or other about infections settled in the lymphatic system — which, God knows, this one was. What did the lower-case "g" mean, though? He studied the glass hypo and saw letters engraved on what looked like a rotating disk at the top of the barrel. They ran from "a" to "i," and there was an index line engraved on the barrel on the opposite side from the calibrations.

Shrugging, old Dr. Full turned the disk until "g" coincided with the index line, and lifted the hypo to eye level. As he pressed in the plunger he did not see the tiny thread of fluid squirt from the tip of the needle. There was a sort of dark mist for a moment about the tip. A closer inspection showed that the needle was not even pierced at the tip. It had the usual slanting cut across the bias of the shaft, but the cut did not expose an oval hole. Baffled, he tried pressing the plunger again. Again *something* appeared around the tip and vanished. "We'll settle this," said the doctor. He slipped the needle into the skin of his forearm. He thought at first that he had missed — that the point had glided over the top of his skin instead of catching and slipping under it. But he saw a tiny blood-spot and realized that somehow he just hadn't felt the puncture. Whatever was in the barrel, he decided, couldn't do him any harm if it lived up to its billing — and if it could come out through a needle that had no hole. He gave himself three cc. and twitched the needle out. There was the swelling — painless, but otherwise typical.

Dr. Full decided it was his eyes or something, and gave three cc. of "g" from hypodermic IV to the feverish child. There was no interruption to her wailing as the needle went in and the swelling rose. But a long instant later, she gave a final gasp and was silent.

Well, he told himself, cold with horror, you did it that time. You killed her with that stuff.

Then the child sat up and said: "Where's my mommy?"

Incredulously, the doctor seized her arm and palpated the elbow. The gland infection was zero, and the temperature seemed normal. The blood-congested tissues surrounding the wound were subsiding as he watched. The child's pulse was stronger and no faster than a child's should be. In the sudden silence of the room he could hear the little girl's mother sobbing in her kitchen, outside. And he also heard a girl's insinuating voice:

"She gonna be okay, doc?"

He turned and saw a gaunt-faced, dirty-blonde sloven of perhaps eighteen leaning in the doorway and eyeing him with amused contempt. She continued: "I heard about you, *Doc-tor* Full. So don't go try and put the bite on the old lady. You couldn't doctor up a sick cat."

"Indeed?" he rumbled. This young person was going to get a lesson she richly deserved. "Perhaps you would care to look at my patient?"

"Where's my mommy?" insisted the little girl, and the blonde's jaw fell. She went to the bed and cautiously asked: "You okay now, Teresa? You all fixed up?"

"Where's my mommy?" demanded Teresa. Then, accusingly, she gestured with her wounded hand at the doctor. "You *poke* me!" she complained, and giggled pointlessly.

"Well —" said the blonde girl, "I guess I got to hand it to you, doc. These loud-mouth women around here said you didn't know your . . . I mean, didn't know how to cure people. They said you ain't a real doctor."

"I *have* retired from practice," he said. "But I happened to be taking this case to a colleague as a favor, your good mother noticed me, and —" a deprecating smile. He touched the lock of the case and it folded up into the little black bag again.

"You stole it," the girl said flatly.

He sputtered.

"Nobody'd trust you with a thing like that. It must be worth plenty. You stole that case. I was going to stop you when I come in and saw you working over Teresa, but it looked like you wasn't doing her any harm. But when you give me that line about taking that case to a colleague I know you stole it. You gimme a cut or I go to the cops. A thing like that must be worth twenty — thirty dollars."

The mother came timidly in, her eyes red. But she let out a whoop of joy when she saw the little girl sitting up and babbling to herself, embraced her madly, fell on her knees for a quick prayer, hopped up to kiss the doctor's hand, and then dragged him into the kitchen, all the while rattling in her native language while the blonde girl let her eyes go cold with disgust. Dr. Full allowed himself to be towed into the kitchen, but flatly declined a cup of coffee and a plate of anise cakes and St. John's Bread.

"Try him on some wine, ma," said the girl sardonically.

"Hyass! Hyass!" breathed the woman delightedly. "You like-a wine, docta?" She had a carafe of purplish liquid before him in an instant, and the blonde girl snickered as the doctor's hand twitched out at it. He drew his hand back, while there grew in his head the old image of how it would smell and then taste and then warm his stomach and limbs. He made the kind of calculation at which he was practiced; the delighted woman would not notice as he downed two tumblers, and he could overawe her through two tumblers more with his tale of Teresa's narrow brush with the Destroying Angel, and then — why, then it would not matter. He would be drunk.

But for the first time in years, there was a sort of counter-image: a blend of the rage he felt at the blonde girl to whom he was so transparent, and of pride at the cure he had just effected. Much to his own surprise, he drew back his hand from the carafe and said, luxuriating in the words: "No, thank you. I don't believe I'd care for any so early in the day." He covertly watched the blonde girl's face, and was gratified at her surprise.

Then the mother was shyly handing him two bills and saying: "Is no much-a money, docta — but you come again, see Teresa?"

"I shall be glad to follow the case through," he said. "But now excuse me — I really must be running along." He grasped the little black bag firmly and got up; he wanted very much to get away from the wine and the older girl.

"Wait up, doc," said she. "I'm going your way." She followed him out and down the street. He ignored her until he felt her hand on the black bag. Then old Dr. Full stopped and tried to reason with her:

"Look, my dear. Perhaps you're right. I might have stolen it. To be perfectly frank, I don't remember how I got it. But you're young and you can earn your own money —"

"Fifty-fifty," she said, "or I go to the cops. And if I get another word outta you, it's sixty-forty. And you know who gets the short end, don't you, doc?"

Defeated, he marched to the pawnshop, her impudent hand still on the handle with his, and her heels beating out a tattoo against his stately tread.

In the pawnshop, they both got a shock.

"It ain't stendard," said Uncle, unimpressed by the ingenious lock. "I ain't nevva seen one like it. Some cheap Jap stuff, maybe? Try down the street. This I nevva could sell."

Down the street they got an offer of one dollar. The same complaint was made: "I ain't a collecta, mista — I buy stuff that got resale value. Who could I sell this to, a Chinaman who don't know medical instruments? Every one of them looks funny. You sure you didn't make these yourself?" They didn't take the one-dollar offer.

The girl was baffled and angry; the doctor was baffled too, but triumphant. He had two dollars, and the girl had a half-interest in something nobody wanted. But, he suddenly marveled, the thing had been all right to cure the kid, hadn't it?

"Well," he asked her, "do you give up? As you see, the kit is practically valueless."

She was thinking hard. "Don't fly off the handle, doc. I don't get this but something's going on all right . . . would those guys know good stuff if they saw it?"

"They would. They make a living from it. Wherever this kit came from —"

She seized on that, with a devilish faculty she seemed to have of eliciting answers without asking questions. "I thought so. You don't know either, huh? Well, maybe I can find out for you. C'mon in here. I ain't letting go of that thing. There's money in it — some way, I don't know how, there's money in it." He followed her into a cafeteria and to an almost-empty corner. She was oblivious to stares and snickers from the other customers as she opened the little black bag — it almost covered a cafeteria table — and ferreted through it. She picked out a retractor from a loop, scrutinized it, contemptuously threw it down, picked out a speculum, threw it down, picked out the lower half of an O.B. forceps, turned it over, close to her sharp young eyes — and saw what the doctor's dim old ones could not have seen.

All old Dr. Full knew was that she was peering at the neck of the forceps and then turned white. Very carefully, she placed the half of the forceps back in its loop of cloth and then replaced the retractor and the speculum. "Well?" he asked. "What did you see?"

"'Made in U.S.A.'" she quoted hoarsely. "'Patent Applied for July 2450.'"

He wanted to tell her she must have misread the inscription, that it must be a practical joke, that —

But he knew she had read correctly. Those bandage shears: they *had* driven his fingers, rather than his fingers driving them. The hypo needle that had no hole. The pretty blue pill that had struck him like a thunderbolt.

"You know what I'm going to do?" asked the girl, with sudden animation. "I'm going to go to charm school. You'll like that, won't ya, doc? Because we're sure going to be seeing a lot of each other."

Old Dr. Full didn't answer. His hands had been playing idly with that plastic card from the kit on which had been printed the rows and columns that had guided him twice before. The card had a slight convexity; you could snap the convexity back and forth from one side to the other. He noted, in a daze, that with each snap a different text appeared on the cards. *Snap.* "The knife with the blue dot in the handle is for tumors only. Diagnose tumors with your Instrument Seven, the Swelling Tester. Place the Swelling Tester —" *Snap.* "An overdose of the pink pills in Bottle 3 can be fixed with one white pill from Bottle —" *Snap.* "Hold the suture needle by the end without the hole in it. Touch it to one end of the wound you want to close and let go. After it has made the knot, touch it —" *Snap.* "Place the top half of the O.B. Forceps near the opening. Let go. After it has entered and conformed to the shape of —" *Snap.*

The slot man saw "FLANNERY 1 — MEDICAL" in the upper left corner of the hunk of copy. He automatically scribbled "trim to .75" on it and skimmed it across the horseshoe-shaped copy desk to Piper, who had been handling Edna Flannery's quack-exposé series. She was a nice youngster, he thought, but like all youngsters she over-wrote. Hence, the "trim."

Piper dealt back a city hall story to the slot, pinned down Flannery's feature with one hand and began to tap his pencil across it, one tap to a word, at the same steady beat as a teletype carriage traveling across the roller. He wasn't exactly reading it this first time. He was just looking at the letters and words to find out whether, as letters and words, they conformed to *Herald* style. The steady tap of his pencil ceased at intervals as it drew a black line ending with a stylized letter "d" through the word "breast" and scribbled in "chest" instead, or knocked down the capital "E" in "East" to lower case with a diagonal, or closed up a split word — in whose middle Flannery had bumped the space bar of her typewriter — with two curved lines like parentheses rotated through ninety degrees. The thick black pencil zipped a ring around the "30" which, like all youngsters, she put at the end of her stories. He turned back to the first page for the second reading. This time the pencil drew lines with the stylized "d's" at the end of them through adjectives and whole phrases, printed big "L's" to mark paragraphs, hooked some of Flannery's own paragraphs together with swooping recurved lines.

At the bottom of "FLANNERY ADD 2 — MEDICAL" the pencil

slowed down and stopped. The slot man, sensitive to the rhythm of his beloved copy desk, looked up almost at once. He saw Piper squinting at the story, at a loss. Without wasting words, the copy reader skimmed it back across the Masonite horseshoe to the chief, caught a police story in return and buckled down, his pencil tapping. The slot man read as far as the fourth add, barked at Howard, on the rim: "Sit in for me," and stumped through the clattering city room toward the alcove where the managing editor presided over his own bedlam.

The copy chief waited his turn while the make-up editor, the press-room foreman and the chief photographer had words with the M.E. When his turn came, he dropped Flannery's copy on his desk and said: "She says this one isn't a quack."

The M.E. read:

FLANNERY 1 — MEDICAL,
by Edna Flannery, *Herald* Staff Writer.

The sordid tale of medical quackery which the *Herald* has exposed in this series of articles undergoes a change of pace today which the reporter found a welcome surprise. Her quest for the facts in the case of today's subject started just the same way that her exposure of one dozen shyster M.D.'s and faith-healing phonies did. But she can report for a change that Dr. Bayard Full is, despite unorthodox practices which have drawn the suspicion of the rightly hypersensitive medical associations, a true healer living up to the highest ideals of his profession.

Dr. Full's name was given to the *Herald*'s reporter by the ethical committee of a county medical association, which reported that he had been expelled from the association on July 18, 1941 for allegedly "milking" several patients suffering from trivial complaints. According to sworn statements in the committee's files, Dr. Full had told them they suffered from cancer, and that he had a treatment which would prolong their lives. After his expulsion from the association, Dr. Full dropped out of their sight — until he opened a midtown "sanitarium" in a brown-stone front which had for years served as a rooming house.

The *Herald*'s reporter went to that sanitarium, on East 89th Street, with the full expectation of having numerous imaginary ailments diag-nosed and of being promised a sure cure for a flat sum of money. She expected to find unkempt quarters, dirty instruments and the mumbo-jumbo paraphernalia of the shyster M.D. which she had seen a dozen times before.

She was wrong.

Dr. Full's sanitarium is spotlessly clean, from its tastefully furnished entrance hall to its shining, white treatment rooms. The attractive, blonde receptionist who greeted the reporter was soft-spoken and correct, asking only the reporter's name, address and the general nature of her complaint. This was given, as usual, as "nagging backache." The receptionist asked the *Herald*'s reporter to be seated, and a short while later conducted her to a second-floor treatment room and introduced her to Dr. Full.

Dr. Full's alleged past, as described by the medical society spokesman, is hard to reconcile with his present appearance. He is a clear-eyed, white-haired man in his sixties, to judge by his appearance — a little above middle height and apparently in good physical condition. His voice was firm and friendly, untainted by the ingratiating whine of the shyster M.D. which the reporter has come to know too well.

The receptionist did not leave the room as he began his examination after a few questions as to the nature and location of the pain. As the reporter lay face down on a treatment table the doctor pressed some instrument to the small of her back. In about one minute he made this astounding statement: "Young woman, there is no reason for you to have any pain where you say you do. I understand they're saying nowadays that emotional upsets cause pains like that. You'd better go to a psychologist or psychiatrist if the pain keeps up. There is no physical cause for it, so I can do nothing for you."

His frankness took the reporter's breath away. Had he guessed she was, so to speak, a spy in his camp? She tried again: "Well, doctor, perhaps you'd give me a physical checkup. I feel run-down all the time, besides the pains. Maybe I need a tonic." This is never-failing bait to shyster M.D.'s — an invitation for them to find all sorts of mysterious conditions wrong with a patient, each of which "requires" an expensive treatment. As explained in the first article of this series, of course, the reporter underwent a thorough physical checkup before she embarked on her quack-hunt, and was found to be in one hundred percent perfect condition, with the exception of a "scarred" area at the bottom tip of her left lung resulting from a childhood attack of tuberculosis and a tendency toward "hyperthyroidism" — overactivity of the thyroid gland which makes it difficult to put on weight and sometimes causes a slight shortness of breath.

Dr. Full consented to perform the examination, and took a number of shining, spotlessly clean instruments from loops in a large board literally covered with instruments — most of them unfamiliar to the reporter. The instrument with which he approached first was a tube with a curved dial in its surface and two wires that ended on flat disks growing from its ends. He placed one of the disks on the back of the reporter's right hand and the other on the back of her left. "Reading the meter," he called out some number which the attentive receptionist took down on a ruled form. The same procedure was repeated several times, thoroughly covering the reporter's anatomy and thoroughly convincing her that the doctor was a complete quack. The reporter had never seen any such diagnostic procedure practiced during the weeks she put in preparing for this series.

The doctor then took the ruled sheet from the receptionist, conferred with her in low tones and said: "You have a slightly overactive thyroid, young woman. And there's something wrong with your left lung — not seriously, but I'd like to take a closer look."

He selected an instrument from the board which, the reporter knew, is called a "speculum" — a scissorlike device which spreads apart body openings such as the orifice of the ear, the nostril and so on, so that a doctor can look in during an examination. The instrument was, however, too large to be an aural or nasal speculum but too small to be anything else. As the *Herald*'s reporter was about to ask further questions, the attending receptionist told her: "It's customary for us to blindfold our patients during lung examinations — do you mind?" The reporter, bewildered, allowed her to tie a spotlessly clean bandage over her eyes, and waited nervously for what would come next.

She still cannot say exactly what happened while she was blindfolded — but X rays confirm her suspicions. She felt a cold sensation at her ribs on the left side — a cold that seemed to enter inside her body. Then there was a snapping feeling, and the cold sensation was gone. She heard Dr. Full say in a matter-of-fact voice: "You have an old tubercular scar down there. It isn't doing any particular harm, but an active person like you needs all the oxygen she can get. Lie still and I'll fix it for you."

Then there was a repetition of the cold sensation, lasting for a longer time. "Another batch of alveoli and some more vascular glue," the *Herald*'s reporter heard Dr. Full say, and the receptionist's crisp response to the order. Then the strange sensation departed and the eye-bandage was removed. The reporter saw no scar on her ribs, and yet the doctor assured her: "That did it. We took out the fibrosis — and a good fibrosis it was, too; it walled off the infection so you're still alive to tell the tale. Then we planted a few clumps of alveoli — they're the little gadgets that get the oxygen from the air you breathe into your blood. I won't monkey with your thyroxin supply. You've got used to being the kind of person you are, and if you suddenly found yourself easygoing and all the rest of it, chances are you'd only be upset. About the backache: just check with the county medical society for the name of a good psychologist or psychiatrist. And look out for quacks; the woods are full of them."

The doctor's self-assurance took the reporter's breath away. She asked what the charge would be, and was told to pay the receptionist fifty dollars. As usual, the reporter delayed paying until she got a receipt signed by the doctor himself, detailing the services for which it paid. Unlike most, the doctor cheerfully wrote: "For removal of fibrosis from left lung and restoration of alveoli," and signed it.

The reporter's first move when she left the sanitarium was to head for the chest specialist who had examined her in preparation for this series. A comparison of X rays taken on the day of the "operation" and those taken previously would, the *Herald*'s reporter then thought, expose Dr. Full as a prince of shyster M.D.'s and quacks.

The chest specialist made time on his crowded schedule for the reporter, in whose series he has shown a lively interest from the planning stage on. He laughed uproariously in his staid Park Avenue examining room as she described the weird procedure to which she had been subjected. But he did not laugh when he took a chest X ray of the reporter, developed it, dried it, and compared it with the ones he had taken earlier. The chest specialist took six more X rays that afternoon, but finally admitted that they all told the same story. The *Herald*'s reporter has it on his authority that the scar she had eighteen days ago from her tuberculosis is now gone and has been replaced by healthy lung-tissue. He declares that this is a happening unparalleled in medical history. He does not go along with the reporter in her firm conviction that Dr. Full is responsible for the change.

The *Herald*'s reporter, however, sees no two ways about it. She concludes that Dr. Bayard Full — whatever his alleged past may have been — is now an unorthodox but highly successful practitioner of medicine, to whose hands the reporter would trust herself in any emergency.

Not so is the case of "Rev." Annie Dimsworth — a female harpy who, under the guise of "faith" preys on the ignorant and suffering who come to her sordid "healing parlor" for help and remain to feed "Rev." Annie's bank account, which now totals up to $53,238.64. Tomorrow's article will show, with photostats of bank statements and sworn testimony that —"

The managing editor turned down "FLANNERY 1 — MEDICAL" and tapped his front teeth with a pencil, trying to think straight. He finally told the copy chief: "Kill the story. Run the teaser as a box." He tore off the last paragraph — the "teaser" about "Rev." Annie — and handed it to the desk man, who stumped back to his Masonite horseshoe.

The make-up editor was back, dancing with impatience as he tried to catch the M.E.'s eye. The interphone buzzed with the red light which indicated that the editor and publisher wanted to talk to him. The M.E. thought briefly of a special series on this Dr. Full, decided nobody would believe it and that he probably was a phony anyway. He spiked the story on the "dead" hook and answered his interphone.

Dr. Full had become almost fond of Angie. As his practice had grown to engross the neighborhood illnesses, and then to a corner suite in an uptown taxpayer building, and finally to the sanitarium, she seemed to have grown with it. Oh, he thought, we have our little disputes —

The girl, for instance, was too much interested in money. She had wanted to specialize in cosmetic surgery — removing wrinkles from wealthy old women and whatnot. She didn't realize, at first, that a thing like this was in their trust, that they were the stewards and not the owners of the little black bag and its fabulous contents.

He had tried, ever so cautiously, to analyze them, but without success. All the instruments were slightly radioactive, for instance, but not quite so. They would make a Geiger-Müller counter indicate, but they would not collapse the leaves of an electroscope. He didn't pretend to be up on the latest developments, but as he understood it, that was just plain *wrong*. Under the highest magnification there were lines on the instruments' superfinished surfaces: incredibly fine lines, engraved in random hatchments which made no particular sense. Their magnetic properties were preposterous. Sometimes the instruments were strongly attracted to magnets, sometimes less so, and sometimes not at all.

Dr. Full had taken X rays in fear and trembling lest he disrupt whatever delicate machinery worked in them. He was *sure* they were not solid, that the handles and perhaps the blades must be mere shells filled with busy little watchworks — but the X rays showed nothing of the sort. Oh, yes — and they were always sterile, and they wouldn't rust. Dust *fell* off them if you shook them: now, that was something he understood. They ionized the dust, or were ionized themselves, or something of the sort. At any rate, he had read of something similar that had to do with phonograph records.

She wouldn't know about that, he proudly thought. She kept the books well enough, and perhaps she gave him a useful prod now and then when he was inclined to settle down. The move from the neighborhood slum to the uptown quarters had been her idea, and so had the sanitarium. Good, good, it enlarged his sphere of usefulness. Let the child have her mink coats and her convertible, as they seemed to be calling roadsters nowadays. He himself was too busy and too old. He had so much to make up for.

Dr. Full thought happily of his Master Plan. She would not like it much, but she would have to see the logic of it. This marvelous thing that had happened to them must be handed on. She was herself no doctor; even though the instruments practically ran themselves, there was more to doctoring than skill. There were the ancient canons of the healing art. And so, having seen the logic of it, Angie would yield; she would assent to his turning over the little black bag to all humanity.

He would probably present it to the College of Surgeons, with as little fuss as possible — well, perhaps a *small* ceremony, and he would like a souvenir of the occasion, a cup or a framed testimonial. It would be a relief to have the thing out of his hands, in a way; let the giants of the healing art decide who was to have its benefits. No, Angie would understand. She was a goodhearted girl.

It was nice that she had been showing so much interest in the surgical side lately — asking about the instruments, reading the instruction card for hours, even practicing on guinea pigs. If something of his love for humanity had been communicated to her, old Dr. Full sentimentally thought, his life would not have been in vain. Surely she would realize that a greater good would be served by surrendering the instruments to wiser hands than theirs, and by throwing aside the cloak of secrecy necessary to work on their small scale.

Dr. Full was in the treatment room that had been the brownstone's front parlor; through the window he saw Angle's yellow convertible roll to a stop before the stoop. He liked the way she looked as she climbed the stairs; neat, not flashy, he thought. A sensible girl like her, she'd understand. There was somebody with her — a fat woman, puffing up the steps, overdressed and petulant. Now, what could she want?

Angie let herself in and went into the treatment room, followed by the fat woman. "Doctor," said the blonde girl gravely, "may I present Mrs. Coleman?" Charm school had not taught her everything, but Mrs. Coleman, evidently *nouveau riche*, thought the doctor, did not notice the blunder.

"Miss Aquella told me *so* much about you, doctor, and your remarkable system!" she gushed.

Before he could answer, Angie smoothly interposed: "Would you excuse us for just a moment, Mrs. Coleman?"

She took the doctor's arm and led him into the reception hall. "Listen," she said swiftly, "I know this goes against your grain, but I couldn't pass it up. I met this old thing in the exercise class at Elizabeth Barton's. Nobody else'll talk to her there. She's a widow. I guess her husband was a black marketeer or something, and she has a pile of dough. I gave her a line about how you had a system of massaging wrinkles out. My idea is, you blindfold her, cut her neck open with the Cutaneous Series knife, shoot some Firmol into the muscles, spoon out some of that blubber with an Adipose Series curette and spray it all with Skintite. When you take the blindfold off she's got rid of a wrinkle and doesn't know what happened. She'll pay five hundred dollars. Now, don't say 'no,' doc. Just this once, let's do it my way, can't you? I've been working on this deal all along too, haven't I?"

"Oh," said the doctor, "very well." He was going to have to tell her about the Master Plan before long anyway. He would let her have it her way this time.

Back in the treatment room, Mrs. Coleman had been thinking things over. She told the doctor sternly as he entered: "Of course, your system is permanent, isn't it?"

"It is, madam," he said shortly. "Would you please lie down there? Miss Aquella, get a sterile three-inch bandage for Mrs. Coleman's eyes." He turned his back on the fat woman to avoid conversation, and pretended to be adjusting the lights. Angie blindfolded the woman, and the doctor selected the instruments he would need. He handed the blonde girl a pair of retractors, and told her: "Just slip the corners of the blades in as I cut —" She gave him an alarmed look, and gestured at the reclining woman. He lowered his voice: "Very well. Slip in the corners and rock them along the incision. I'll tell you when to pull them out."

Dr. Full held the Cutaneous Series knife to his eyes as he adjusted the little slide for three centimeters depth. He sighed a little as he recalled that its last use had been in the extirpation of an "inoperable" tumor of the throat.

"Very well," he said, bending over the woman. He tried a tentative pass through her tissues. The blade dipped in and flowed through them, like a finger through quicksilver, with no wound left in the wake. Only the retractors could hold the edges of the incision apart.

Mrs. Coleman stirred and jabbered: "Doctor, that felt so peculiar! Are you sure you're rubbing the right way?"

"Quite sure, madam," said the doctor wearily. "Would you please try not to talk during the massage?"

He nodded at Angie, who stood ready with the retractors. The blade sank in to its three centimeters, miraculously cutting only the dead horny tissues of the epidermis and the live tissue of the dermis, pushing aside mysteriously all major and minor blood vessels and muscular tissue, declining to affect any system or organ except the one it was — tuned to, could you say? The doctor didn't know the answer, but he felt tired and bitter at this prostitution. Angie slipped in the retractor blades and rocked them as he withdrew the knife, then pulled to separate the lips of the incision. It bloodlessly exposed an unhealthy string of muscle, sagging in a dead-looking loop from blue-grey ligaments. The doctor took a hypo, number IX, pre-set to "g" and raised it to his eye level. The mist came and went. There probably was no possibility of an embolus with one of these gadgets, but why take chances? He shot one cc. of "g" — identified as "Firmol" by the card — into the muscle. He and Angie watched as it tightened up against the pharynx.

He took the Adipose Series curette, a small one, and spooned out yellowish tissue, dropping it into the incinerator box, and then nodded to Angie. She eased out the retractors and the gaping incision slipped together into unbroken skin, sagging now. The doctor had the atomizer — dialed to "Skintite" — ready. He sprayed, and the skin shrank up into the new firm throat line.

As he replaced the instruments, Angie removed Mrs. Coleman's bandage and gayly announced: "We're finished! And there's a mirror in the reception hall —"

Mrs. Coleman didn't need to be invited twice. With incredulous fingers she felt her chin, and then dashed for the hall. The doctor grimaced as he heard her yelp of delight, and Angie turned to him with a tight smile. "I'll get the money and get her out," she said. "You won't have to be bothered with her any more."

He was grateful for that much.

She followed Mrs. Coleman into the reception hall, and the doctor dreamed over the case of instruments. A ceremony, certainly — he was *entitled* to one. Not everybody, he thought, would turn such a sure source of money over to the good of humanity. But you reached an age when money mattered less, and when you thought of these things you had done that *might* be open to misunderstanding if, just if, there chanced to be any of that, well, that judgment business. The doctor wasn't a religious man, but you certainly found yourself thinking hard about some things when your time drew near —

Angie was back, with a bit of paper in her hands. "Five hundred dollars," she said matter-of-factly. "And you realize, don't you, that we could go over her an inch at a time — at five hundred dollars an inch?"

"I've been meaning to talk to you about that," he said.

There was bright fear in her eyes, he thought — but why?

"Angie, you've been a good girl and an understanding girl, but we can't keep this up forever, you know."

"Let's talk about it some other time," she said flatly. "I'm tired now."

"No — I really feel we've gone far enough on our own. The instruments —"

"Don't say it, doc!" she hissed. "Don't say it, or you'll be sorry!" In her face there was a look that reminded him of the hollow-eyed, gaunt-faced, dirty-blonde creature she had been. From under the charm-school finish there burned the guttersnipe whose infancy had been spent on a sour and filthy mattress, whose childhood had been play in the littered alley and whose adolescence had been the sweatshops and the aimless gatherings at night under the glaring street lamps.

He shook his head to dispel the puzzling notion. "It's this way," he patiently began. "I told you about the family that invented the O.B. forceps and kept them a secret for so many generations, how they could have given them to the world but didn't?"

"They knew what they were doing," said the guttersnipe flatly.

"Well, that's neither here nor there," said the doctor, irritated. "My mind is made up about it. I'm going to turn the instruments over to the College of Surgeons. We have enough money to be comfortable. You can even have the house. I've been thinking of going to a warmer climate, myself." He felt peeved with her for making the unpleasant scene. He was unprepared for what happened next.

Angie snatched the little black bag and dashed for the door, with panic in her eyes. He scrambled after her, catching her arm, twisting it in a sudden rage. She clawed at his face with her free hand, babbling curses. Somehow, somebody's finger touched the little black bag, and it opened grotesquely into the enormous board, covered with shining instruments, large and small. Half a dozen of them joggled loose and fell to the floor.

"*Now* see what you've done!" roared the doctor, unreasonably. Her hand was still viselike on the handle, but she was standing still, trembling with choked-up rage. The doctor bent stiffly to pick up the fallen instruments. Unreasonable girl! he thought bitterly. Making a scene —

Pain drove in between his shoulderblades and he fell face-down. The light ebbed. "Unreasonable girl!" he tried to croak. And then: "They'll know I tried, anyway —

Angie looked down on his prone body, with the handle of the Number Six Cautery Series knife protruding from it. "— will cut through all tissues. Use for amputations before you spread on the Re-Gro. Extreme caution should be used in the vicinity of vital organs and major blood vessels or nerve trunks —"

"I didn't mean to do that," said Angie, dully, cold with horror. Now the detective would come, the implacable detective who would reconstruct the crime from the dust in the room. She would run and turn and twist, but the detective would find her out and she would be tried in a courtroom before a judge and jury; the lawyer would make speeches, but the jury would convict her anyway, and the headlines would scream: "BLONDE KILLER GUILTY!" and she'd maybe get the chair, walking down a plain corridor where a beam of sunlight struck through the dusty air, with an iron door at the end of it. Her mink, her convertible, her dresses, the handsome man she was going to meet and marry —

The mist of cinematic clichés cleared, and she knew what she would do next. Quite steadily, she picked the incinerator box from its loop in the board — a metal cube with a different-textured spot on one side. "— to dispose of fibroses or other unwanted matter, simply touch the disk —" You dropped something in and touched the disk. There was a sort of soundless whistle, very powerful and unpleasant if you were too close, and a sort of lightless flash. When you opened the box again, the contents were gone. Angie took another of the Cautery Series knives and went grimly to work. Good thing there wasn't any blood to speak of — She finished the awful task in three hours.

She slept heavily that night, totally exhausted by the wringing emotional demands of the slaying and the subsequent horror. But in the morning, it was as though the doctor had never been there. She ate breakfast, dressed with unusual care — and then undid the unusual care. Nothing out of the ordinary, she told herself. Don't do one thing different from the way you would have done it before. After a day or two, you can phone the cops. Say he walked out spoiling for a drunk, and you're worried. But don't rush it, baby — *don't rush it.*

Mrs. Coleman was due at 10:00 A.M. Angie had counted on being able to talk the doctor into at least one more five-hundred-dollar session. She'd have to do it herself now — but she'd have to start sooner or later.

The woman arrived early. Angie explained smoothly: "The doctor asked me to take care of the massage today. Now that he has the tissue-firming process beginning, it only requires somebody trained in his methods —" As she spoke, her eyes swiveled to the instrument case — open! She cursed herself for the single flaw as the woman followed her gaze and recoiled.

"What are those things!" she demanded. "Are you going to cut me with them? I *thought* there was something fishy —"

"Please, Mrs. Coleman," said Angie, "please, *dear* Mrs. Coleman — you don't understand about the . . . the massage instruments!"

"Massage instruments, my foot!" squabbled the woman shrilly. "That doctor *operated* on me. Why, he might have killed me!"

Angie wordlessly took one of the smaller Cutaneous Series knives and passed it through her forearm. The blade flowed like a finger through quicksilver, leaving no wound in its wake. *That* should convince the old cow!

It didn't convince her, but it did startle her. "What did you do with it? The blade folds up into the handle — that's it!"

"Now look closely, Mrs. Coleman," said Angie, thinking desperately of the five hundred dollars. "Look very closely and you'll see that the, uh, the sub-skin massager simply slips beneath the tissues without doing any harm, tightening and firming the muscles themselves instead of having to work through layers of skin and adipose tissue. It's the secret of the doctor's method. Now, how can outside massage have the effect that we got last night?"

Mrs. Coleman was beginning to calm down. "It *did* work, all right," she admitted, stroking the new line of her neck. "But your arm's one thing and my neck's another! Let me see you do that with your neck!"

Angie smiled —

Al returned to the clinic after an excellent lunch that had almost reconciled him to three more months he would have to spend on duty. And then, he thought, and then a blessed year at the blessedly super-normal South Pole working on his specialty — which happened to be telekinesis exercises for ages three to six. Meanwhile, of course, the world had to go on and of course he had to shoulder his share in the running of it.

Before settling down to desk work he gave a routine glance at the bag board. What he saw made him stiffen with shocked surprise. A red light was on next to one of the numbers — the first since he couldn't think when. He read off the number and murmured "Okay, 674,101. That fixes *you*." He put the number on a card sorter and in a moment the record was in his hand. Oh, yes — Hemingway's bag. The big dummy didn't remember how or where he had lost it; none of them ever did.

There were hundreds of them floating around.

Al's policy in such cases was to leave the bag turned on. The things practically ran themselves, it was practically impossible to do harm with them, so whoever found a lost one might as well be allowed to use it. You turn it off, you have a social loss — you leave it on, it may do some good. As he understood it, and not very well at that, the stuff wasn't "used up." A temporalist had tried to explain it to him with little success that the prototypes in the transmitter had been transducted through a series of point-events of transfinite cardinality. Al had innocently asked whether that meant prototypes had been stretched, so to speak, through all time, and the temporalist had thought he was joking and left in a huff.

"Like to see him do this," thought Al darkly, as he telekinized himself to the combox, after a cautious look to see that there were no medics around. To the box he said: "Police chief," and then to the police chief: "There's been a homicide committed with Medical Instrument Kit 674,101. It was lost some months ago by one of my people, Dr. John Hemingway. He didn't have a clear account of the circumstances."

The police chief groaned and said: "I'll call him in and question him." He was to be astonished by the answers, and was to learn that the homicide was well out of his jurisdiction.

Al stood for a moment at the bag board by the glowing red light that had been sparked into life by a departing vital force giving, as its last act, the warning that Kit 674,101 was in homicidal hands. With a sigh, Al pulled the plug and the light went out.

"Yah," jeered the woman. "You'd fool around with my neck, but you wouldn't risk your own with that thing!"

Angie smiled with serene confidence a smile that was to shock hardened morgue attendants. She set the Cutaneous Series knife to three centimeters before drawing it across her neck. Smiling, knowing the blade would cut only the dead horny tissue of the epidermis and the live tissue of the dermis, mysteriously push aside all major and minor blood vessels and muscular tissue —

Smiling, the knife plunging in and its microtomesharp metal shearing through major and minor blood vessels and muscular tissue and pharynx, Angie cut her throat.

In the few minutes it took the police, summoned by the shrieking Mrs. Coleman, to arrive, the instruments had become crusted with rust, and the flasks which had held vascular glue and clumps of pink, rubbery alveoli and spare grey cells and coils of receptor nerves held only black slime, and from them when opened gushed the foul gases of decomposition.

THEORY OF ROCKETRY

Mr. Edel taught six English classes that year at Richard M. Nixon High School, and the classes averaged seventy-five pupils each. That was four hundred and fifty boys and girls, but Mr. Edel still tried to have the names down cold by at least the third week of the semester. As English 308 stormed into his room he was aware that he was not succeeding, and that next year he would even stop trying, for in 1978 the classes would average eighty-two pupils instead of seventy-five.

One seat was empty when the chime sounded; Mr. Edel was pleased to notice that he remembered whose it was. The absent pupil was a Miss Kahn, keyed into his memory by "Kahnsti-pated," which perhaps she was, with her small pinched features centered in a tallow acre of face. Miss Kahn slipped in some three seconds late; Edel nodded at his intern, Mrs. Giovino, and Mrs. Giovino coursed down the aisle to question, berate and possibly demerit Miss Kahn. Edel stood up, the Modern Revised Old Testament already open before him.

"You're blessed," he read, "if you're excused for your wrongdoing and your sin is forgiven. You're blessed if God knows that you're not evil and sly any more. I, King David, used to hide my sins from God while I grew old and blustered proudly all day. But all day and all night too your hand was heavy on me, God ..."

It would be the flat, crystal-clear, crystal-blank M.R.O.T. all this week; next week he'd read (with more pleasure) from the Roman Catholic Knox translation; the week after that, from the American Rabbinical Council's crabbed version heavy with footnotes; and the week after that, back to M.R.O.T. Thrice blessed was he this semester that there were no Moslems, Buddhists, militant atheists or miscellaneous cultists to sit and glower through the reading or exercise their legal right to wait it out in the corridor. This semester the classes were All-American: Protestant, Catholic, Jewish — choice of one.

"Amen," chorused the class, and they sat down; two minutes of his fifty-minute hour were gone forever.

Soft spring was outside the windows, and they were restless. Mr. Edel "projected" a little as he told them, "This is the dreaded three-minute impromptu speech for which English Three Oh Eight is notorious, young ladies and gentlemen. The importance of being able to speak clearly on short notice should be obvious to everybody. You'll get nowhere in your military service if you can't give instructions and verbal orders. You'll get less than nowhere in business if you can't convey your ideas crisply and accurately." A happy thought struck him: great chance to implement the Spiritual-Values Directive. He added, "You may be asked to lead in prayer or say grace on short notice." (He'd add that one to his permanent repertoire; it was a natural.) "We are not asking the impossible. Anybody can talk interestingly, easily and naturally for three minutes if they try. Miss Gerber, will you begin with a little talk on your career plans?"

Miss Gerber ("Grapefruit" was the mnemonic) rose coolly and driveled about the joys of motherhood until Mrs. Giovino passed her card to Edel and called time.

"You spoke freely, Miss Gerber, but perhaps not enough to the point," said Edel. "I'm pleased, though, that you weren't bothered by any foolish shyness. I'm sure everybody I call on will be able to talk right up like you did." (He liked that "like" the way you like biting on a tooth that aches; he'd give them Artificial-Grammar De-emphasis …) "Foster, may we hear from you on the subject of your coming summer vacation?" He jotted down a C for the Grapefruit.

Foster ("Fireball") rose and paused an expert moment. Then in a firm and manly voice he started with a little joke ("If I survive English Three Oh Eight …"), stated his theme ("A vacation is not a time for idling and wasted opportunity"), developed it ("harvest crew during the day for physical — my Science Search Project during the evenings for mental"), elevated it ("no excuse for neglecting one's regular attendance at one's place of worship") and concluded with a little joke ("should be darned glad to get back to school!").

The speech clocked 2:59. It was masterly; none of the other impromptus heard that morning came close to it.

"And," said Mr. Edel at lunch to his semi-crony Dr. Fugua, biology, "between classes I riffled through the grade cards again and found I'd marked him F. Of course I changed it to A. The question is, why?"

"Because you'd made a mistake," said Fuqua absently. Something was on his mind, thought Edel.

"No, no. Why did I make the mistake?"

"Well, Fured, in *The Psychology of Everyday* —"

"Roland, please, I know all that. Assume I do. Why do I unconsciously dislike Foster? I should get down on my knees and thank God for Foster."

Fugua shook his head and began to pay attention. "Foster?" he said. "You don't know the half of it. I'm his faculty adviser. Quite a boy, Foster."

"To me just a name, a face, a good recitation every time. You know:

seventy-five to a class. What's he up to here at dear old Tricky Dicky?"

"Watch the funny jokes, Edel," said Fuqua, alarmed.

"Sorry. It slipped out. But Foster?"

"Well, he's taking an inhuman pre-engineering schedule. Carrying it with ease. Going out for all the extracurricular stuff the law allows. R.O.T.C. Drill Team, Boxing Squad, Math Club, and there I had to draw the line. He wanted on the Debating Team too. I've seen him upset just once. He came to me last year when the school dentist wanted to pull a bad wisdom tooth he had. He made me make the dentist wait until he had a chance to check the dental requirements of the Air Force Academy. They allow four extractions, so he let the dentist yank it. Fly boy. Off we go into the whatsit. He wants it bad."

"I see. Just a boy with motivation. How long since you've seen one, Roland?"

Dr. Fuqua leaned forward, his voice low and urgent. "To hell with Foster, Dave. I'm in trouble. Will you help me?"

"Why, of course, Roland. How much do you need?" Mr. Edel was a bachelor and had found one of the minor joys of that state to be "tiding over" his familied friends.

"Not that kind of trouble, Dave. Not yet. They're sharpening the ax for me. I get a hearing this afternoon."

"Good God! What are you supposed to have done?"

"Everything. Nothing. It's one of those 'best interests' things. Am I taking the Spiritual-Values Directive seriously enough? Am I thinking about patting any adolescent fannies? Exactly why am I in the lowest quarter for my seniority group with respect to voluntary hours of refresher summer courses? Am I happy here?"

Edel said, "These things always start somewhere. Who's out to get you?"

Fuqua took a deep breath and said in a surprisingly small voice, "Me, I suppose."

"Oh?"

Then it came out with a rush. "It was the semester psychometrics. I'd been up all night almost, fighting with Beth. She does not understand how to handle a fifteen-year-old boy — never mind. I felt sardonic, so I did something sardonic. And stupid. Don't ever get to feeling sardonic, Dave. I took the psychometric and I checked their little boxes and I told the goddamned truth right down the line. I checked them where I felt like checking them and not where a prudent biology teacher ought to check them."

"You're dead," Mr. Edel said after a pause.

"I thought I could get a bunch of the teachers to say they lie their way through the psychometrics. Start a real stink."

"I'd make a poor ditch digger, Roland, but — if you can get nine others, I'll speak up. No, make that six others. I don't think they could ignore eight of us."

"You're a good man," Dr. Fuqua said. "I'll let you know. There's old McGivern — near retirement. I want to try him." He gulped his coffee and headed across the cafeteria.

Edel sat there, mildly thunderstruck at Fuqua's folly and his own daring. Fuqua had told them the kind of bird he was by checking "Yes" or "No" on the silly-clever statements. He had told them that he liked a drink, that he thought most people were stupider than he, that he talked without thinking first, that he ate too much, that he was lazy, that he had an eye for a pretty ankle — that he was a human being not much better or worse than any other human being. But that wasn't the way to do it, and damned well Fuqua had known it. You simply told yourself firmly, for the duration of the test, "I am a yuk. I have never had an independent thought in my life; independent thinking scares me. I am utterly monogamous and heterosexual. I go bowling with the boys. Television is the greatest of the art forms. I believe in installment purchasing. I am a yuk."

That these parlor games were taken seriously by some people was an inexplicable but inexorable fact of life in the twentieth century. Edel had yukked his way through scholarships, college admissions, faculty appointment and promotions and had never thought the examination worse than a bad cold. Before maturity set in, in the frat house, they had eased his qualms about psychometric testing with the ancient gag "You ain't a man until you've had it three times."

Brave of him, pretty brave at that, to back up Fuqua — if Roland could find six others.

Roland came to him at four o'clock to say he had not even found one other. "I don't suppose — No. I'm not asking you to, Dave. Two — it wouldn't be any good."

He went into the principal's office.

The next day a bright young substitute was teaching biology in his place and his student advisees had been parceled out among other teachers. Mr. Edel found that young Foster had now become his charge.

The seventy-two pupils in his English 114 class sat fascinated and watched the television screen. Dr. Henley Ragen was teaching them *Macbeth*, was teaching about nine hundred English 114 classes throughout the state *Macbeth*, and making them like it. The classroom rapport was thick enough to cut and spread with a shingle. The man's good, Edel thought, but that good? How much is feedback from their knowing he's famous for his rapport, how much is awe of his stupendous salary, still nowhere equal to nine hundred teachers' salaries?

Dr. Henley Ragen, el magnifico, portentously turned a page; there was grim poetry in the gesture. He transfixed the classroom (nine hundred classrooms) with Those Eyes. Abruptly he became Macbeth at the Banquet prepar'd. With nervous hilarity he shouted at his guests, "You know your own degrees; sit down! At first and last, the hearty welcome!" Stock still at a lectern he darted around the table, bluffly rallying the company, slipped off to chat, grimly merry, with the First Murtherer at the door, returned to the banquet, stood in chilled horror at the Ghost in the chair, croaked, "The table's full."

Mr. Edel studied the faces of his seventy-two English 114ers. They were in hypnotic states of varying depths, except Foster. The Fireball was listening and learning, his good mind giving as well as taking. The intelligent face was alive, the jaw firm, and around him eyes were dull and jaws went slack. Foster could speak and write an English sentence, which perhaps was the great distinguishing mark between him and the rest of English 114. Blurted fragments of thought came from them, and the thoughts were cliches a hundred times out of a hundred.

Dr. Henley Ragen growled at them, "We are yet but young in deed …" and his eyes said the rest, promising horrors to come. He snapped the book shut like a pistol's bang; the 114ers popped out of their trances into dazed attentiveness. "Notebooks!" said Ragen (qua Ragen) and, seventy-two gunfighters quick on the draw, they snapped out books and poised their pens. Ragen spoke for ten minutes about the scene; every so often Those Eyes and an intensification of That Voice cued them to write a word or a phrase, almost without glancing at the paper. (Later each would look at his notes and not be surprised to find them lucid, orderly, even masterful summations of the brief lecture.)

As Dr. Henley Ragen bluffly delivered a sort of benediction from the altar of learning, Mr. Edel thought, Well, they've got the Banquet Scene now; they'll own it forever. The way they own the Prologue to *The Canterbury Tales*, the "Ode to the West Wind," Adam Smith. A good deal better than nothing; *pauca sed matura*. Or so he supposed.

That afternoon from three to five Mr. Edel was available to his advisees. It was a period usually devoted to catching up on his paperwork; beyond making out the students' assignment schedule, a task traditionally considered beyond the capacity of the young, he had done no advising in years. And Foster appeared.

His handshake was manly, his grin was modest but compelling. He got to the point. "Mr. Edel, do you think I could swing an Enrichment Project in English?"

The teacher hardly knew what he meant. "Enrichment? Well, we haven't been doing that lately, Foster. I suppose it's still in the optional curriculum —"

"Yes, sir, Form Sixty-eight, English, Paragraph Forty-five, Section Seven. 'Opportunities shall be afforded to students believed qualified by advisers to undertake projects equivalent to College Freshman English term papers, and the grades therefor shall be entered on the students' records and weighed as evidence in assigning students' positions in the graduating class.'"

Mr. Edel had found Foster's card by then and was studying it. The boy's schedule was brutal, but his grade average was somewhere between B-plus and A. "Foster," he told him, "there's such a thing as a breaking point. I — I understand you want very much to go to Colorado Springs." (Poor Fuqua! What had become of ... ?)

"Very much, sir. They expect the best — they have a right to expect the best. I'm not complaining, Mr. Edel, but there are girls with straight-A averages who aren't working as hard as I am. Well, I've just got to beat them at their own game."

Mr. Edel understood. It wasn't just girls, though mostly it was. There was a type of student who was no trouble, who did the work, every smidgen of it, who read every word of every assigned page, who turned in accurate, curiously dead, echoless, unresonant papers which you could not in decency fault though you wanted to tear them up and throw them in their authors' bland faces. You had a curious certainty that the adeptly memorized data they reeled back on demand vanished forever once the need for a grade was gone, that it never by any chance became bone of their bone to strengthen them against future trials. Often enough when you asked them what they hoped to be they smilingly said, "I am going to teach."

Foster, now. A boy who fought with the material and whipped it. He said, "Why so strong, Foster? What's it about?"

The boy said, "Space, partly. And my father. Two big challenges, Mr. Edel. I think I'm a very lucky fellow. Here I am with a new frontier opening up, but there are lots of fellows my age who don't see it. I see it because of my father. It's wonderful to have a challenge like that: Can I be the man he is? Can I learn even more, be a better leader, a better engineer?"

Mr. Edel was moved deeply. "Your father just missed space flight, is that it?"

"By a whisker," Foster said regretfully. "Nothing can be done about it except what I'm doing."

"He's an aeroengineer?"

"He can do anything," Foster said positively. "And he has!"

A picture of the elder Foster was forming in Mr. Edel's mind — young Fireball grown taller, solider and grizzled, the jaw firmed and controlled, the voice more powerful and sure. And, unquestionably, leather puttees.

Foster's card said he had no mother, which made it more understandable. This fine boy was hard material honed to an edge, single-purposed. Did he have a young Hap Arnold here in his office? A Curtis LeMay? They had to come from somewhere, those driving, wide-ranging leaders and directors of millions. The slow-rolling conquest of space needed such men, first to navigate and pilot so no navigator or pilot would ever be able to snow them, then to move up step by step through research to command, then to great command.

"I'll bet on you, Foster," he said abruptly. "We can't let the — the future English teachers outpoint you with their snap courses. You'll do me a term paper on … on *Henry V*. First, read it. Read hell out of it and take notes. Get in touch with me when you think you're ready to talk it over. I happen to be a bachelor; I have time in the evenings. And talk it over with your father, if you can persuade him to read along with you."

Foster laughed. "I'm afraid Dad's much too busy for Shakespeare, but I'll try. Thanks, Mr. Edel." He left.

Mr. Edel, with considerable trouble, found a pad of forms in his desk which covered Enrichment Projects, English, Adviser's Permission for. He filled one out for Foster, looked it over and said, surprised, "Again, damn it!" He had checked the box for "Permission denied." He tore up the form — it was discolored anyway from being so long on the top of the pad — and meticulously made out another, checking the various boxes with exquisite care.

That night after dinner he tried to telephone Roland Fuqua, but service to his number had been discontinued. Alarmed, he buzzed over on his scooter to Fuqua's apartment, one of a quarter million in the Dearborn Village Development of Metropolitan Life and Medical. Roland's hulking, spoiled and sullen boy Edward (who had unilaterally changed his name last year to Rocky) was the only person there, and he was on his way out — "to an orgy with some pigs," if you believed him. He said "Little Rollo" was now a night-shift lab assistant in a pet-food company's quality-control department and this was his mother's Bingo night. "You want I should give a message?" he asked satirically, overplaying the role of intolerably burdened youth.

"If it won't break your back," Mr. Edel said, "please ask your father to give me a ring sometime."

Again in his own small apartment, Mr. Edel thought of many things. Of the ancient papyrus which, when decoded, moaned: "Children are not now as respectful and diligent as they were in the old days." Of *Henry V*. Of Dr. Fuqua drudging away on petfood protein determinations and lucky to be doing that. Of his own selfish, miserable, lonely comfort in his castle. Of Foster, the hero-king to be, and of himself, Aristotle to the young Alexander. Had there been a dozen such in his twenty years? There had not. Marie Perrone still sent him her novels, and they were almost popular and very bad. Jim Folwell had gone to Princeton and into the foreign service and that was that. Janice Reeves and Ward Dreiman were married and both teaching at Cornell. What had happened to the hundred thousand others he had taught only God and themselves knew. If they all dropped dead at this instant, tomorrow morning some trucks would not roll for an hour or two, some advertising agencies would come near to missing a few deadlines, some milk would sour and some housewives would bang, perplexed, on the doors of shops that should be open, a few sales would languish unclosed, a few machines would growl for lack of oil. But Foster might land on the moons of Jupiter.

Therefore let him learn, make him learn, how to be great. He would meet his Pistols, Bardolphs, Fluellens, a few Exeters, and without doubt his Cambridges and Scroops: clowns, fuss-budgets, friends and traitors. It could matter to nobody except herself if her agent ripped poor arty Marie Perrone up her back; it might matter a great deal to — he shied at the alternatives — to, let us say, man, if Foster trusted a Pistol to do his work, or passed over a Fluellen for his mannerisms, or failed to know a Scroop when he saw one.

We will arm the young hero-king, he thought comfortably just before sleep claimed him.

Roland Fuqua had been transferred to Toledo by the pet-food company. He wrote to Edel:

> Instinct tells me not to queer my luck by talking about it, but anyway — I really believe I'm moving up in the organization. The other day a party from Sales came through the QC labs and one of them, just an ordinary-looking Joe, stopped to talk to me about the test I was running — asked very intelligent questions. You could have knocked me over with a Folin-Wu pipette when they told me who he was afterward: just John McVey himself, Assistant Vice-President in Charge of Sales!

Unaccustomed as I am to pipe dreams, it can't be a coincidence that it was me he talked to instead of half a dozen other lab men with seniority; I don't know what he has in mind exactly, maybe some kind of liaison job between QC and Sales, which would put me on Staff level instead of Hourly-Rated. ...

Mr. Edel felt sick for him. He would have to answer the letter at once; if he put it off he would put it off again and their correspondence would peter out and Fuqua would be betrayed. But what could he tell him — that he was pipe-dreaming, that "coincidences" like that happen to everybody a hundred times a day, that Roland Fuqua, Ph.D., would never, at forty-five, move from the quality-control lab to the glittering world of sales?

He stalled for time by stamping and addressing the envelope first, then hung over the typewriter for five minutes of misery. It was Wednesday night; Foster was due for the twelfth and last of his Enrichment sessions. Mr. Edel tried not to cause Fuqua pain by dwelling on the world of teaching he had lost — but what else was there to write about?

I'm sure you remember Foster — the fly boy? I've been taking him, on one of those Enrichment things, through Henry V. This is supposed to win him .001 of a place higher on the graduating-class list and get him into the Academy, and I suppose it will. Things are very simple for Foster, enviably so. He has a titan of engineering for a father who appears to commute between the Minas Gerais power station in Brazil, his consulting service in the city and trouble spots in the I. T. and T. network — maybe I should say commutate. I honestly do not believe that Foster has to lie his way through the personality profiles like the rest of us mortals —

Now, there was a hell of a thing to put down. He was going to rip the page out and start again, then angrily changed his mind. Fuqua wasn't a cripple; it wasn't Bad Form to mention his folly; it would be merely stupid to pretend that nothing had happened. He finished out the page with a gush of trivia. Sexy little Mrs. Dickman who taught Spanish was very visibly expecting. New dietician in the cafeteria, food cheaper but worse than ever. Rumored retirement of Old Man Thelusson again and one step up for history teachers if true. Best wishes good luck regards to Beth and the youngster, Dave. He whipped the page into folds, slipped it into the envelope and sealed the flap fast, before he could change his mind again. It was time to stop treating Fuqua like a basket case; if convalescence had not begun by now it never would.

His bell rang: Foster was on time, to the minute.

They shook hands rather formally. "Like a cup of coffee, Foster?" Mr. Edel asked.

"No thank you, sir."

"I'll make one for myself, then. Brought your paper? Good. Read it to me."

While he compounded coffee Foster began to read. After much discussion they had settled on "Propaganda and Reality in *Henry V*" as his topic. The boy had read Holinshed where relevant, articles in *The Dictionary of National Biography* and appropriate history texts. Beyond suggesting these, Mr. Edel had left him alone in the actual treatment of his paper. He did not quite know what to expect from Foster beyond careful organization and an absence of gross blunders; he waited with interest.

The paper was a short one — fifteen hundred words, by request. Nevertheless it gave Mr. Edel a few painful shocks. There were two sneers at "deluded groundlings," much reveling in the irony of the fictional Henry's affection for his Welsh captain as against the real Henry who had helped to crush Glendower and extinguish the Welsh as a nation, and fun with the Irishman Macmorris who came loyally from Shakespeare's pen in 1599 while "the general of our gracious empress" was doing his best to extinguish the Irish as a nation. Henry's "we have now no thoughts in us but France (save those to God)" was evaluated as "the poet's afterthought." The massacre of the French prisoners at Agincourt, Henry's brutal practical joke with the pretended glove of a French nobleman, his impossibly compressed and eloquent courtship of Katharine, were all somehow made to testify to a cynical Shakespeare manipulating his audience's passions.

The great shock was that Foster approved of all this. "It was a time of troubles and England was besieged from without and threatened from within. The need of the time was a call to unity, and this Shakespeare provided in good measure. The London mob and the brotherhood of apprentices, always a potential danger to the Peace, no doubt were inspired and pacified for a time by the Shakespearean version of a successful aggressor's early career."

Modestly Foster folded his typescript.

It was ground into Mr. Edel that you start by saying whatever words of praise are possible and then go on to criticize. Mechanically he said warm things about the paper's organization, its style, its scholarly apparatus. "But — aren't you taking a rather too utilitarian view of the play? It is propaganda to some extent, but should you stop short with the propaganda function of the play? I'm aware that you're limited by your topic and length, but I wish there had been some recognition of the play's existence as a work of art."

Foster said, smiling, "Well, I'm new at this, Mr. Edel. I didn't know I was supposed to stray. Should I revise it?"

"Oh, no," Mr. Edel said quickly. "I didn't mean to imply that you're unarguably mistaken in anything you said. I don't know why I'm fussing at you about it at all. I suppose you've taken a sort of engineering approach to literature, which is natural enough. Did you ever succeed in engaging your father in the project?"

"I'm afraid not, Mr. Edel. You can imagine."

"He's been away?"

"Why, no." Foster was surprised. But didn't his father go away now and then? He thought Foster had said — or almost said — He took the paper from him and leafed through it. "This is quite good enough for a pass, Foster. It'll be read by somebody in the English chairman's office, but that's a formality. Let's say you've completed your Enrichment Option." He stuck out his hand and Foster took it warmly. "That, then, is that. Do you have to run now?"

"With all rods out," Foster said. "I've got to prepare for the Math Team meet, a hundred things. Can I mail that for you?"

It was the letter to Fuqua on his desk. "Why, thanks."

"Thank you, Mr. Edel, for the time you've taken with me."

Well worth it, son, Mr. Edel thought after the door closed. There aren't many like you. The paper was a little cold and cynical, but you'll learn. Criticism's heady stuff. Speaking quite objectively, you've done a piece thoroughly consistent with College Freshman English work, and that's what you were supposed to do. If it helps get you into Colorado Springs, I've done my job.

He turned in the paper the next day to the English chairman's office and the assistant chairman read it while he waited, mumbled "Seems quite competent" and entered a "Completed" on Foster's grade card. He let his eyes run over the other grades and whistled. "A beaver," he said.

"All rods out," Mr. Edel smugly corrected him, and went to the door. A freshman girl who knew him, on messenger duty with the principal's office, intercepted him in the corridor. The message: he would please report at once to the principal; Mrs. Giovino would be advised to take such classes as he might be obliged to miss.

"Classes?" he asked the girl, unbelievingly.

She knew nothing.

The assistant principal for teaching personnel received him at once, alone in his two-window office. He was a gray man named Sturgis whose pride was getting to the point. "Edel," he asked, "are you sure you're happy here?"

Mr. Edel said, recognizing a sheet of typing on Sturgis' desk, "May I ask how you got that letter of mine?"

"Surely. Your young friend Foster turned it in."

"But why? Why?"

"I shall quote: 'I honestly do not believe that Foster has to lie his way through the personality profiles like the rest of us mortals.' If you believed this, Edel, why did you counsel him to lie? Why did you show him this letter as proof that you lied yourself?"

"Counsel him to lie? I never. I never."

His stammering was guilt; his sweating was guilt. Sturgis pitied him and shook his head. "He kept a little record," Sturgis said. "Ha, a 'log' he called it — he's quite space-minded; did you know?"

"I know. I demand a hearing, goddammit!"

Sturgis was surprised. "Oh, you'll get a hearing, Edel. We always give hearings; you know that."

"I know that. Can I get back to my classes now?"

"Better not. If you're not happy here ..."

Mr. Edel and Foster met that afternoon in the soda shop two blocks from the school. Mr. Edel had been waiting for him, and Foster saw the teacher staring at him from a booth. He excused himself politely from the Math Team crowd around him and joined Mr. Edel.

"I feel I owe you an explanation, sir," Foster said.

"I agree. How could you — why — ?"

Foster said apologetically, "They like you to be a little ruthless at the Academy. This will stand out on my record as a sign of moral fiber. No, Mr. Edel, don't try to hit me. It'll make things look that much worse at the hearing. Goodbye, sir."

He rejoined his handsome, quiet crowd at the counter; in a moment they were talking busily about elliptic functions and Fourier series. Mr. Edel slunk from the place knowing that there was only one court of appeal.

3379 Seneca Avenue turned out to be a shocking slum tenement back of a municipal bus garage. The apartment, Mr. Edel thought, after his initial surprise, would be one of those "hideaways" — probably a whole floor run together, equipped with its own heating and air-conditioning, plumbing replaced … after all, would Foster Senior give a damn about a fancy address? Not that engineer.

But the Foster apartment, or so said a card tacked to a rust-stiffened bell-pull, was only one of a dozen like it on the cabbage-reeking fifth floor. And the paunchy, unshaven, undershirted man who came to the door and stood reeling in the doorway said: "Yah, I'm Ole Foster. Yah, I got a boy in Nixon High. What the crazy kid do now? He's crazy, that kid. Maybe I get a little drunk sometime, I got a little pension from I hurt my back driving the buses, people don't appreciate, don't realize. You wanna drink? What you say you come for?"

"About your son …"

"So I beat him up!" the man yelled, suddenly belligerent. "Ain't I his father? He talks smart to me, I got a right to beat him some, ain't I? People don't appreciate …"

Old Foster lost interest and, mumbling, closed the door.

Mr. Edel walked slowly down the stairs, not able to forgive, but feeling at least the beginnings of eventual ease from the knowledge of why he was being destroyed.

MAKE MINE MARS

"X is for the ecstasy she ga-a-ave me;
E is for her eyes — one, two, and three-ee;
T is for the teeth with which she'd sha-a-ave me;
S is for her scales of i-vo-ree-ee-ee . . ."

Somebody was singing, and my throbbing head objected. I seemed to have a mouthful of sawdust.

"T is for her tentacles ah-round me;
J is for her jowls — were none soo-oo fair;
H is for the happy day she found me;
Fe is for the iron in her hair..."

I ran my tongue around inside my mouth. It was full of sawdust — spruce and cedar, rocketed in from Earth.

"Put them all to-gether, they spell Xetstjhfe ..."

My eyes snapped open, and I sat up, cracking my head on the underside of the table beneath which I was lying. I lay down and waited for the pinwheels to stop spinning. I tried to sort it out. Spruce and cedar... Honest Blogri's Olde Earthe Saloon ... eleven stingers with a Sirian named Wenjtkpli . . .

"A worrud that means the wur-r-l-l-d too-oo mee-ee-ee!"

Through the fading pinwheels, I saw a long and horrid face, a Sirian face, peering at me with kindly interest under the table. It was Wenjtkpli.

"Good morning, little Earth chum," he said. "You feel not so tired now?"

"Morning?" I yelled, sitting up again and cracking my head again and lying down again to wait for the pinwheels to fade again.

"You sleep," I heard him say, "fourteen hours — so happy, so peaceful!"

"I gotta get out of here," I mumbled, scrambling about on the imported sawdust for my hat. I found I was wearing it and climbed out, stood up, and leaned against the table, swaying and spitting out the last of the spruce and cedar.

"You like another stinger?" asked Wenjtkpli brightly. I retched feebly.

"Fourteen hours," I mumbled. "That makes it 0900 Mars now, or exactly ten hours past the time I was supposed to report for the nightside at the bureau."

"But last night you talk different," the Sirian told me in surprise. "You say many times how bureau chief McGillicuddy can take lousy job and jam —"

"That was last night," I moaned. "This is this morning."

"Relax, little Earth chum. I sing again song you taught me:

"X is for the ecstasy she ga-a-ave me; E is for —"

My throbbing head still objected. I flapped good-by at him and set a course for the door of Blogri's joint. The quaint period mottoes — "QUAFFE YE NUT-BROWN AYLE" "DROPPE DEAD TWYCE" and so on — didn't look so quaint by the cold light of the Martian dawn.

An unpleasant little character, Venusian or something, I'd seen around the place oozed up to me.

"Head hurt plenty, huh?" he simpered.

"This is no time for sympathy," I said. "Now one side or flipper off — I gotta go to work."

"No sympathy," he said, his voice dropping to a whisper. He fumbled oddly in his belt, then showed me a little white capsule. "Clear your head, huh? Work like lightning, you bet!"

I was interested. "How much?"

"For you, friend, nothing. Because I hate seeing fellows suffer with big head."

"Beat it," I told him and shoved past through the door.

That pitch of his with a free sample meant he was pushing J-K-B. I was in enough trouble without adding an unbreakable addiction to the stuff. If I'd taken his free sample, I would have been back to see him in 12 hours, sweating blood for more. And that time he would have named his own price.

I fell into an eastbound chair and fumbled a quarter into the slot. The thin, cold air of the pressure dome was clearing my head already. I was sorry for all the times I'd cussed a skinflint dome administration for not supplying a richer air mix or heating the outdoors more lavishly. I felt good enough to shave, and luckily had my razor in my wallet. By the time the chair was gliding past the building where Interstellar News had a floor, I had the whiskers off my jaw and most of the sawdust out of my hair.

The floater took me up to our floor while I tried not to think of what McGillicuddy would have to say.

The newsroom was full of noise, as usual. McGillicuddy was in the copydesk slot chewing his way through a pile of dispatches due to be filed on the pressure dome split for A.M. newscasts in four minutes by the big wall clock. He fed his copy, without looking, to an operator battering the keys of the old-fashioned radioteletype that was good enough to serve for local clients.

"Two minutes short!" he yelled at one of the men on the "Gimme a brightener! Gimme a god-damned brightener!" The rim man raced to the receiving ethertypes from Cammadion, Betelgeuse, and the other Interstellar bureaus. He yanked an item from one of the clicking machines and threw it at McGillicuddy, who slashed at it with his pencil and passed it to the operator. The tape the operator was coding started through the transmitter-distributor, and on all local clients' radioteletypes appeared:

FIFTEEN-MINUTE INTERSTELLAR NEWSCAST A.M.
MARS PRESSURE DOMES

Everybody leaned back and lit up. McGillicuddy's eye fell on me, and I cleared my throat.

"Got a cold?" he asked genially.

"Nope. No cold."

"Touch of indigestion? Flu, maybe? You're tardy today."

"I know it."

"Bright boy."

He was smiling. That was bad.

"Spencer," he told me. "I thought long and hard about you. I thought about you when you failed to show up for the nightside. I thought about you intermittently through the night as I took your shift. Along about 0300 I decided what to do with you. It was as though Providence had taken a hand. It was as though I prayed 'Lord, what shall I do with a drunken, no-good son of a spacecook who ranks in my opinion with the boils of Job as an affliction to man?' Here's the answer, Spencer."

He tossed me a piece of ethertype paper, torn from one of our inter-stellar-circuit machines. On it was the following dialogue:

ANYBODY TTHURE I MEAN THERE

THIS MARSBUO ISN GA PLS

WOT TTHUT I MEAN WOT THAT MEAN PLEASE

THIS IS THE MARS BUREAU OF INTERSTELLAR NEWS. WHO ARE YOU AND WHAT ARE YOU DOING HORSING AROUND ON OUR KRUEGER 60-B CIRCUIT TELETYPE QUESTIONMARK WHERE IS REGULAR STAFFER GO AHEAD

THATK WOT I AM CALLING YOU ABBOUUT. KENNEDY DIED THIS MORNING PNEUMONIA. I AM WEEMS EDITOR PHOENIX. U SENDING REPLLACEMENT KENNEDY PLEAS

THIS MCGILLICUDDY, MARSBUO ISN CHIEF. SENDING REPLACEMENT KENNEDY SOONEST. HAVE IDEAL MAN FOR JOB END

That was all. It was enough.

"Chief," I said to McGillicuddy. "Chief, you can't. You wouldn't — *would* you?"

"Better get packed," he told me, busily marking up copy, "Better take plenty of nice, warm clothing. I understand Krueger 60-B is about one thousand times dimmer than the sun. That's absolute magnitude, of course — Frostbite's in quite close. A primitive community, I'm told. Kennedy didn't like it. But of course the poor old duffer wasn't good enough to handle anything swifter than a one-man bureau on a one-planet split. Better take *lots of* warm clothing."

"I quit," I said.

"Sam," said somebody, in a voice that always makes me turn to custard inside.

"Hello, Ellie," I said. "I was just telling Mr. McGillicuddy that he isn't going to shoot me off to Frostbite to rot."

"Freeze," corrected McGillicuddy with relish. "Freeze. Good morning, Miss Masters. Did you want to say a few parting words to your friend?"

"I do," she told him and drew me aside to no man's land where the ladies of the press prepared strange copy for the softer sex. "Don't quit, Sam," she said in that voice. "I could never love a quitter. What if it *is* a minor assignment?"

"Minor," I said. "What a gem of understatement *that* is!"

"It'll be good for you," she insisted. "You can show him that you've got on the ball. You'll be on your own except for the regular dispatches to the main circuit and your local unit. You could dig up all sorts of cute feature stories that'd get your name known." And so on. It was partly her logic, partly that voice and partly her promise to kiss me good-by at the port.

"I'm going to take it," I told McGillicuddy.

He looked up with a pleased smile and murmured: "The power of prayer …"

The good-by kiss from Ellie was the only thing about the journey that wasn't nightmarish. ISN's expense account stuck me on a rusty bucket that I shared with glamorous freight like yak kids and ten-penny nails. The little yaks blatted whenever we went into overdrive to break through the speed of light. The Greenhough Effect — known to readers of the science features as "supertime" — scared hell out of them. On ordinary rocket drive, they just groaned and whimpered to each other, the yak equivalent of, "Tibet was never like this!"

The Frostbite spaceport wasn't like the South Pole, but it'd be like Greenland. There was a bunch of farmers waiting for their yaks, beating their mittened hands together and exhaling long plumes of vapor. The collector of customs, a rat-faced city boy, didn't have the decency to hand them over and let the hayseeds get back to the administration building. I watched through a porthole and saw him stalling and dawdling over a sheaf of papers for each of the farmers. Oddly enough, the stalling and dawdling stopped as soon as the farmers caught on and passed over a few dollars. Nobody even bothered to slip it shamefacedly from one hand to another. They just handed it over, not caring who saw — Rat-Face sneering, the farmers dumbly accepting the racket.

My turn came. Rat-Face came aboard and we were introduced by the chief engineer. "Harya," he said. "Twenny bucks."

"What for?"

"Landing permit. Later at the administration you can pay your visitor's permit. That's twenny bucks too."

"I'm not a visitor. I'm coming here to work."

"Work, schmurk. So you'll need a work permit — twenny bucks." His eyes wandered. "Whaddaya got there?"

"Ethertype parts. May need them for replacements."

He was on his knees in front of the box, crooning, "Triple *ad va-*

lorem plus twenny dollars security bond for each part plus twenny dollars inspection fee plus twenny dollars for decontamination plus twenny dollars for failure to declare plus —"

"Break it up, Joe," said a new arrival — a grey-mustached little man, lost in his parka. "He's a friend of mine. Extend the courtesies of the port."

Rat-Face — Joe — didn't like it, but he took it. He muttered about doing his duty and gave me a card.

"Twenny bucks?" I asked, studying it.

"Nah," he said angrily. "You're free-loading." He got out.

"Looks as if you saved ISN some money," I said to the little man. He threw back the hood of his parka in the relative warmth of the ship.

"Why not? We'll be working together. I'm Chenery from the *Phoenix.*"

"Oh, yeah — the client."

"That's right," he agreed, grinning. *"The* client. What exactly did you do to get banished to Frostbite?"

Since there was probably a spacemail aboard from McGillicuddy telling him exactly what I did, I told him.

"Chief thought I was generally shiftless."

"You'll do here," he said. "It's a shiftless, easy-going kind of place. I have the key to your bureau. Want me to lead the way?"

"What about my baggage?"

"Your stuff's safe. Port officers won't loot it when they know you're a friend of the *Phoenix.*"

That wasn't exactly what I'd meant; I'd always taken it for granted that port officers didn't loot anybody's baggage, no matter whose friends they were or weren't. As Chenery had said, it seemed to be a shiftless, easy-going place.

I let him lead the way. He had a jeep waiting to take us to the administration building, a musty, too-tight hodgepodge of desks. A lot of them were vacant, and the dowdy women and fattish men at the others didn't seem to be very busy. The women were doing their nails or reading; the men mostly were playing blotto with pocket-size dials for small change. A couple were sleeping.

From the administration building, a jet job took us the 20 kilos to town. Frostbite, the capital of Frostbite, housed maybe 40,000 people. No pressure dome. Just the glorious outdoors, complete with dust, weather, bisects, and a steady, icy wind. Hick towns seem to be the same the universe over. There was a main street called Main Street with clothing shops and restaurants, gambling houses, and more or less fancy saloons, a couple of vaudeville theaters, and dance halls. At the unfashionable end of Main Street were some farm implement shops, places to buy surveying instruments and geologic detectors, and the building that housed the Inter-Stellar News Service's Frostbite Bureau. It was a couple of front rooms on the second floor with a mechanical dentist, an osteopath above, and a "ride-up-and-save" parka emporium to the rear.

Chenery let me in, and it was easy to see at once why Kennedy had died of pneumonia. Bottles. The air conditioning must have carried away every last sniff of liquor, but it seemed to me that I could smell the rancid, homebrew stuff he'd been drinking. They were everywhere, the relics of a shameless, hopeless alcoholic who'd been good for nothing better than Frostbite. Sticky glasses and bottles everywhere told the story.

I slid open the hatch of the incinerator and started tossing down bottles and glasses from the copy desk, the morgue, the ethertype. Chenery helped and decently kept his mouth shut. When we'd got the place kind of cleaned up, I wanted to know what the daily routine was like.

Chenery shrugged. "Anything you make it, I guess. I used to push Kennedy to get more low-temperature agriculture stories for us. And those yaks that landed with you started as a civic-betterment stunt the *Phoenix* ran. It was all tractors until our farm editor had a brainstorm and brought in a pair. It's a hell of a good idea — you can't get milk, butter, and meat out of a tractor. Kennedy helped us get advice from some Earthside agronomy station to set it up, and he helped get clearance for the first pair, too. I don't have much idea of what copy he filed back to ISN. Frankly, we used him mostly as a contact man."

I asked miserably: "What the hell kind of copy *can* you file from a hole like this?"

He laughed and cheerfully agreed that things were pretty slow.

"Here's today's *Phoenix,*" he said, as the faxer began to hum. A neat, 16-page tabloid, stapled, pushed its way out in a couple of seconds. I flipped through it and asked: "No color at *all*?"

Chenery gave me a wink. "What the subscribers and advertisers don't know won't hurt them. Sometimes we break down and give them a page-one color pic."

I studied the *Phoenix.* Very conservative layout — naturally. It's competition that leads to circus makeup, and the *Phoenix* was the only sheet on the planet. The number-one story under a modest two-column head was an ISN farm piece on fertilizers for high-altitude agriculture, virtually unedited. The number-two story was an ISN piece on the current United Planets assembly.

"Is Frostbite in the UP, by the way?" I asked.

"No. It's the big political question here. The *Phoenix* is against applying. We figure the planet can't afford the assessment in the first place, and if it could, there wouldn't be anything to gain by joining."

"Um." I studied the ISN piece closer and saw that the *Phoenix* was very much opposed indeed. The paper had doctored our story plenty. I hadn't seen the original, but ISN is — in fact and according to its charter — as impartial as it's humanly possible to be. But our story, as it emerged in the *Phoenix,* consisted of a paragraph about an undignified, wrangling debate over the Mars-excavation question, a fist-fight between a Titanian and an Earth delegate in a corridor, a Sirian's red-hot denunciation of the UP as a power-politics instrument of the old planets, and a report of UP administrative expenses — without a corresponding report of achievements.

"I suppose," I supposed, "that the majority of the planet is stringing along with the *Phoenix*?"

"Eight to one, the last time a plebiscite was run off," said Chenery proudly.

"You amaze me."

I went on through the paper. It was about 70 percent ads, most of them from the Main Street stores we'd passed. The editorial page had an anti-UP cartoon showing the secretary-general of the UP as the greasy, affable conductor of a jetbus jammed to the roof with passengers. A sign on the bus said: "Fare, $15,000,000 and up per year." A road sign pointing in the direction the bus was heading said, "To Nowhere." The conductor was saying to a small, worried-looking man in a parka labeled "New Agricultural Planets" that, "There's always room for one more!" The outline said: "But is there — and is it worth it?"

The top editorial was a glowing tribute from the *Phoenix* to the *Phoenix* for its pioneering work in yaks, pinned on the shipment that arrived today. The second editorial was anti-UP, echoing the cartoon and quoting from the Sirian in the page-one ISN piece.

It was a good, efficient job of the kind that turns a working newsman's stomach while he admires the technique.

"Well, what do you think of it?" asked Chenery proudly.

I was saved from answering by a *brrp* from the ethertype.

"GPM FRB GA PLS" it said. "Good-afternoon, Frostbite Bureau — go ahead, please."

What with? I hunted around and found a typed schedule on the wall that Kennedy had evidently once drawn up in a spasm of activity.

"MIN PLS" I punched out on the ethertype, and studied the sked.

It was quite a document.

0900-1030: BREAKFAST
1030-1100: PHONE WEEMS FOR BITCHES RE SVS
1100-1200: NOTE MARSBUO RE BITCHES
1200-1330: LUNCH
1330-1530: RUN DROPS TO WEEMS: GAB WITH CHENERY
1530-1700: CLIP PHOENIX, REWRITE PUNCH & FILE
SUNDAYS 0900-1700: WRITE AND FILE ENTERPRISERS.

Chenery spared my blushes by looking out the window as I read the awful thing. I hadn't quite realized how low I'd sunk until then.

"Think it's funny?" I asked him — unfairly, I knew. He was being decent. It was decent of him not to spit in my eye and shove me off the sidewalk for that matter. I had hit bottom.

He didn't answer. He was embarrassed, and in the damn-fool way people have of finding a scapegoat, I tried to make him feel worse. Maybe if I rubbed it in real hard, he'd begin to feel almost as bad as I did.

"I see," I told him, "that I've wasted a morning. Do you or Weems have any bitches for me to messenger-boy to Mars?"

"Nothing special," he said. "As I said, we always like low-temperature and high-altitude agriculture stuff. And good farm-and-home material."

"You'll get it," I told him. "And now I see I'm behind clipping and rewriting and filing stories from your paper."

"Don't take it so hard," he said unhappily. "It's not such a bad place. I'll have them take the bureau stuff here and your personal stuff to the Hamilton House. It's the only decent hotel in town except the *Phoenix* and that's kind of high —"

He saw that I didn't like him jumping to such accurate conclusions about my paycheck and beat it with an apologetic grimace of a smile.

The ethertype went *brrp* again and said "GB FRB CU LTR" "Goodby, Frostbite. See you later." There must have been many days when old Kennedy was too sick or too sick at heart to rewrite pieces from the lone client. Then the machine began beating out news items which I'd tear off eventually and run over to the *Phoenix*.

"Okay, sweetheart," I told the clattering printer. "You'll get copy from Frostbite. You'll get copy that'll make the whole damned ISN sit up and take notice —" and I went on kidding myself in that vein for a couple of minutes, but it went dry very soon.

Good God, but they've got me! I thought. If I'm no good on the job, they'll keep me here because there's nothing lower. And if I'm good on the job, they'll keep me here because I'm good at it. Not a chance in a trillion to *do* anything that'll get noticed — just plain stuck on a crummy planet with a crummy political machine that'll never make news in a million years!

I yanked down Kennedy's library — "YOUR FUTURE ON FROSTBITE," which was a C. of C. recruiting pamphlet, "MANUAL OF ETHERTYPE MAINTENANCE AND REPAIR," an ISN house handbook, and "THE UNITED PLANETS ORGANIZATION SECRETARIAT COMMITTEE INTERIM REPORT ON HABIT-FORMING DRUGS IN INTERPLANETARY COMMERCE," a grey-backed UP monograph that got to Frostbite God knew how. Maybe Kennedy had planned to switch from home brew to something that would kill him quicker.

The Chamber of Commerce job gave a thumbnail sketch of my new home. Frostbite had been colonized about five generations ago for the usual reason. Somebody had smelled money. A trading company planted a power reactor — still going strong — at the South Pole in exchange for choice tracts of land which they'd sold off to homesteaders, all from Earth and Earth-colonized planets. In fine print the pamphlet gave lip service to the UP ideal of interspecific brotherhood, *but —*

Apparently Frostbite, in typical hick fashion, thought only genus homo was good enough for its sacred soil and that all non-human species were more or less alarming monsters.

I looked at that editorial-page cartoon in the *Phoenix* again and really noticed this time that there were Sirians, Venusians, Martians, Lyrans, and other non-human beings jammed into the jetbus, and that they were made to look sinister. On my first glance, I'd taken them in casually, the way you would on Earth or Mars or Vega's Quembrill, but here they were supposed to scare me stiff, and I was supposed to go around saying, "Now, don't get me wrong, some of my best friends are Martians, *but —*"

Back to the pamphlet. The trading company suddenly dropped out of the chronology. By reading between the lines, I could figure out that it was one of the outfits which had overextended itself planting colonies so it could have a monopoly hauling to and from the new centers. A lot of them had gone smash when the Greenhough Effect took interstellar flight out of the exclusive hands of the supergiant corporations and put it in the reach of medium-sized operators like the rusty-bucket line that had hauled in me, the yaks, and the ten-penny nails.

In a constitutional convention two generations back, the colonists had set up a world government of the standard type, with a president, a unicameral house, and a three-step hierarchy of courts. They'd adopted the United Planets model code of laws except for the bill of rights — to keep the slimy extra-terrestrials out — with no thanks to the UP.

And that was it, except for the paean of praise to the independent farmer, the backbone of his planet, beholden to no man, etc.

I pawed through the ethertype handbook. The introduction told me that the perfection of instantaneous transmission had opened the farthest planets to the Interstellar News Service, which I knew; that it was knitting the colonized universe together with bonds of understanding, which I doubted; and that it was a boon to all human and non-human intelligences, which I thought was a bare-faced lie. The rest of it was "see Fig. 76 3b," "Wire 944 will slip easily through orifice 459," "if Knob 545 still refuses to turn, take Wrench 31 and gently, without forcing —" Nothing I couldn't handle.

The ethertype was beating out:

> FARM NOTE FROSTBITE
> NOME, ALASKA, EARTH — ISN — HOUSEWIVES OF THE COLDER FARM PLANETS WOULD DO WELL TO TAKE A LEAF FROM THE BOOK OF THE PRIMITIVE AMERINDIAN SEAMSTRESS. SO SAYS PROFESSOR OF DOMESTIC SCIENCE MADGE MCGUINESS OF THE UNIVERSITY OF NOME'S SCHOOL OF LOW-TEMPERATURE AGRONOMY. THE INDIAN MAID BY SEWING LONG, NARROW STRIPS OF FUR AND BASKET-WEAVING THEM INTO A BLANKET TURNED OUT COVERINGS WITH TWICE THE WARMTH AND HALF THE WEIGHT OF FUR ROBES SIMPLY SEWED EDGE TO EDGE —

That was my darling, with her incurable weakness for quote leads and the unspeakable "so says." Ellie Masters, I thought, you're a lousy writer, but I love you and I'd like to wring your neck for helping McGillicuddy con me into this. "Dig up all sorts of cute feature stories," you told me, and you made it sound sensible. Better I should be under the table at Blogri's with a hangover and sawdust in my hair than writing little byliners about seventeen tasty recipes for yak manure, which is all that's ever going to come out of this Godforsaken planet.

Rat-Face barged in without knocking; a moronic-looking boy was with him toting the box of ethertype spare parts.

"Just set it anywhere," I said. "Thanks for getting it right over here.

Uh, Joe, isn't it? — Joe, where could I get me a parka like that? I like those lines. Real mink?"

It was the one way to his heart. "You betcha. Only the best mink lining on Frostbite. Ya notice the lapels? Look!" He turned them forward and showed me useless little hidden pockets with zippers that looked like gold.

"I can see you're a man with taste."

"Yeah. Not like some of these bums. If a man's Collector of the Port, he's got a position to live up to. Look, I hope ya didn't get me wrong there, at the field. Nobody told me you were coming. If you're right with the *Phoenix,* you're right with the Organization. If you're right with the Organization, you're right with Joe Downing. I'm regular."

He said that last word the way a new bishop might say, "I am consecrated."

"Glad to hear that. Joe, when could I get a chance to meet some of the other regular boys?"

"Ya wanna get in, huh?" he asked shrewdly. "There's been guys here a lot longer than you, Spencer."

"In, out," I shrugged. "I want to play it smart. It won't do me any harm."

He barked with laughter. "Not a bit," he said. "Old man Kennedy didn't see it that way. You'll get along here. Keep ya nose clean and we'll see about The Boys." He beckoned the loutish porter and left me to my musings.

That little rat had killed his man, I thought — but where, why, and for whom?

I went out into the little corridor and walked into the "ride-up-and-save" parka emporium that shared the second floor with me. Leon Portwanger, said the sign on the door. He was a fat old man sitting cross-legged, peering through bulging shell-rimmed glasses at his needle as it flashed through fur.

"Mr. Portwanger? I'm the new ISN man, Sam Spencer."

"So?" he grunted, not looking up.

"I guess you knew Kennedy pretty well."

"Never. Never."

"But he was right in front there —"

"Never," grunted the old man. He stuck himself with the needle, swore, and put his finger in his mouth. "Now see what you made me do?" he said angrily and indistinctly around the finger. "You shouldn't bother me when I'm working. Can't you see when a man's working?"

"I'm sorry," I said and went back into the newsroom. A man as old as Leon, tailoring as long as Leon, didn't stick himself. He didn't even wear a thimble — the forefinger was calloused enough to be a thimble itself. He didn't stick himself unless he was very, very excited — or unless he wanted to get rid of somebody. I began to wish I hadn't fired those bottles of Kennedy's home brew down to the incinerator so quickly.

At that point, I began a thorough shakedown of the bureau. I found memos torn from the machine concerning overfiling or failure to file, clippings from the *Phoenix,* laundry lists, style memos from ISN, paid bills, blacksheets of letters to Marsbuo requesting a transfer to practically anywhere but Frostbite, a list of phone numbers, and a nasty space-mailed memo from McGillicuddy.

It said: "Re worldshaker, wll blv whn see. Meanwhile sggst keep closer sked avoid wastage costly wiretime. Reminder guppy's firstest job offhead orchid bitches three which bypassed u yestermonth. How? McG"

It was typical of McGillicuddy to memo in cablese. Since news bureaus began — as "wire services;" see his archaic "wiretime" — their executives have been memoing underlings in cablese as part of one-of-the-working-press-Jones-boys act that they affect. They also type badly so they can slash up their memo with copyreader symbols. This McGillicuddy did too, of course. The cablese, the bad typing, and the copyreading made it just about unintelligible to an outsider.

To me it said that McGillicuddy doubted Kennedy's promise to file a worldshaking story, that he was sore about Kennedy missing his scheduled times for filing on the ether-type, and that he was plenty sore about Kennedy failing to intercept complaints from the client *Phoenix,* three of which McGillicuddy had been bothered by during the last month.

So old Kennedy had dreamed of filing a worldshaker. I dug further into the bureau files and the desk drawers, finding only an out of date "WHO'S WHO IN THE GALAXY." No notes, no plans, no lists of interviewees, no tipsters — no blacksheet, I realized, of the letter to which McGillicuddy's cutting memo was a reply.

God only knew what it all meant.

I was hungry, sleepy, and sick at heart. I looked up the number of the Hamilton House and found that helpful little Chenery had got me a reservation, and that my luggage had arrived from the field. I headed for a square meal and my first night in bed for a week without yaks blatting at me through a thin bulkhead.

It wasn't hard to fit in. Frostbite was a swell place to lose your ambition and acquire a permanent thirst. The sardonic sked posted on the bureau wall — I had been planning to tear it down for a month, but the inclination became weaker and weaker. It was so true to life.

I would wake up the Hamilton House, have a skimpy breakfast, and get down to the bureau. Then there'd be a phone conversation with Weems during which he'd nag me for more and better Frostbite-slant stories. In an hour of "wire-time" I'd check in with Marsbuo. At first I risked trying to sneak a chat with Ellie, but the jokers around Marsbuo cured me of that. One of them pretended he was Ellie on the other end of the wire and before I caught on had me believing that she was six months pregnant with a child by McGillicuddy and was going to kill herself for betraying me. Good clean fun, and after that I stuck to space-mail for my happy talk.

After lunch, at the Hamilton House or more often in a tavern, I'd tear up the copy from the printer into neat sheets and deliver them to the *Phoenix* building on the better end of Main Street. (If anything big had come up, I would have phoned them to hold the front page open. If not, local items filled it, and ISN copy padded out the rest of their sheet.) As in Kennedy's sked, I gabbed with Chenery or watched the compositors or proof pullers or transmittermen at work and then went back to the office to clip my copy rolling out of the faxer. On a good day, I'd get four or five items — maybe a human interester about a yak mothering an orphaned baby goat, a new wrinkle on barn insulation with native materials that the other cold-farming planets we served could use, a municipal election or a murder trial verdict to be filed just for the record.

Evenings I spent at a tavern talking and sopping up home brew, or at one of the two-a-day vaudeville houses, or at the Clubhouse. I once worked on the Philadelphia *Bulletin,* so the political setup was nothing new to me. After Joe Downing decided I wouldn't get pushy, he took me around to meet The Boys.

The Clubhouse was across the street from the three-story capitol building of Frostbite's World Government. It was a little bigger than the capitol and in much better repair. Officially, it was the headquarters of the Frostbite Benevolent Society, a charitable, hence tax-free, organization. Actually it was the headquarters of the Frostbite Planetary Party, a standard gang of brigands. Down on the wrong end of Main Street somewhere was an upper room where the Frostbite Interplanetary Party, made up of liberals, screwballs, and disgruntled ex-members of the Organization but actually run by stooges of that Organization, hung out.

The Boys observed an orderly rotation of officers based on seniority. If you got in at the age of 18, didn't bolt and didn't drop dead, you'd be president someday. To the party you had to bring loyalty, hard work — not on your payroll job, naturally, but on your electioneering — and cash. You kept bringing cash all your life; salary kickbacks, graft kickbacks, contributions for gold dinner services, tickets to testimonial banquets, campaign chest assignments, widows' and orphans' fund contributions, burial insurance, and dues, dues, dues.

As usual, it was hard to learn who was who. The President of Frostbite was a simple-minded old boy named Witherspoon, so far gone in senile decay that he had come to believe the testimonial-banquet platitudes he uttered. You could check him off as a wheelhorse. He was serving the second and last year of his second and last term, and there was a mild battle going on between his Vice-President and the Speaker of the House as to who would succeed him. It was a traditional battle and didn't mean much; whoever lost would be next in line. When one of the contestants was so old or ill that he might not live to claim his term if he lost, the scrap would be waived in a spirit of good sportsmanship that the voters would probably admire if they ever heard of it.

Joe Downing was a comer. His sponsorship of me meant more than the friendship of Witherspoon would have. He was Chenery's ally; they were the leadership of the younger, sportier element. Chenery's boss Weems was with the older crowd that ate more, talked more, and drank less.

I had to join a committee before I heard of George, though. That's the way those things work.

It was a special committee for organizing a testimonial banquet for Witherspoon on his 40th year in the party. I wound up in the subcommittee to determine a testimonial gift for the old guffer. I knew damned well that we'd be expected to start the subscription for the gift rolling, so I suggested a handsome — and inexpensive — illuminated scroll with a sentiment lettered on it. The others were scandalized. One fat old woman called me "cheap" and a fat male pay-roller came close to accusing me of irregularity, at which I was supposed to tremble and withdraw my suggestion. I stood on my rights, and wrote a minority report standing up for the scroll while the majority of the subcommittee agreed on an inscribed sterling tea service.

At the next full committee meeting, we delivered our reports and I thought it would come to a vote right away. But it seemed they weren't used to there being two opinions about anything. They were flustered, and the secretary slipped out with both reports during a five-minute adjournment. He came back and told me, beaming, "Chenery says George liked your idea." The committee was reconvened, and because George liked my idea, my report was adopted and I was appointed a subcommittee of one to procure the scroll.

I didn't learn any more about George after the meeting except that some people who liked me were glad I'd been favorably noticed, and others were envious about the triumph of the Johnny-come-lately.

I asked Chenery in the bar. He laughed at my ignorance and said, "George *Parsons*."

"Publisher of the *Phoenix*? I thought he was an absentee owner."

"He doesn't spend a lot of time on Frostbite. At least, I don't think he does. As a matter of fact, I don't know a lot about his comings and goings. Maybe Weems does."

"He swings a lot of weight in the Organization."

Chenery looked puzzled. "I guess he does at that. Every once in a while he does speak up, and you generally do what he says. It's the paper, I suppose. He could wreck any of the boys."

Chenery wasn't being irregular: newsmen are always in a special position.

I went back to the office and, late as it was, sent a note to the desk to get the one man subcommittee job cleaned up:

ATTN MCGILLICUDDY RE CLIENT RELATIONS NEED SOONEST ILLUMINATED SCROLL PRESENT HOMER WITHERSPOON PRESIDENT FROSTBITE HONORING HIM 40 YEARS MEMBERSHIP FROSTBITE PLANETARY PARTY USUAL SENTIMENTS NOTE MUST BE TERRESTRIAL STYLE ART IF NOT ACTUAL WORK EARTHER ACCOUNT ANTIBEM PREJUDICE HERE FRBBUO END.

That happened on one of those Sundays which, according to Kennedy's sardonic sked, was to be devoted to writing and filing enterprisers.

The scroll came through with a memo from McGillicuddy: "Fyi ckng with clnt et if this gag wll hv ur hide. Reminder guppy's firstest job offheading orchid bitches one which bypassed u yesterweek. How? McG"

There was a sadly sweet letter from Ellie aboard the same rust-bucket. She wanted me to come back to her, but not a broken man. She wanted me to do something really big on Frostbite to show what I had in me. She was sure that if I really looked there'd be something more to file than the copy I'd been sending in. Yeah.

Well, the big news that week would be the arrival of a loaded immigrant ship from Thetis of Procyon, a planet whose ecology had been wrecked beyond repair in a few short generations by DDT, hydraulic mining, unrestricted logging, introduction of rabbits and house cats, and the use of poison bait to kill varmints. In a few thousand years maybe the planet would have topsoil, cover crops, forests, and a balanced animal population again, but Thetis as of now was a ruin whose population was streaming away to whatever havens it could find.

Frostbite had agreed to take 500 couples, provided they were of terrestrial descent and could pass a means test — that is, provided they had money to be fleeced of. They were arriving on a bottom called *Esmeralda.* According to my year-old *Lloyds' Shipping Index* — "exclusive accurate and up-to-date, being the result of daily advices from every part of the galaxy" — *Esmeralda* was owned by the Frimstedt Atomic Astrogation Company, Gammadion, gross tonnage 830,000, net tonnage 800,000, class GX — "freighter/steerage passengers" — insurance rating: hull A, atomics A. The tonnage difference meant real room for only about 850. If she took the full thousand, she'd be jammed. She was due to arrive at Frostbite in the very early morning. Normally I would have kept a deathwatch, but the AA rating lulled me, and I went to the Hamilton House to sleep.

At 4:30, the bedside phone chimed.

"This Willie Egan," a frightened voice said. "You remember — on the desk at the *Phoenix.*"

Desk, hell — he was a 17-year-old copyboy I'd tipped to alert me on any hot breaks.

"There's some kind of trouble with the *Esmeralda,*" he said. That big immigrant ship. They had a welcoming committee out, but the ship's overdue. I thought there might be a story in it. You got my home address? You better send the check there. Mr. Weems doesn't like us to do string work. How much do I get?"

"Depends," I said, waking up abruptly. "Thanks, kid."

I was into my clothes and down the street in five minutes. It looked good, mighty good. The ship was overcrowded, the AA insurance rating I had was a year old — maybe it had gone to pot since then and we'd have a major disaster on our hands. I snapped on the newsroom lights and grabbed the desk phone, knocked down one toggle on the key box, and demanded: "Space operator! Space operator!"

"Yes, sir. Let me have your call, please?"

"Gimme the bridge of the *Esmeralda*, due to dock at the Frostbite spaceport today. While you're setting up the call, gimme interplanetary and break in when you get the *Etmeralda*."

"Yes, sir." *Click-click-click.* "Interplanetary operator."

"Gimme Planet Gammadion. Person-to-person, to the public relations officer of the Frimstedt Atomic Astrogation Company. No, I don't know his name. No, I *don't* know the Gammadion routing. While you're setting up the call, gimme the local operator and break in when you get my party."

"Yes, sir."

Click-click-click.

"Your call, please."

"Person-to-person, captain of the spaceport."

"Yes, sir." *Click-click-click.* "Here is *Esmeralda*, sir."

"Who's calling?" yelled a voice. "This is the purser's office, who's calling?"

"Interstellar News, Frostbite Bureau. What's up about the ship being late?"

"I can't talk now! Oh, my God! I can't talk now! They're going crazy in the steerage —"

He hung up, and I swore a little.

"Space operator!" I yelled. "Get me *Esmeralda* again — if you can't get the bridge, get the radio shack, the captain's cabin, anything inboard!"

"Yes, sir." *Click-click-click.* "Here is your party, sir."

"Captain of the port's office," said the phone.

"This is Interstellar News. What's up about *Esmeralda?* I just talked to the purser in space, and there's some trouble aboard."

"I don't know anything more about it than you boys," said the captain of the port. But his voice didn't sound right.

"How about those safety-standard stories?" I fired into the dark.

"That's a tomfool rumor!" he exploded. "Her atomics are perfectly safe!"

"Still," I told him, fishing, "it *was* an engineer's report —"

"Eh? What was? I don't know what you're talking about." He realized he'd been had. "Other ships have been an hour late before and there are always rumors about shipping. That's absolutely all I have to say — absolutely all!"

He hung up.

Click-click-click. "Interplanetary operator. I am trying to place your call, sir." She must be too excited to plug in the right hole on her switchboard. A Frostbite-Gammadion call probably cost more than her annual salary, and it was a gamble at that on the feeble and mysteriously erratic sub-radiation that carried voices across segments of the galaxy.

But there came a faint *harrumph* from the phone.

"This is Captain Gulbransen. Who is calling, please?"

I yelled into the phone respectfully: "Captain Gulbransen, this is Interstellar News Service on Frostbite." I knew the way conservative shipping companies have of putting ancient, irritable astrogators into public-relations berths after they are ripe to retire from space. "I was wondering, sir," I shouted, "if you'd care to comment on the fact that *Esmeralda* is overdue at Frostbite with 1,000 immigrants."

"Young man," wheezed Gulbransen dimly, "it is clearly stated in our tariffs filed with the ICC that all times of arrival are to be read as plus or minus eight Terrestrial Hours, and that the company assumes no liability in such cases as —"

"Excuse me, sir, but I'm aware that the eight-hour leeway is traditional. But isn't it a fact that the average voyage hits the E.T.A. plus or minus only fifteen minutes T.H.?"

"That's so, but —"

"Please excuse me once more, sir — I'd like to ask just one more question. There is, of course, no reason for alarm in the lateness of *Esmeralda,* but wouldn't you consider a ship as much as one hour overdue as possibly in danger? And wouldn't the situation be rather alarming?"

"Well, one full hour, perhaps you would. Yes, I suppose so — but the eight-hour leeway, you understand —"

I laid the phone down quietly on the desk and ripped through the *Phoenix* for yesterday. In the business section it said "*Esmeralda* due 0330." And the big clock on the wall said 0458.

I hung up the phone and sprinted for the ethertype, with the successive stories clear in my head, ready to be punched and fired off to Marsbuo for relay on the galactic trunk. I would beat out IS clanging bells on the printer and follow them with

INTERSTELLAR FLASH
IMMIGRANT SHIP ESMERALDA SCHEDULED TO LAND FROSTBITE WITH 1,000 FROM THETIS PROCYON ONE AND ONE HALF HOURS OVERDUE: OWNER ADMITS SITUATION "ALARMING" CRAFT "IN DANGER."

And immediately after that a five-bell bulletin:

INTERSTELLAR BULLETIN

FROSTBITE — THE IMMIGRANT SHIP ESMERALDA, DUE
TODAY AT FROSTBITE FROM THETIS PROCYON WITH 1,000
STEERAGE PASSENGERS ABOARD, IS ONE AND ONE HALF
HOURS OVERDUE. A SPOKESMAN FOR THE OWNERS, THE
FRIMSTEDT ATOMIC ASTROGATION COMPANY, SAID SUCH A
SITUATION IS "ALARMING" AND THAT THE CRAFT MIGHT BE
CONSIDERED "IN DANGER."

ESMERALDA IS AN 830 THOUSAND-TON FREIGHTER-
STEERAGE PASSENGER CARRIER.

THE CAPTAIN OF THE PORT AT FROSTBITE ADMITTED
THAT THERE HAVE BEEN RUMORS CIRCULATING ABOUT THE
CONDITION OF THE CRAFTS ATOMICS THOUGH THESE WERE
RATED "A" ONE YEAR AGO. THE PURSER OF THE SPACESHIP,
CONTACTED IN SPACE, WAS AGITATED AND INCOHERENT
WHEN QUESTIONED. HE SAID —

"Get up, Spencer, get away from the machine."

It was Joe Downing, with a gun in his hand.

"I've got a story to file," I said blankly.

"Some other time." He stepped closer to the ethertype and let out a
satisfied grunt when he saw the paper was clean. "Port captain called
me," he said. "Told me you were nosing around."

"Will you get out of here?" I asked, stupefied. "Man, I have flash and
bulletin matter to clear. Let me alone!"

"I said to get away from that machine or I'll cut ya down, boy."

"But why? *Why?*"

"George don't want any big stories out of Frostbite."

"You're crazy. Mr. Parsons is a newsman himself. Put that damn-
fool gun away and let me get this out!"

I turned to the printer when a new voice said, "No! Don't do it, Mr.
Spencer. He is a Nietzschean. He'll kill you, all right. He'll kill you."

It was Leon Portwanger, the furrier, my neighbor, the man who
claimed he never knew Kennedy. His fat, sagging face, his drooping
white mustache, his sad black eyes enormous behind the bull's-eye
spectacles, were very matter-of-fact. He meant what he said. I got up
and backed away from the ethertype.

"I don't understand it," I told them.

"You don't have to understand it," said the rat-faced collector of the port. "All you have to understand is that George don't like it."

He fired one bullet through the printer, and I let out a yelp. I'd felt that bullet going right through me.

"Don't," the steady voice of the furrier cautioned. I hadn't realized that I was walking toward Downing and that his gun was now on my middle. I stopped.

"That's better," said Downing. He kicked the phone connection box off the baseboard, wires snapping and trailing. "Now go to the Hamilton House and stay there for a couple of days."

I couldn't get it through my head. "But *Esmeralda's* a cinch to blow up," I told him. "It'll be a major space disaster. *Half of them are women!* I've got to get it out!"

"I'll take him back to his hotel, Mr. Downing," said Portwanger. He took my arm in his flabby old hand and led me out while that beautiful flash and bulletin and the first lead disaster and the new lead disaster went running through my head to a futile obbligato of "They can't *do* this to me!" But they did it.

Somebody gave me a drink at the hotel, and I got sick, and a couple of bellboys helped me to bed. The next thing I knew I was feeling very clear-headed and wakeful and Chenery was hovering over me looking worried.

"You've been out cold for forty-eight hours," he said. "You had a high fever, chills, the works. What happened to you and Downing?"

"How's *Esmeralda*?" I demanded.

"Huh? Exploded about half a million miles off. The atomics went."

"Did anybody get it to ISN for me?"

"Couldn't. Interplanetary phones are out again. You seem to have got the last clear call through to Gammadion. And you put a bullet through your ethertype —"

"*I* did? Like hell — Downing did!"

"Oh? Well, that makes better sense. The fact is, Downing's dead. He went crazy with that gun of his, and Chief Selig shot him. But old Portwanger said you broke the ethertype when you got the gun away from Downing for a minute — no, that doesn't make sense. What's the old guy up to?"

"I don't give a damn. You see my pants anywhere? I want to get that printer fixed."

He helped me dress. I was a little weak on my legs, and he insisted on pouring expensive eggnog into me before he'd let me go to the bureau.

Downing hadn't done much of a job, or maybe you can't do much of a job on an ethertype without running it through an induction furnace. Everything comes apart, everything's replaceable. With a lot of thumbing through the handbook, I had all the busted bits and pieces out and new ones in. The adjustment was harder, needing two pairs of eyes. Chenery watched the meters while I turned the screws. In about four hours, I was ready to call. I punched out:

NOTE MARSBUO ISN. FRBBUO RESTORED TO SVC AFTR MECHNCL TRBL ETILLNESS.

The machine spat back:

NOTE FRBBUO. HW ELLNSS COINCDE WTH MJR DISSTR YR TRRTRY? FYI GAMMADION BUO ISN OUTRCHD FR ESMERALDA AFTR YR INXPLCBL SLNCE ETWS BDLY BTN GAMMADION BUGS COMPTSHN. MCG END.

He didn't want to hear any more about it. I could see him stalking away from the printer to the copydesk slot to chew his way viciously through wordage for the major splits. I wished I could see in my mind's eye Ellie slipping over to the Krueger 60-B circuit sending printer and punching out a word or two of kindness — the machine stirred again. It said: "SAM SAM COULD YOU? ELLIE"

Oh, God.

"Leave me alone, will you?" I asked Chenery.

"Sure — sure. Anything you say," he humored me, and slipped out.

I sat for a while at the desk, noticing that the smashed phone connection had been installed again, that the place had been policed up.

Leon Portwanger came waddling in with a bottle in his hand. "I have here some prune brandy," he said.

Things began to clear up. "*You* gave me that mickey," I said slowly. "And you've been lying about me. You said I wrecked the ethertype."

"You are a determinist, and I was trying to save your life," he said, setting down two glasses and filling them. "Take your choice and I will have the other. No mickeys."

I picked one and gulped it down — nasty, too-sweet stuff that tasted like plum peelings. He sipped his and seemed to enjoy it.

"I thought," he said, "that you were in with their gang. What *was* I to think? They got rid of poor Kennedy. Pneumonia! You too would have pneumonia if they drenched you with water and put you on the roof in your underwear overnight. The bottles were planted here. He used to drink a little with me, he used to get drunk now and then — so did I — nothing bad."

"You thought I was in their gang," I said. "What gang are you in?"

"The Frostbite Interplanetary Party," he said wryly. "I would smile with you if the joke were not on me. I know, I know — we are Outs who want to be Ins, we are neurotic youngsters, we are led by stooges of the Planetary Party. So what should I do — start a one-man party alone on a mountain-top, so pure that I must blackball everybody except myself from membership? I am an incorrigible reformer and idealist whether I like it or not — and sometimes, I assure you, I don't like it very well.

"Kennedy was no reformer and idealist. He was a pragmatist, a good man who wanted a good news story that would incidentally blow the present administration up. He used me, I used him. He got his story and they killed him and burglarized the bureau to remove all traces of it. Or did they?"

"I don't know," I muttered. "Why did you dope me? Did Downing really go crazy?"

"I poisoned you a little because Downing did *not* go crazy. Downing was under orders to keep you from sending out that story. Probably, after he had got you away from the ethertype, he would have killed you if I had not poisoned you with some of my heart medicine. They realized while you were ill and feverish that it might as well be one as another. If they killed you, there would only be another newsman sent out to be inveigled into their gang. If they killed Downing, they could blame everything on him, you would never be able to have anything more than suspicions, and — there are a lot more Downings available, are there not?"

My brain began to click. "So your mysterious 'they' didn't want a top-drawer story to center around Frostbite. If it did, there'd be follow-ups, more reporters, ICC people investigating the explosion. Since the news break came from Gammadion, that's where the reporters would head, and that's where the ICC investigation would be based. But what have they got to hide? The political setup here smells to high heaven, but it's no worse than on fifty other planets. Graft, liquor, vice, drugs, gambling —"

"No drugs," said the furrier.

"That's silly," I told him. "Of course they have drugs. With everything else, why not drugs?"

He shrugged apologetically. "Excuse me," he said. "I told you I was a reformer and an idealist. I did not mention that I used to be an occasional user of narcotics. A little something to take the pressure off — those very small morphine sulphate tablets. You can imagine my horror when I emigrated to this planet twenty-eight years ago and found there were no drugs — literally. Believe me when I tell you that I — *looked hard.* Now, of course, I am grateful. But I had a few very difficult weeks."

He shuddered, finished his prune brandy and filled both our glasses again. He tossed down his glass.

"Damn it all!" he exploded. "Must I rub your nose in it? Are you going to figure it out for yourself? And are you going to get killed like my poor friend, Kennedy? Look here! And here!" He lurched to his feet and yanked down *Who's Who in the Galaxy* and the *United Planets Drug Committee Report.*

His pudgy finger pointed to:

"PARSONS, George Warmerdam, organic chemist, news-ppr pubr, b. Gammadion 172, s. Henry and Dolores (Warmerdam) P., studied Gammadion Chem. Inst. B.Ch 191, M.Ch 193, D.Ch 194; empl. dir research Hawley Mfg Co. (Gammadion) 194-198; founded Parsons Chem Mfg Labs (Gammadion) 198, headed same 198-203; removed Frostbite 203; founded newspaper Frostbite *Phoenix* 203. Author, tech papers organ chem 193-196. Mem Univ Organ Chem Soc. Address c/o Frostbite *Phoenix,* Frostbite."

And in the other book:

"— particular difficulty encountered with the stupefiant known as 'J-K-B.' It was first reported on Gammadion in the year 197, when a few isolated cases presented themselves for medical treatment. The problem rapidly worsened through the year 203, by which time the drug was in widespread illicit interplanetary commerce. The years 203-204 saw a cutting-off of the supply of J-K-B for reasons unknown. Prices soared to fantastic levels, unnumbered robberies and murders were committed by addicts to obtain possession of the minute quantities remaining on the market, and other addicts, by the hundreds of thousands presented themselves to the authorities hoping more or less in vain for a 'cure.' J-K-B appeared again in the year 205, not confined to any segment of the inhabited galaxy. Supplies have since remained at a constant level — enough to brutalize, torment, and shorten the lives of the several score million terrestrial and extra-terrestrial beings who have come into its grip. Interrogation of peddlers intercepted with J-K-B has so far only led back through a seemingly endless chain of middlemen. The nature of the drug is such that it cannot be analyzed and synthesized —"

My head spun over the damning parallel trails. Where Parsons tried his wings in chemistry, J-K-B appeared. When he went on his own, the quantity increased. When he moved to another planet, the supply was cut off. When he was established, the supply grew to a constant level and stayed there.

And what could be sweeter than a thoroughly corrupt planet to take over with his money and his newspaper? Dominate a machine and the members' "regularity" will lead them to kill for you — or to kill killers if need be. Encourage planetary ignorance and isolationism; keep the planet unattractive and depressed by letting your freebooters run wild — that'll discourage intelligent immigration. Let token parties in, fleece them fast and close, let them spread the word that Frostbite's no place for anybody with brains.

"A reformer and idealist I am," said Portwanger calmly. "Not a man of action. What should be done next?"

I thought it over and told him; "If it kills me, and it might, I am going to send a rash of flashes and bulletins from this Godforsaken planet. My love life depends on it. Leon, do you know anybody on Mars?"

"A Sirian fellow named Wenjtkpli — a philosophical anarchist. An unreal position to take. Who is he to say —"

I held up my hand. "I know him, too." I could taste that eleventh stinger again; by comparison, the prune brandy was mellow. I took a gulp. "Do you think you could go to Mars without getting bumped off?"

"A man could try."

The next two weeks were agonizing. Those Assyrian commissars or Russian belshazzars or whatever they were who walked down prison corridors waiting to be shot in the back of the head never went through what I did. I walked down the corridor for fourteen days.

First Leon got off all right on a bucket of bolts. I had no guarantee that he wouldn't be plugged by a crew member who was in on the party. Then there was a period of waiting for the first note that I'd swap you for a mad tarantula.

It came:

NOTE FRBBUO HOW *WELL* XPCT KP CLNT IF UN-ABL DROP

COPY? MCG MARSBUO.

I'd paved the way for that one by drinking myself into a hangover on home brew and lying in bed and groaning when I should have been delivering the printer copy to the *Phoenix*. I'd been insulting as possible to Weems to insure that he'd phone a squawk to McGillicuddy — I hoped. The tipoff was "hell." Profanity was never, ever used on our circuits — I hoped. "Hell" meant "Portwanger contacted me, I got the story, I am notifying United Planets Patrol in utmost secrecy."

Two days later came:

NOTE FRBBUO BD CHMN WNTS KNO WOT KIND DAMN KNUCKLHED FILING ONLY FOURFIVE ITMS DAILY FM XPNSVE ONEMAN BUO. XPCT UP-STEP PRDCTN IMMY, RPT IMMY MCG MARSBUO.

"Damn" meant "Patrol contacted, preparing to raid Frostbite." "Fourfive" meant "fourfive" — days from message.

The next note would have got ISN in trouble with the Interplanetary Communications Commission if it hadn't been in a good cause. I'm unable to quote it. But it came as I was in the bureau about to leave for the Honorable Homer Witherspoon's testimonial banquet. I locked the door, took off my parka, and rolled up my sleeves. I was going to sweat for the next few hours.

When I heard the multiple roar of the Patrol ships on rockets, I very calmly beat out fifteen bells and sent:

INTERSTELLAR FLASH
UNITED PLANETS PATROL DESCENDING ON FROSTBITE, KRUEGER 60-B'S ONLY PLANET, IN UNPRECEDENTED MASS RAID ON TIP OF INTERSTELLAR NEWS SERVICE THAT WORLD IS SOLE SOURCE OF DEADLY DRUG J-K-B.

INTERSTELLAR BULLETIN
THE MASSED PATROL OF THE UNITED PLANETS ORGA-NIZATION DESCENDED ON THE ONLY PLANET OF KRUEGER 60-B, FROSTBITE, IN AN UNPRECEDENTED MASS RAID THIS EVENING. ON INFORMATION FURNISHED BY INTERSTEL-LAR NEWS REPORTER SAM SPENCER. THE PATROL HOPES TO WIPE OUT THE SOURCE OF THE DEADLY DRUG J-K-B, WHICH

HAS PLAGUED THE GALAXY FOR 20 YEARS. THE CHEMI-
CAL GENIUS SUSPECTED OF INVENTING AND PRODUCING
THE DRUG IS GEORGE PARSONS, RESPECTED PUBLISHER OF
FROSTBITE'S ONLY NEWSPAPER.

INTERSTELLAR FLASH
FIRST UNITED PLANETS PATROL SHIP LANDS IN FROST-
BITE CAPITAL CITY OF PLANET.
INTERSTELLAR FLASH
PATROL COMMANDER PHONES EXCLUSIVE INTERVIEW
TO INTERSTELLAR NEWS SERVICE FROSTBITE BUREAU RE-
PORTING ROUND-UP OF PLANETARY GOVERNMENT LEAD-
ERS AT TESTIMONIAL DINNER (WITH FROSTBITE) FROST-
BITE — ISN — ONE INTERSTELLAR NEWS REPORTER HAS
ALREADY GIVEN HIS LIFE IN THE CAMPAIGN TO EXPOSE
THE MAKER OF J-K-B. ED KENNEDY, ISN BUREAU CHIEF, WAS
ASSASSINATED BY AGENTS OF DRUGMAKER GEORGE PAR-
SONS THREE MONTHS AGO. AGENTS OF PARSONS STRIPPED
KENNEDY AND EXPOSED HIM OVERNIGHT TO THE BITTER
COLD OF THIS PLANET, CAUSING HIS DEATH BY PNEUMO-
NIA. A SECOND INTERSTELLAR NEWS SERVICE REPORTER,
SAM SPENCER, NARROWLY ESCAPED DEATH AT THE HANDS
OF A DRUG-RING MEMBER WHO SOUGHT TO PREVENT HIM
FROM SENDING NEWS OVER THE CIRCUITS OF THE INTER-
STELLAR NEWS SERVICE.

INTERSTELLAR FLASH
PATROL SEIZES PARSONS INTERSTELLAR BULLETIN
FROSTBITE — IN A TELEPHONE MESSAGE TO INTERSTEL-
LAR NEWS SERVICE A PATROL SPOKESMAN SAID GEORGE
PARSONS HAD BEEN TAKEN INTO CUSTODY AND UNMIS-
TAKABLY IDENTIFIED. PARSONS HAD BEEN LIVING A LIE ON
FROSTBITE, USING THE NAME CHENERY AND THE GUISE OF
A COLUMNIST FOR PARSONS NEWSPAPER. SAID THE PATROL
SPOKESMAN; — "IT IS A TYPICAL MANEUVER. WE NEVER
GOT SO FAR ALONG THE CHAIN OF J-K-B PEDDLERS THAT
WE NEVER FOUND ONE MORE. APPARENTLY THE SOURCE
OF THE DRUG HIMSELF THOUGHT HE COULD PUT HIMSELF
OUT OF THE REACH OF INTERPLANETARY JUSTICE BY AS-
SUMING A FICTITIOUS PERSONALITY. HOWEVER, WE HAVE
ABSOLUTELY IDENTIFIED HIM AND EXPECT A CONFESSION

WITHIN THE HOUR. PARSONS APPEARS TO BE A J-K-B AD-
DICT HIMSELF.

    INTERSTELLAR FLASH
    PARSONS CONFESSES
    (FIRST LEAD FROSTBITE)
    FROSTBITE — ISN — THE UNITED PLANETS PATROL AND
THE INTERSTELLAR NEWS SERVICE JOINED HANDS TODAY
IN TRIUMPH AFTER WIPING OUT THE MOST VICIOUS NEST
OF DRUGMAKERS IN THE GALAXY. J-K-B, THE INFAMOUS
NARCOTIC WHICH HAS MENACED —

I ground out nearly thirty thousand words of copy that night. Bleary-
eyed at the end of the run, I could barely read a note that came across:

    NOTE FRBBUO: WELL DONE. RETURN MARS JMMY:
SNDNG REPLCEMNT. MARSBUO MCG.

The Patrol flagship took me back in a quick, smooth trip with lots of
service and no yaks. After a smooth landing I took an eastbound chair
from the field and whistled as the floater lifted me to the ISN floor. The
newsroom was quiet for a change, and the boys and girls stood up for
me.

McGillicuddy stepped out from the copy table slot to say: "Welcome back. Frankly, I didn't think you had it in you, but you proved me
wrong. You're a credit to the profession and the ISN."

Portwanger was there, too. "A pragmatist, your McGillicuddy," he
muttered. "But you did a good job."

I didn't pay very much attention; my eyes were roving over no
man's land. Finally I asked McGillicuddy: "Where's Miss Masters?
Day off?"

"How do you like that?" laughed McGillicuddy. "I forgot to tell you.
She's your replacement on Frostbite. Fired her off yesterday. I thought
the woman's angle — where do you think *you're* going?"

"Honest Blogri's Olde Earthe Saloon," I told him with dignity. "If
you want me, I'll be under the third table from the left as you come in.
With sawdust in my hair."

TIME BUM

Harry Twenty-Third Street suddenly burst into laughter. His friend and sometimes roper Farmer Brown looked inquisitive.

"I just thought of a new con," Harry Twenty-Third Street said, still chuckling.

Farmer Brown shook his head positively. "There's no such thing, my man," he said. "There are only new switches on old cons. What have you got — a store con? Shall you be needing a roper?" He tried not to look eager as a matter of principle, but everybody knew the Farmer needed a connection badly. His girl had two-timed him on a badger game, running off with the chump and marrying him after an expensive, month-long buildup.

Harry said, "Sorry, old boy. No details. It's too good to split up. I shall rip and tear the suckers with this con for many a year, I trust, before the details become available to the trade. Nobody, but nobody, is going to call copper after I take him. It's beautiful and it's mine. I will see you around, my friend."

Harry got up from the booth and left, nodding cheerfully to a safe-blower here, a fixer there, on his way to the locked door of the hangout. Naturally he didn't nod to such small fry as pickpockets and dope peddlers. Harry had his pride.

The puzzled Farmer sipped his lemon squash and concluded that Harry had been kidding him. He noticed that Harry had left behind him in the booth a copy of a magazine with a space ship and a pretty girl in green bra and pants on the cover.

"A furnished ... bungalow?" the man said hesitantly, as though he knew what he wanted but wasn't quite sure of the word.

"Certainly, Mr. Clurg," Walter Lachlan said. "I'm sure we can suit you. Wife and family?"

"No," said Clurg. "They are . . . far away." He seemed to get some secret amusement from the thought. And then, to Walter's horror, he sat down calmly in empty air beside the desk and, of course, crashed to the floor looking ludicrous and astonished.

Walter gaped and helped him up, sputtering apologies and wondering privately what was wrong with the man. There wasn't a chair there. There was a chair on the other side of the desk and a chair against the wall. But there just wasn't a chair where Clurg had sat down.

Clurg apparently was unhurt; he protested against Walter's apologies, saying: "I should have known, Master Lachlan. It's quite all right; it was all my fault. What about the bang — the bungalow?"

Business sense triumphed over Walter's bewilderment. He pulled out his listings and they conferred on the merits of several furnished bungalows. When Walter mentioned that the Curran place was especially nice, in an especially nice neighborhood — he lived up the street himself — Clurg was impressed.

"I'll take that one," he said. "What is the . . . feoff?" Walter had learned a certain amount of law for his real-estate license examination; he recognized the word. "The *rent* is seventy-five dollars," he said. "You speak English very well, Mr. Clurg." He hadn't been certain that the man was a foreigner until the dictionary word came out. "You have hardly any accent."

"Thank you," Clurg said, pleased. "I worked hard at it. Let me see — seventy-five is six twelves and three." He opened one of his shiny-new leather suitcases and calmly laid six heavy little paper rolls on Walter's desk. He broke open a seventh and laid down three mint-new silver dollars. "There I am," he said. "I mean, there you are."

Walter didn't know what to say. It had never happened before. People paid by check or in bills. They just didn't pay in silver dollars. But it was money — why shouldn't Mr. Clurg pay in silver dollars if he wanted to? He shook himself, scooped the rolls into his top desk drawer, and said: "I'll drive you out there, if you like. It's nearly quitting time anyway."

Walter told his wife Betty over the dinner table: "We ought to have him in some evening. I can't imagine where on Earth he comes from. I had to show him how to turn on the kitchen range. When it went on he said, 'Oh, yes — electricity!' and laughed his head off. And he kept ducking the question when I tried to ask him in a nice way. Maybe he's some kind of a political refugee."

"Maybe ..." Betty began dreamily and then shut her mouth. She didn't want Walter laughing at her again. As it was, he made her buy her science-fiction magazines downtown instead of at neighborhood newsstands. He thought it wasn't becoming for his wife to read them. *He's so eager for success,* she thought sentimentally.

That night while Walter watched a television variety show, she read a story in one of her magazines. (Its cover, depicting a space ship and a girl in green bra and shorts, had been prudently torn off and thrown away.) It was about a man from the future who had gone back in time, bringing with him all sorts of marvelous inventions. In the end the Time Police punished him for unauthorized time traveling. They had come back and got him, brought him back to his own time. She smiled. It *would* be nice if Mr. Clurg, instead of being a slightly eccentric foreigner, were a man from the future with all sorts of interesting stories to tell and a satchelful of gadgets that could be sold for millions and millions of dollars.

After a week they did have Clurg over for dinner. It started badly. Once more he managed to sit down in empty air and crash to the floor. While they were brushing him off he said fretfully: "I *can't* get used to not —" and then said no more.

He was a picky eater. Betty had done one of her mother's specialties, veal cutlet with tomato sauce, topped by a poached egg. He ate the egg and sauce, made a clumsy attempt to cut up the meat, and abandoned it. She served a plate of cheese, half a dozen kinds, for dessert, and Clurg tasted them uncertainly, breaking off a crumb from each, while Betty wondered where that constituted good manners. His face lit up when he tried a ripe cheddar. He popped the whole wedge into his mouth and said to Betty: "I will have that, please."

"Seconds?" asked Walter. "Sure. Don't bother, Betty. I'll get it." He brought back a quarter-pound wedge of the cheddar.

Walter and Betty watched silently as Clurg calmly ate every crumb of it. He sighed.

"Very good. Quite like —"

The word, Walter and Betty later agreed, was *see-mon-joe*. They were able to agree quite early in the evening, because Clurg got up after eating the cheese, said warmly, "Thank you so much!" and walked out of the house.

Betty said, "*What* — on — *Earth!*"

Walter said uneasily, "I'm sorry, doll. I didn't think he'd be quite that peculiar —"

"— But after *all!*"

"— Of course he's a foreigner. What was that word?"

He jotted it down.

While they were doing the dishes, Betty said, "I think he was drunk. Falling-down drunk."

"No," Walter said. "It's exactly the same thing he did in my office. As though he expected a chair to come to him instead of him going to a chair." He laughed and said uncertainly, "Or maybe he's royalty. I read once about Queen Victoria never looking around before she sat down, she was so sure there'd be a chair there."

"Well, there isn't any more royalty, not to speak of," she said angrily, hanging up the dish towel. "What's on TV tonight?"

"Uncle Miltie. But . . . uh . . . I think I'll read. Uh . . . where do you keep those magazines of yours, doll? Believe I'll give them a try."

She gave him a look that he wouldn't meet, and she went to get him some of her magazines. She also got a slim green book which she hadn't looked at for years. While Walter flipped uneasily through the magazines, she studied the book. After about ten minutes she said: "Walter. *Seemonjoe.* I think I know what language it is!"

He was instantly alert. "Yeah? What?"

"It should be spelled c-i-m-a-n-g-o, with little jiggers over the C and G. It means 'Universal food' in Esperanto."

"Where's Esperanto?" he demanded.

"Esperanto isn't anywhere. It's an artificial language. I played around with it a little once. It was supposed to end war and all sorts of things. Some people called it the language of the future." Her voice was tremulous.

Walter said, "I'm going to get to the bottom of this."

He saw Clurg go into the neighborhood movie for the matinee. That gave him about three hours.

Walter hurried to the Curran bungalow, remembered to slow down, and tried hard to look casual as he unlocked the door and went in. There wouldn't be any trouble — he was a good citizen, known and respected — he could let himself into a tenant's house and wait for him to talk about business if he wanted to.

He tried not to think of what people would think if he should be caught rifling Clurg's luggage, as he intended to do. He had brought along an assortment of luggage keys. Surprised by his own ingenuity, he had got them at a locksmith's by saying his own key was lost and he didn't want to haul a heavy packed bag downtown.

But he didn't need the keys. In the bedroom closet the two suitcases stood, unlocked.

There was nothing in the first except uniformly new clothes, bought locally at good shops.

The second was full of the same. Going through a rather extreme sports jacket, Walter found a wad of paper in the breast pocket. It was a newspaper page. A number had been penciled on a margin; apparently the sheet had been torn out and stuck into the pocket and forgotten. The dateline on the paper was July 18th, 2403.

Walter had some trouble reading the stories at first, but found it was easy enough if he read them aloud and listened to his voice.

One said:

TAIM KOP NABD: PROSKYOOTR ASKS DETH

Patrolm'n Oskr Garth V thi Taim Polis w'z arest'd toodei at hiz hom, 4365 9863th Suit, and bookd at 9768th Prisint on m——. tchardg'z 'v Polis-Ekspozh'r. Thi aledjd Ekspozh'r okurd hwaile Garth w'z on dooti in thi Twenti-Furst Sentch'ri. It konsist'd 'v hiz admish'n too a sit'zen 'v thi Twenti-Furst Sentch'ri that thi Taim Polis ekzisted and woz op'rated fr'm thi Twenti-Fifth Sentch'ri. Thi Proskypot'rz Ofis sed thi deth pen'lti wil be askt in vyoo 'v thi heinus neitch'r 'v thi ofens, hwitch thret'nz thi hwol fabrik 'v Twenti-Fifth-Sentch'ri eksiztens.

There was an advertisement on the other side:

BOIZ AND YUNG MEN!

SERV EUR SENTCH'RI!
ENLIST IN THI TAIM POLIS RSURV NOW!

RIMEMB'R — 'V THI AJEZ! ONLY IN THI TAIM POLIS KAN EU PROTEKT EUR SIVILIZASHON FR'M VARENS! THEIR IZ NO HAIER SERVIS TOO AR KULTCH'R! THEIR IZ NO K'REER SO FAS'NATING AZ A K'REER IN THI TAIM POLIS!

Underneath it another ad asked:

HWAI BI ASHEEMPD UV EUR TCHAIRZ?
GET ROLFASTS!

No uth'r tcheir haz thi immidjit respons uv a Rolfast. Sit enihweir — eur Rolfast iz ther! Eur Rolfast metl partz ar solid gold to avoid tairsum polishing. Eur Rolfast beirings are thi fain'st six-intch dupliks di'mondz for long wair.

Walter's heart pounded. Gold — to avoid tiresome polishing! Six-inch diamonds — for long wear!

And Clurg must be a time policeman. "Only in the time police can you see the pageant of the ages!" What did a time policeman do? He wasn't quite clear about that. But what they *didn't* do was let anybody else — anybody earlier — know that the Time Police existed. He, Walter Lachlan of the Twentieth Century, held in the palm of his hand Time Policeman Clurg of the Twenty-Fifth Century — the Twenty-Fifth Century where gold and diamonds were common as steel and glass in this!

He was there when Clurg came back from the matinee. Mutely, Walter extended the page of newsprint. Clurg snatched it incredulously, stared at it, and crumpled it in his fist. He collapsed on the floor with a groan.

"I'm done for!" Walter heard him say.

"Listen, Clurg," Walter said. "Nobody ever needs to know about this — *nobody*."

Clurg looked up with sudden hope in his eyes. "You will keep silent?" he asked wildly. "It is my life!"

"What's it worth to you?" Walter demanded with brutal directness. "I can use some of those diamonds and some of that gold. Can you get it into this century?"

"It would be missed. It would be over my mass-balance," Clurg said. "But I have a Duplix. I can copy diamonds and gold for you; that was how I made my feoff money."

He snatched an instrument from his pocket — a fountain pen, Walter thought.

"It is low in charge. It would Duplix about five kilograms in one operation —"

"You mean," Walter demanded, "that if I brought you five kilograms of diamonds and gold you could duplicate it? And the originals wouldn't be harmed? Let me see that thing. Can I work it?"

Clurg passed over the "fountain pen." Walter saw that within the case was a tangle of wires, tiny tubes, lenses — he passed it back hastily.

Clurg said, "That is correct. You could buy or borrow jewelry and I could duplix it. Then you could return the originals and retain the copies. You swear by your contemporary God that you would say nothing?"

Walter was thinking. He could scrape together a good thirty thousand dollars by pledging the house, the business, his own real estate, the bank account, the life insurance, the securities. Put it all into diamonds, of course and then — *doubled! Overnight!*

"I'll say nothing," he told Clurg. "If you come through." He took the sheet from the twenty-fifth-century newspaper from Clurg's hands and put it securely in his own pocket. "When I get those diamonds duplicated," he said, "I'll burn this paper and forget the rest. Until then, I want you to stay close to home. I'll come around in a day or so with the stuff for you to duplicate."

Clurg nervously promised.

The secrecy, of course, didn't include Betty. He told her when he got home, and she let out a yell of delight. She demanded the newspaper, read it avidly, and then demanded to see Clurg.

"I don't think he'll talk," Walter said doubtfully. "But if you really want to . . ."

She did, and they walked to the Curran bungalow. Clurg was gone, lock, stock and barrel, leaving not a trace behind. They waited for hours, nervously.

At last Betty said, "He's gone back."

Walter nodded. "He wouldn't keep his bargain, but by God I'm going to keep mine. Come along. We're going to the *Enterprise*."

"Walter," she said. "You wouldn't — would you?"

He went alone, after a bitter quarrel.

At the *Enterprise* office, he was wearily listened to by a reporter, who wearily looked over the twenty-fifth-century newspaper. "I don't know what you're peddling, Mr. Lachlan," he said, "but we like people to buy their ads in the *Enterprise*. This is a pretty bare-faced publicity grab."

"But —" Walter sputtered.

"Sam, would you please ask Mr. Morris to come up here if he can?" the reporter was saying into the phone. To Walter he explained, "Mr. Morris is our press-room foreman."

The foreman was a huge, white-haired old fellow, partly deaf. The reporter showed him the newspaper from the twenty-fifth century and said, "How about this?"

Mr. Morris looked at it and smelled it and said, showing no interest in the reading matter: "American Type Foundry Futura number nine, discontinued about ten years ago. It's been hand-set. The ink — hard to say. Expensive stuff, not a news ink. A book ink, a job-printing ink. The paper, now, I know. A nice linen rag that Benziger jobs in Philadelphia."

"You see, Mr. Lachlan? It's a fake." The reporter shrugged.

Walter walked slowly from the city room. The press-room foreman *knew*. It was a fake. And Clurg was a faker. Suddenly Walter's heels touched the ground after twenty-four hours and stayed there. Good God, the diamonds! Clurg was a conman! He would have worked a package switch! He would have had thirty thousand dollars' worth of diamonds for less than a month's work!

He told Betty about it when he got home, and she laughed unmercifully. "Time Policeman" was to become a family joke between the Lachlans.

Harry Twenty-Third Street stood, blinking, in a very peculiar place. Peculiarly, his feet were firmly encased, up to the ankles, in a block of clear plastic.

There were odd-looking people, and a big voice was saying: "May it please the court. The People of the Twenty-Fifth Century versus Harold Parish, alias Harry Twenty-Third Street, alias Clurg, of the Twentieth Century. The charge is impersonating an officer of the Time Police. The Prosecutor's Office will ask the death penalty in view of the heinous nature of the offense, which threatens the whole fabric —"

A KORNBLUTH BIBLIOGRAPHY

The following bibliography is, as usual, as complete as I can make it given the print and online resources to which I have access. Also as usual, I welcome any and all additions and corrections. Because of the number of collaborations and pseudonyms herein, I have opted to list all the stories together in chronological order rather than breaking it up. Just to keep my sanity, I have placed an arbitrary cut-off coinciding with the publication of *The Best of C. M. Kornbluth*, i.e. 1976. In addition to those listed below, he also used the pennames Earl Balons and Carl F. Burke. There are also at least another dozen and a half mystery stories I could find no citation for.

Short Stories and Articles

"Stepsons of Mars" — April 1940 *Astonishing Stories* (with Richard Wilson, as by Ivar Towers)

"Hollow of the Moon" — May 1940 *Super Science Stories* (as by Gabriel Barclay)

"King Cole of Pluto" — May 1940 *Super Science Stories* (as by S. D. Gottesman)

"Before the Universe" — July 1940 *Super Science Stories* (with Frederik Pohl, as by S. D. Gottesman)

"Nova Midplane" — November 1940 *Super Science Stories* (with Frederik Pohl, as by S. D. Gottesman)

"Trouble in Time" — December 1940 *Astonishing Stories* (with Frederik Pohl, as by S. D. Gottesman)

"Vacant World" — January 1941 *Super Science Stories* (with Frederik Pohl and Dirk Wylie, under Wylie's name)

"Dead Center" — February 1941 *Stirring SF* (as by S. D. Gottesman)

"Thirteen O'Clock" — February 1941 *Stirring SF* (as by Cecil Corwin)

"Callistan Tomb" — Spring 1941 *SF Quarterly* (with Frederik Pohl, as by Paul Dennis Lavond)

"The Psychological Regulator" — March 1941 *Comet Stories* (with E. Balter, Robert W. Lowndes, John Michel, and Donald Wollheim, as by Arthur Cooke)

"The Martians Are Coming" — March 1941 *Cosmic Stories* (with Robert W. Lowndes, under Lowndes' name)

"New Directions" — March 1941 *Cosmic Stories* (article, as by Walter C. Davies)

"Return from M-15" — March 1941 *Cosmic Stories* (as by S. D. Gottesman)

"The Reversible Revolutions" — March 1941 *Cosmic Stories* (as by Cecil Corwin)

"Exiles of New Planet" — April 1941 *Astonishing Stories* (with Frederik Pohl, Robert W. Lowndes and Dirk Wylie, as by Paul Dennis Lavond)

"The Rocket of 1955" — April 1941 *Stirring SF* (as by Cecil Corwin)

"The Castle on the Outerplanet" — April 1941 *Stirring SF* (with Frederik Pohl and Robert W. Lowndes, as by S. D. Gottesman)

"A Prince of Pluto" — April 1941 *Future SF* (with Frederik Pohl, as by Paul Dennis Lavond)

"Best Friend" — May 1941 *Super Science Stories* (with Frederik Pohl, as by S. D. Gottesman)

"Dimension of Darkness" — May 1941 *Cosmic Stories* (as by S. D. Gottesman)

"No Place to Go" — May 1941 *Cosmic Stories* (as by Edward J. Bellin)

"What Sorghum Says" — May 1941 *Cosmic Stories* (as by Cecil Corwin)

"Forgotten Tongue" — June 1941 *Stirring SF* (as by Walter C. Davies)

"Kazam Collects" — June 1941 *Stirring SF* (as by S. D. Gottesman)

"Mr. Packer Goes to Hell" — June 1941 *Stirring SF* (as by Cecil Corwin)

"The Words of Guru" — June 1941 *Stirring SF* (as by Kenneth Falconer)

"Fire Power" — July 1941 *Cosmic Stories* (as by S. D. Gottesman)

"Interference" — July 1941 *Cosmic Stories* (as by Walter C. Davies)

"The City in the Sofa" — July 1941 *Cosmic Stories* (as by Cecil Corwin)

"Mars-Tube" — September 1941 *Astonishing Stories* (with Frederik Pohl, as by S. D. Gottesman)

"Sir Mallory's Magnitude" — Winter 1941-42 *SF Quarterly* (as by S. D. Gottesman)

"Crisis!" — Spring 1942 *SF Quarterly* (as by Cecil Corwin)

"Einstein's Planetoid" — Spring 1942 *SF Quarterly* (with Frederik Pohl, Robert W. Lowndes and Dirk Wylie, as by Paul Dennis Lavond)

"The Embassy" — March 1942 *Astounding* (with Donald Wollheim, as by Martin Pearson)

"The Golden Road" — March 1942 *Stirring SF* (as by Cecil Corwin)

"Masquerade" — March 1942 *Stirring SF* (as by Kenneth Falconer)

"The Perfect Invasion" — March 1942 *Stirring SF* (as by S. D. Gottesman)

"The Core" — April 1942 *Future SF* (as by S. D. Gottesman)

"An Old Neptunian Custom" — August 1942 *Super Science Stories* (with Frederik Pohl, as by Scott Mariner)

"The Extrapolated Dimwit" — October 1942 *Future SF* (with Frederik Pohl and Robert W. Lowndes, as by S. D. Gottesman)

"Blood on the Campus" — June 1948 *Detective Story* (mystery)

"The Only Thing We Learn" — July 1949 *Startling Stories*

"The Little Black Bag" — July 1950 *Astounding*

"Iteration" — September/October 1950 *Future*

"The Silly Season" — Fall 1950 *F&SF*

"The Mindworm" — December 1950 *Worlds Beyond*

"Friend to Man" — Spring 1951 *Thrilling Wonder Stories*

"The Marching Morons" — April 1951 *Galaxy*

"Mars Child" — serial, May-July 1951 *Galaxy* (with Judith Merril, as by Cyril Judd)

"With These Hands" — December 1951 *Galaxy*

"That Share of Glory" — January 1952 *Astounding*

"Gunner Cade" — serial, March-May 1952 *Astounding* (with Judith Merril, as by Cyril Judd)

"The Luckiest Man in Denv" — June 1952 *Galaxy* (as by Simon Eisner)

"Gravy Planet" — serial, June-August 1952 *Galaxy* (with Frederik Pohl)

"Make Mine Mars" — November 1952 *SF Adventures*

"The Altar at Midnight" — November 1952 *Galaxy*

"The Goodly Creatures" — December 1952 *F&SF*

"The Mask of Demeter" — January 1953 *F&SF* (as by Cecil Corwin and Martin Pearson, pseuds. of Kornbluth and Donald Wollheim respectively)

"Time Bum" — January/February 1953 *Fantastic*

"Sea Change" — March 1953 *Dynamic SF* (with Judith Merril, as by Cyril Judd)

"The Adventurer" — May 1953 *Space SF*

"Dip Detail" — July 1953 *Private Eye* (mystery)

"The Meddlers" — September 1953 *SF Adventures*

"Everybody Knows Joe" — October/November 1953 *Future*

"The Syndic" — serial, December 1953-February 1954 *SF Adventures* (with Judith Merril, as by Cyril Judd)

"I Never Ast No Favors" — April 1954 *F&SF*

"Takeoff" — serial, April-June 1954 *New Worlds* (#22-24)

"Gladiator At Law" — serial, June-August 1954 *Galaxy* (with Frederik Pohl)

"Dominoes" — in *Star SF Stories*, ed. Frederik Pohl; Ballantine 16 (simul. hardback and paperback), 1953

"The Remorseful" — in *Star SF Stories #2*, ed. Frederik Pohl; Ballantine 55 (simul. hardback and paperback), 1954

"The Adventurers" — February 1955 *SF Quarterly*

"Gomez" — February 1955 *New Worlds* (#32)

"Not This August" — serial, May-June 1955 *MacLean's*

"The Cosmic Charge Account" — January 1956 *F&SF*

"The Engineer" — February 1956 *Infinity* (with Frederik Pohl)

"The Education of Tigress Macardle" — July 1957 *Venture*

"MS. Found In a Chinese Fortune Cookie" — July 1957 *F&SF*

"The Unfortunate Topologist" — verse, July 1957 *F&SF* (as by S. D. Gottesman)

"The Slave" — September 1957 *SF Adventures*

"The Last Man Left in the Bar" — October 1957 *Infinity*

"Wolfbane" — serial, October-November 1957 *Galaxy* (with Frederik Pohl)

"Requiem for a Scientist" — article, December 1957 *Fantastic Universe*

"Passion Pills" — in *A Mile Beyond the Moon*, Doubleday 1958 (hardback only)

"The Events Leading Down to the Tragedy" — January 1958 *F&SF*

"Virginia" — March 1958 *Venture*

"Reap the Dark Tide" — June 1958 *Venture*

"Theory of Rocketry" — July 1958 *F&SF*

"Two Dooms" — July 1958 *Venture*

"The Advent on Channel Twelve" — in *Star SF Stories #4*, ed. Frederik Pohl; Ballantine 272K, 1958

"Nightmare With Zeppelins" — December 1958 *Galaxy* (with Frederick Pohl)

"A Gentle Dying" — June 1961 *Galaxy* (with Frederik Pohl)

"The Quaker Cannon" — August 1961 *Astounding* (with Frederik Pohl)

"The World of Myrion Flowers" — October 1961 *F&SF* (with Frederik Pohl)

"Critical Mass" — February 1962 *Galaxy* (with Frederik Pohl)

Collections and Novels

Gunner Cade — with Judith Merril, as by Cyril Judd; Simon & Schuster 1952; Ace D-277, 1957

Naked Storm — as by Simon Eisner; Lion 109, 1952 (mystery)

Outpost Mars — with Judith Merril, as by Cyril Judd; Abelard, 1952; Dell 760, 1954

Half — as by Jordan Park; Lion 135, 1953 (mystery)

Takeoff — Doubleday, 1952; Pennant P15, 1953

Valerie — as by Jordan Park; Lion 176, 1953 (mystery)

Space Merchants — with Frederik Pohl; Ballantine 21 (simul. hardback and paperback), 1952

The Syndic — Doubleday, 1953; Bantam 1317, 1955

The Explorers — Ballantine 86, 1954 (coll.)

Search the Sky — with Frederik Pohl; Ballantine 61 (simul. hardback and paperback), 1954

Gladiator-at-Law — with Frederik Pohl; Ballantine 107 (simul. hardback and paperback), 1955

Mindworm and Other Stories — M. Joseph, 1955 (UK coll.)

A Town is Drowning — with Frederik Pohl; Ballantine 123 (simul. hardback and paperback), 1955

Not This August — Doubleday 1955; Bantam A1492, 1956

Presidential Year — with Frederik Pohl; Ballantine 144 (simul. hardback and paperback), 1955

Sorority House — with Frederik Pohl, as by Jordan Park; Lion Library 97, 1956 (lesbiana)

A Man of Cold Rages — as by Jordan Park; Pyramid G368, 1958 (mystery)

A Mile Beyond the Moon — Doubleday, 1958; McFadden 40-100, 1962 (coll.)

The Marching Morons — Ballantine 303K, 1959 (coll.)

Wolfbane — with Frederik Pohl; Ballantine 335K, 1959

The Wonder Effect — with Frederik Pohl; Ballantine F638, 1962 (coll.)

Best Science Fiction Stories — Faber, 1968 (UK coll.)

Thirteen O'Clock — ed. James Blish, Dell 8731, 1970 (coll.)

The Best of C. M. Kornbluth — SF Book Club, 1976; Ballantine 25461, 1976 (coll.)

In addition to the above, Pohl mentions two unpublished Kornbluth novels in his introduction to *The Best of C. M. Kornbluth*, but cites only one title: *The Crater*. Again, if anyone out there knows what the other title is, I invite you to share with the class.

— Bud Webster